THE HITLER
WEREWOLF MURDERS

THE HITLER WEREWOLF MURDERS

Leo Kessler

This first world edition published in Great Britain 1994 by
SEVERN HOUSE PUBLISHERS LTD of
9–15 High Street, Sutton, Surrey SM1 1DF.
First published in the USA 1994 by
SEVERN HOUSE PUBLISHERS INC., of
425 Park Avenue, New York, NY 10022.

British Library Cataloguing in Publication Data
Kessler, Leo
  Hitler werewolf Murders
  I. Title
  823.914 [F]

  ISBN 0-7278-4662-0

Typeset by Hewer Text Composition Services, Edinburgh.
Printed and bound in Great Britain by
Hartnolls, Ltd, Bodmin, Cornwall.

"Even if we could not conquer, we should drag half the world into destruction with us and leave no one to triumph over Germany . . . We may be destroyed, but if we are, we shall drag a world with us – *a world in flames*!"

Josef Goebbels.

AUTHOR'S NOTE

In the second half of the 20th century we live in the age of the guerrilla. Even as I write guerrillas are in action everywhere, from Ireland to Bosnia.

Once they were seen by the Establishment as the exponents of immature violence in an "emerging" world. Today we know that is no longer true. Once the guerrillas discovered the value – in terms of publicity – of the hijacked airliner, the kidnapped foreign consul, the murdered politician, they realized that the real battle for the public's "heart and mind" was not to be fought in some obscure jungle or against some nameless authority. No, it was to be waged in the city and against some particular individual.

Surprisingly enough it was the Establishment, in particular, the British Establishment, which started it all. Back in 1941, the wartime British government forced the Czech Government-in-Exile into dropping two parachutists, Jan Kubis and Josef Gabcik, on their occupied homeland. Their mission was to murder the German overlord, Reinhard Heydrich, whose efforts had convinced the ordinary man in the street to collaborate with their German masters. The two Czechs carried out their mission well enough. Heydrich was ambushed and murderd. The enraged Germans retaliated with the notorious Lidice Massacre. Thereafter, the Czechs didn't collaborate any longer. The first urban guerrilla action had been eminently successful.

After that year guerrilla movements started and flourished all over Europe. Even little Luxembourg, with a population of only 300,000, had a very active partisan organization which harassed the German occupiers everywhere it could. In the "cause of freedom", from one end of Europe to the other, the German occupiers were kidnapped and murdered, their installations and machines of war destroyed and sabotaged so that in the end the *Wehrmacht* was forced to fight pitched battles with the guerrillas in such countries as Poland and France.

Yet what of Germany, the oppressor? When in the winter of 1944/45 the allies crossed Germany's frontiers to west and east, where was a German resistance movement? In that country, which Minister of Propaganda, Josef Goebbels, boasted "would never surrender", how did the Germans resist? Where were the German urban guerrillas?

This is their story. It is a bloody and not pretty one. But in those days there were no pretty stories.

L.K. Reinbek/Germany, 1994.

ONE

Hitler's Werewolves

"WERE-WOLF: a prehistoric WGmc compound whose constituents are represented by OE we-man-and OE Wulf-wolf; a person transformed into a wolf or capable of assuming a wolf's form.

Webster's New Collegiate Dictionary.

ONE

Now the Flying Fortress started to swing in from the North Sea. Somewhere below there lay the Belgian port of Antwerp. But although Antwerp had been in Allied hands for six months now, the port was still strictly blacked out. A searchlight flicked on. The first pilot at the controls of the big four-engined American bomber tensed. Its icy white light swept across the night sky and rested on the bomber. For a moment the cabin was flooded with the blinding light. Then as abruptly as it had appeared, the light disappeared again. The enemy down below was satisfied. It was an Allied plane.

"*Mensch*," the co-pilot gasped, a note of relief in his voice, "*die haben's geglaubt!*"

The first pilot nodded, but said nothing. He was concentrating on his instruments. The drop had to be absolutely accurate. The "chief", as everyone called the mysterious SS general, had briefed him personally, telling him more than once, "the whole success of the operation depends on a one hundred per cent accurate drop just over the border."

He started to lose height. To his right there was a cluster of lights. Brussels, the Belgian capital, he told himself. The blackout wasn't too hot there. Suddenly he remembered the great days of victory back in '40 when he had been stationed down there. God in heaven, in those days there had been champers for breakfast and a new woman every night! He sniffed ruefully and told himself, now five years later in poor old battered Germany, a man was lucky to get a cup of ersatz "nigger sweat" for breakfast and most of the women were too weary and bomb-happy even to think of spreading their legs.

A long, flowing silver sheen started to loom up. The Meuse, he told himself. Quickly he checked his position. He was just south of Liege. He turned to the co-pilot. "All right, Otto," he snapped. "Better stand them to. Ten minutes, I estimate, to the DZ."

Otto took off his leather flying helmet and clambered out of his seat. He staggered back to where they sat on their parachutes in the captured American bomber and, shouting above the roar of the engines, said: "Buckle on your chutes! Ten minutes to the DZ – dropping zone!"

They nodded and rose to their feet, including the woman.

She wasn't pretty, but he knew under her bulky overall, she had a nice pair of tits. "Do you want me to help you, Fraulein?" he asked hopefully. He hadn't had a feel at a pair of female tits for a while now; they had been too busy preparing for this mission – and dodging enemy planes, which seemed to be everywhere over the Reich these days.

She looked at him with those stern eyes of hers. "No thank you, *Herr Leutnant*, I can manage quite well by myself."

The blond Hitler Youth boy – he was only sixteen, the pilot knew – sniggered and said, "She's quite a handful, our Ilse is, or haven't you noticed?" He licked his lips suggestively, then seeing the look on the officer's face, began buckling on his chute.

They were slowing down now, as they approached the frontier with the Reich, where most of the enemy anti-aircraft guns were located. Up in the cockpit, the pilot switched on his position lights so that the Allied flak gunners could see Fortress' outline quite clearly. The pilot bit his bottom lip tensely. There was, he knew, a whole American anti-aircraft brigade down there. If the ruse didn't work, they'd knock him right out of the night sky.

Nothing happened. The gunners must have been taken in. Now he shouted to the co-pilot down in the fuse-lage, "All right, we're nearly there." He switched on the red light.

With a grunt, the co-pilot opened the hatch. The plane was flooded with icy air. The wind buffeted the co-pilot as

4

he balanced there, watching the ground go by. "On your feet!" he shouted above the roar.

Obediently, the four men, the boy and the woman with the big tits got to their feet and shuffled forward awkwardly, as they had been taught.

The co-pilot stared at the red light intently. He willed it to turn to green.

Abruptly it did. He slapped the first man on the shoulder and shouted *"Go!"*

Without hesitation the man flung himself out of the big plane and disappeared into the night.

Rapidly, the rest followed, till only the woman was left. The co-pilot wondered for an instant whether she was going to back out. But he was wrong. She drew a deep breath and then she, too went. Rapidly the co-pilot closed the hatch and yelled to the pilot at the controls. "All gone. The Ascension Day commando has gone!"

The pilot nodded his understanding. Yes, Otto, was right, he told himself. The six of them *were* on a one-way mission, trying to carry out their assignment nearly two hundred kilometres behind enemy lines. Then he dismissed them and concentrated on getting the big bomber back to base . . .

Down below the wind howled around the girl as she fell at a tremendous speed. The very breath was dragged from her lungs and she found herself gasping for air. Frantically, she sought for the ring-pull. After what seemed an eternity, she found it. She tugged hard. With a clap like thunder, the canopy opened. That terrifying descent at speed ceased. Abruptly her mad fall ended. Now as she swayed gently from side to side, she caught glimpses of the moonlit countryside beneath. To the one side there were hills covered with spiked lines of firs. To the other, there were flat meadows, with here and there patches of frozen snow which glistened and sparkled in the spectral silver light. She nodded her approval. The terrain looked right to her.

Reaching up carefully she started to work the shroud lines as she had been taught to do in training. The pendulum movement ceased. She was now coming down in the target

5

area in a relatively straight line heading for the thick forest on the heights to her left.

She flashed a quick last look around. There was not a light or a building to be seen. The winter countryside seemed completely deserted. Naturally the curfew would keep people indoors till daylight. But what about patrols? Did the *Amis* as they called their American occupiers, and their Dutch allies still patrol this border region when their fighting armies were already on the Rhine? Her instructors had been unable to tell her. She hoped they didn't.

The moonlit ground was now beginning to loom up larger and larger. Resisting the urge to tense her body, she clapped her legs together as she had been taught. She was almost there.

Suddenly, with a crash she was down. The snapping branches of a fir broke her fall and she hardly felt the impact as she hit the ground. All the same she was winded and for a moment she lay there, swamped by her parachute, fighting for breath and subconsciously taking in the faint drone of the departing bomber. She pushed aside the parachute silk. She peered into the darkness. No one. She was all alone.

Now she went to work with the aid of a faint blue-shaded torch clipped to the front of her overall. Hastily she folded the chute, and covered it with leaves and fir branches. She flashed the light on her work. It wasn't perfect, but it would do. Now she stripped off her overall to reveal the baggy black pants and thick man's jacket beneath. The overall she wrapped round her shoulders as extra protection against the freezing cold. She'd dump it later. Finally she untied the pistol with its silencer, which she had strapped between her breasts, and put it in her right pocket, telling herself she wouldn't hesitate to use it if she were challenged. Dressed as she was now in civilian clothes, she knew they'd condemn her to death as a spy if she were taken.

Clambering up the nearest bank by what looked like an animal track, she began to walk slowly through the fir forest, flashing her torch for three seconds every five minutes. The others couldn't be far, she reasoned, but she must have walked at least ten minutes before she caught a glimpse of an answering blue light. For a moment, she did not trust her own eyes. But there it was! On and off and on again. She did not shout, but kept her light on so that they could see her.

Moments later they were all together, talking in an excited manner, recounting the details of their own drops until Wenzel, the SS officer, who was their leader, exclaimed in an angry whisper. "Now stop all this chat! They can hear you all the way to America! Now, let's find out where we are. I want to be over the border and into Aachen by dawn. It's better to do a dive where there are a lot of people than out in the country where you're always spotted as a stranger. Come on. *Los*!"

Suddenly silent, they set off in single file, with the woman bringing up the rear. They moved quickly, but carefully, heads moving from side to side as they sought to penetrate the silver gloom, all aware that their lives were forfeit if they were captured. They crossed a firebreak, turned a corner in the trail and emerged into a larger one, paved with thin logs strapped together by wood. Wenzel said: "*Ami* road. I've seen them before. Their engineers make them. Keep your eyes peeled."

Bent a little now, as if walking against the wind, their hearts thumping, they set off again, knowing well that this American-made trail through the forest might be used for their traffic, bringing supplies up to the front. The *Amis* were moving huge amounts of equipment, shells, petroleum, food and the like, ready for the great crossing of the Rhine.

By now the moon was beginning to wane and the girl told herself it must be slowly getting towards dawn, but there was still no sign of the border with Germany. Wenzel, she told herself, would have to make a decision soon. They'd have to find some sort of hiding place.

Five minutes later Wenzel, in the lead, halted. He raised his hand and pointed. "The border," the Hitler Youth said. "There's the border pole.'

She looked. It was: a red-and-white striped pole, with the Dutch lion painted on an enamel plate in its centre. To its

7

right there was a slotted sentry box, which probably had once been used by the border guards.

Wenzel said: "Well, that's good. It's Vaals. That means we're just seven kilometres from Aachen – ". He broke off abruptly and crouched. Immediately the others did the same. There was someone coming down the trail towards them and he was whistling as if he didn't have a care in the world on this freezing March night.

Wenzel thrust with both arms to left and right. It was the approved ambush technique they had been taught in that remote training school. As one they dived into the drainage ditches on each side of the road. Three in each ditch.

They waited tensely, hearts thumping painfully, weapons at the ready.

A moment later a lone soldier, dressed in English uniform, hands in his greatcoat pockets, rifle slung carelessly over his shoulder, came round the bend, walking in the centre of the trail.

He walked fairly quickly, but it was obvious he was on some kind of patrol because he looked keenly to left and right, though every aspect of his manner indicated that he wasn't expecting trouble on this cold March night; after all, the front was kilometres away.

Now he was moving by them as they crouched low in the drainage ditch, faces bent away from the silver light. The woman licked her suddenly parched lips. The soldier was almost level with her now. In a moment he would be past her and gone round the next bend in the trail.

That wasn't to be. Suddenly the soldier stopped and sniffed the air. The woman cursed to herself. Just before they had finished training the parachute instructor, who could not keep his hands off her breasts when he was "demonstrating parachuting technique" had given her a small bottle of scent. She had put some on just before the operational jump. It masked the smell of her sweat. Now the enemy soldier had smelled it.

The man sniffed again. She could imagine that his face was creasing in a puzzled frown up above her on the trail, wondering how the devil the odour of scent came to be here in the middle of this remote forest just before dawn.

Suddenly her heart leapt. She heard the slither of his rifle being taken off his shoulder. A moment later she heard the sharp click of a safety catch being snapped off. He was coming to investigate!

For one moment she hesitated. Then she made up her mind. She jerked the silenced pistol from her pocket. Jaw clenched, she sprang to her feet. The soldier was standing in the centre of the trail, rifle poised only metres away. He saw her. "*Gott verdamm –*" he began to curse. She pressed the trigger. A soft plop. Next moment the slug hit the fir tree just to the soldier's left. *She'd missed*!

His rifle spat flame. A slug howled by. It missed too.

The Hitler Youth sprang from his hiding place. He'd brought a folding Schmeisser with him for the mission. He pressed the trigger. Slugs cut the air in sudden fury. Leaves and branches rained down. Still the lone soldier wasn't hit.

Now he realized his danger. He dropped his rifle and started to run. He seemed to bear a charmed life. Slugs slashed the air all around him, but none found their target. The woman cursed. She stood very straight, one hand behind her back, the other with the pistol held rigid, as if she were back on the firing range. She controlled her breathing. She took first pressure, then fired. The running man staggered. His head tilted back. His hands clawed the air, as if he were climbing the rungs of an invisible ladder. Next moment he flopped down, dead before he hit the ground.

The woman let her shoulders slump, breathing hard. But there was no time for relaxing now. Shouts were coming from the forest. Someone was shrilling a whistle urgently. "*Alarm . . . alarm*," a voice was crying, somewhere close by.

Wenzel cried: "Scatter . . . scatter . . . We'll rendezvous Aachen . . . Main Station . . . tomorrow . . ." And then he was off, pelting through the forest, as if the Devil himself was after him. For a moment the others hesitated. None of the men had been soldiers like Wenzel. The woman made up their minds for them. "Come on, you fools," she shrieked contemptuously. "Standing round like farts in a trance! Run for it." With that she was off, too, heading for the east and Aachen.

TWO

The woman stopped. The dawn mist had rolled away over the frozen fields. Now she could see the ruined city. She could see the damaged spires of the cathedral with the wrecks of the 18th century houses all around it. Before the war, as a young apprentice, she had spent many happy hours in the old imperial city. Now, Aachen was in ruins and occupied by the hated enemy.

She was cold and shivering, but the thought of the great German city, which housed the bones of Charlemagne himself, in enemy hands made her hot with anger. The chief traitor, who made it possible for the *Amis* to rule Aachen, would have to be eliminated. Then the world would see that Germany, even at this, the eleventh hour, could still strike back. Even in the heart of the enemy camp, there was no safety for those treacherous renegades, those slimy turncoats who had thrown in their lot with the enemy.

Warmed now, her strong, heavy-breasted body filled with new purpose, the woman tugged her rucksack higher and set off across the fields towards the city and her date with destiny.

The others were not waiting for her at the shattered *Hauptbahnhof*. The square outside was packed, but there were few civilians. Mostly, they were American GI's back from the front, waiting for the leave train which would take them to the rest centres in Belgium and France. They were dirty and unshaven, with muddy boots and stained uniforms. They were hollow-eyed and weary, too. Still they had the strength to wolf whistle at the lone woman with the big

11

breasts and cry in broken German. "Hey Frolein, Ich give *Schokolade*. You Schlafen mit mich?".

She felt herself grow red with anger. She turned hastily and left. She knew the drill from the training school. If they missed on rendezvous, they would return to the same place the next day. Now she decided she would spend this day finding the chief traitor.

She turned down one of the shattered sidestreets, the pavements filled with brick rubble, the houses mostly without their roofs, windows filled with shattered glass. The street was deserted. Hastily, she stepped inside one of the houses and, pulling aside some of the bricks, she hid the rucksack filled with her iron rations and extra ammunition for her pistol. She spotted a battered shopping basket. On impulse she picked it up and slung it over her arm. A moment later she was outside once more, looking like any other suburban housewife, off to stand for hours in a long shopping queue for whatever rations were available.

The first woman she stopped middle-aged, wearing army boots and carrying a round loaf of bread under her arm told her all she wanted – to know. The chief burgomaster of Aachen and the arch traitor was named Oppenhoff – Franz Oppenhoff, and he lived in the Eupener Strasse. The woman with the loaf asked her if she knew where that was.

She nodded quickly. She didn't want anyone to know she wasn't from the city. "Yes, it's on the road to the Belgian frontier, . . . near the border post," she said swiftly.

"Yes, that's it."

"And the number?" she asked, as a jeep filled with over-weight *Ami* military police wearing shining white helmets went by slowly. Hastily she averted her eyes.

The woman with the loaf didn't seem to notice. She answered: "Number two hundred and fifty-one. One of those villas out there on the hill. *Wiedersehen*."

"Wiedersehen," the woman said automatically, as the other one scuttled off with her precious rationed loaf of bread.

Her mind raced. Should she carry out the mission herself?

12

She felt capable of doing it. Oppenhoff wouldn't be armed; she was. She hated him with a passion, though she had never met him, for he was a traitor who had to be liquidated as a symbol of vengeance to all the traitors now working for the enemy in Occupied Germany.

In the end she decided she'd do a reconnaissance of the Oberburgomaster's house. The basket discarded now, she set off for the Eupener Strasse. Slowly, she walked through the ruined town, past the tall grey, shell-pocked bunkers where the last German garrison had held out to the last in the previous year's fighting, and started the long climb up the Eupener Strasse.

There were few people about, she noted with satisfaction. Occasionally, she met an old crone or old man bent under a load of branches and twigs from the nearby forest, pulling a little wooden cart. Once, a truck filled with Americans. Despite the penalties laid down by the Americans for having any dealings with German women, they whistled and hollered at her and made obscene gestures. One even undid his flies and flashed his penis. She didn't even blush. She simply looked the other way.

The Eupener Strasse was a very long road. On one side it was bordered with open fields, which might offer a chance of a quick escape. In the middle of the cobbled, shell-holed road there were the tramlines which, in the old days, had brought Belgian workers over the frontier to work in Aachen's factories. Now it was rusty and overgrown with weeds. To her left were the villas, all very large and spaced out at fifty metre intervals. The woman noted with satisfaction that all of the villas were protected from the curious eyes of passers-by by tall hedges or rows of tightly packed firs. Once anyone had managed to penetrate these houses, she told herself, they would be able to do what they wanted, concealed from the road.

Two hundred and fifty-two Eupener Strasse! She slowed down. It was the traitor's villa. For a few moments she was undecided. Then the woman made up her mind. She crossed the street, skirting the shell-holes, and opened the gate. The villa was two metres above the street level and she had to climb seven steps to reach the door, which was located at the side of the house, fronted by a broad wooden-railed balcony running the length of the house. She made a mental note of the layout of the place.

Swiftly she ran her gaze down the list of names pinned on the doors of the occupants, as laid down by the *Amis*. There were six or seven on it. There were a couple she didn't recognize. But those she sought were there all right: '*Oppenhoff, Franz, Oppenhoff, Irmgard*', followed by the names of their three children.

So the arch traitor had three children, she thought, but it didn't alter her determination one bit. He should have thought of the consequences to his family before he had sold his soul to the enemy.

She knocked on the door. There was the sound of footsteps. The door squeaked open. A pretty, dark-haired woman of her own age stood there. "*Sie wünschen*?" she asked politely.

Behind the maid there was a full-length mirror and she caught a glimpse of herself: tall, erect and those big breasts of hers straining to burst out of the poor synthetic material of her pullover. "You're all titties," her teenage girlfriend Karla had used to say, as they lay in bed together as girls, and then she had leaned over to kiss the nipples and she had taken Karla to her like a fond mother of a beloved infant.

She forgot Karla and said: "I've been walking a long time. I'm thirsty. Do you think I could have a glass of water."

The maid smiled and did a little curtsey. "Of course, Fraulein. Follow me."

To the woman's surprise, the maid walked by her and down the steps to the cellar door below. "We've lost the key to the front door. During the fighting. We don't want to break the door down, so we go through the cellar. You know at night you've got to lock up . . . the American soldiers." She flashed the woman a little smile.

They entered a dark tiled hall. There were 18th century prints on the walls. From upstairs came the noise of children.

14

The maid clicked her tongue. "Those kids couldn't make more noise if they tried, could they," she exclaimed.

The woman nodded absently, her eyes busy taking in everything. This would be the entrance then, she told herself. At night the windows would be covered by the blackout and nearly all the windows still retained their glass, so there was no way they could get through them without making too much noise. So, it would have to be the cellar door.

"I'll go and get your water," the maid said and hurried away, just as a much younger girl came into the cellar. "*Guten Tag*," the girl said as the woman started. She recognized the girl. She had been in her troop of the Hitler's Maidens two years before. Did the girl recognize her?

Seemingly, the girl didn't. For they chatted for a few moments until the maid returned with the glass of water, which the woman drained quickly. Then, with a hurried "thank you", she was off again, down the hill in the direction of Aachen, anxious to get away from the Oppenhoff house before the girl recalled who she was.

Suddenly she heard hurrying footsteps behind her. She felt her heart began to thump, She panicked. Desperately she pulled herself together. Her first inclination was to run for it. But she mustn't. The feet caught up with her. She turned. It was the girl, smiling up at her with her bright innocent face. "I know you," she said. "You were – "

– "I've just come back from the other side of the Rhine," she stopped the girl short, knowing that she had been about to say: "you were my old group leader". "But my flat's been bombed out here. I've got nowhere to sleep for the night. Tomorrow I'll decide what to do next."

The girl's innocent young face relaxed. It seemed she had already forgotten that the woman had once been one of the most fanatical Nazis in the Rhineland, always urging the girls in her charge to ever greater efforts for "Folk, Fatherland and Fuhrer". "Why don't you come and spend the night in our place?" she indicated a fairly battered large house further down the road. "I should imagine we can put you up for the night." Fraid we can't feed you though. We've used up our bread and potato ration for this week."

The woman patted the girl's pretty face fondly. She remembered how, once before, she had received the call to active service for the Fatherland. She had once loved girls and now felt the old ache of longing and desire. "Don't worry about the food," she said. "I've got a whole tin of *Ami* corned beef here," she patted her other pocket. "I'll share it with you tonight, if you like."

"*Ach du meine Güte!*" the girl exclaimed and clapped her hands together in sheer delight. "I haven't had meat for ages. Please, let me show the way." The girl thrust her arm through the woman's and, like two lifelong friends, they strolled away.

Two hours later, the woman who had come to Aachen to murder a traitor, was busily occupied helping the 16-year old girl to clean and dust a room in the big house, her normally deathly pale face flushed with the exertion of washing windows and sweeping floors. Franz Oppenhoff, Senior Burgomaster of the occupied city, would live another twenty-four hours.

In the bed they shared that night, she fought to keep her hands off the girl's nubile, plump body. She feigned sleep, but the girl, excited at having a companion, would go on talking. She said the *Amis* had already started publishing a paper in German in Aachen. In it she had read they had already captured Bonn, Koblenz and the whole of Cologne on this side of the Rhine. Soon they would cross the Rhine – the girl said they had been moving up men and material for weeks now – and then the war would be over; Germany would be defeated. "*Defeated*", she said the word several times with pleasure, as if she were glad that her native country would be beaten.

The woman told herself that the silly girl had fallen for the enemy propaganda hook, line and sinker. But she daren't tell her that. She might start asking awkward questions about the reason for her return to Aachen. In the end she could stand the stupid child's defeatist babble no longer and let her hand rest almost casually on the girls' lap.

She gave a little giggle of delight and stopped chattering at once, as if she had been waiting for this move all along. She flung up her nightdress and parted her legs eagerly. The woman gave a grunt of pleasure and then began to work on her with her finger . . .

THREE

"*Damn*," Colonel Sterling said, as the medics dropped the blanket over the dead civilian's tortured face, "that's the third Kraut stiff this week." He turned to the bull-like MP lieutenant who towered above him "Anything?" he asked.

The MP took his gaze from the crowd of half-starved German civilians who were staring as if hypnotized at the shrouded body of their dead burgomaster. He shook his head. "Not much, Colonel, sir. The locals said whoever did it, did it after curfew. The Krauts have to be off the streets by zero eighteen hundred – "

– "Yeah, I know, "Colonel Sterling broke in impatiently." It's my job to know, isn't it? Carry on."

"Well, Colonel, sir, the locals say he was alive just before curfew because a couple of 'em went to his office to get permission to put out a couple of hogs onto the communal pasture. Thereafter no one saw him alive again."

"What about his wife – and family?"

"As burgomaster, he had a pass to move about after curfew. They didn't. So they stayed at home to wait for him to come back from the office." He indicated the corpse with a callous jerk of his thumb. "He didn't."

Colonel Sterling tugged at the end of his big nose, a nose which was robust and red, and strangely out of keeping with his rather delicate and intelligent face. "Were there any . . . er . . . signs?" he asked carefully. As a long-term counter-intelligence officer he was wary of asking direct questions. In suspects at least; it gave them a clue to the way the interrogator's mind was working.

"Yeah, sure," the MP replied. "Over there near that

18

honey dew pile." He indicated the pile of steaming animal manure across the village street. As usual, in these primitive Rhineland villages, the manure was stacked underneath the kitchen window and Colonel Sterling always swore the villagers stored it there to impress their neighbours: the bigger the pile, the more animals they possessed. "We only found it because it had been freshly painted during the night."

"Let's have a look," Sterling said and crossed the cobbled street, while the villagers gawped and the women in their dirty white aprons leaned further out of their windows to get a better look. They had grown used to the *Amis*, by now. They saw them simply as providers of black market cigarettes and coffee and sometimes as rapists, when they had drunk too much. But this was something else. The *Amis* were actually investigating the murder of a village burgomaster. Normally when a German was killed, as they often were by the black Army drivers racing their huge trucks through the villages on the way to the front with supplies, the *Amis* would give the sorrowing relatives a kilo of coffee and a couple of cans of food and that would be that. Today, however, a whole column of jeeps had appeared to look into poor Fritz's murder and the *Amis* now crossing the *Hauptstrasse* were obviously high-ranking officers.

Sterling wrinkled his nose at the stink coming from the "honey dew" pile steaming in the cold morning air and stared at the crumbling wall and the sign.

"You can see, Colonel," the MP commented, "the killers – if it was them? . . ."

"It was," Sterling said grimly.

"Were in a hurry. The paint dripped down at the corner there. You can see it."

Sterling stared at the sign painted in black on the wall, under the old fading one dating back to 1944. He guessed at – "*Sieg oder Siberien*"* It was like two "V"s, almost joined together to form what looked like a Germanic "W".

* Victory or Siberia". *Transl.*

The MP shrugged, puzzled, and said, "Can't make head or tail of it, Colonel. What do you think it signifies, sir?"

Sterling, who had seen a similar sign near the scene of a murder three times in the last month, didn't answer. Instead he said: "There must have been at least two of them to carve up the stiff the way they did – God, it was sheer butchery! Then they did the sign. What then?"

"They took off on pushbikes. It hadn't rained before curfew, but we found tyre marks leading out of the village and it rained during the night. That's the way they went."

Sterling nodded his understanding, delicate features wrinkled in a frown. Before the war he had been Professor of Germanic Studies at College Park, Maryland, and his students had come to know the look well. "Ole Sterling, the German", as they nicknamed him behind his back, is going into his weisheimer act, they'd say. "*Get ready for a profound thought.*"

"So you didn't find any further trace of them, did you?" he asked softly.

"No sir, Colonel."

"So what do you conclude from that, eh?"

"Well our guys are allowed after curfew," the MP blustered, going red in the face with the effort of thinking. "But I sure don't think they'd use pushbikes."

Colonel Sterling nodded encouragingly. "So?"

"So, they must have been Krauts."

Again Sterling nodded, his clever mind way ahead of the bumbling, red-faced policeman.

"But for the life of me, I can't figure Krauts would want to kill a Kraut burgomaster," he confessed, shame-faced.

Colonel Sterling allowed himself a tight little smile before he said: "*Why*? Because we appointed that particular Kraut burgomaster, Lieutenant, that's why." He signalled his jeep to come forward and then said: "All right, Lieutenant, clear the place up. Get the interpreter and question each one of the villagers. Closely. They might know something. And," he looked warningly at the big MP officer, "no knocking them about, do you understand? No third degree methods. We're supposed to be fighting for democracy, you know. At least, that's what the President and General Eisenhower say." He grinned.

The lieutenant grinned back and clenched his fist, which was like a small steam shovel. "Democracy in action, sir," he said. "When I'm through with them they'll be singing like little dickey-birds."

"I'm quite sure of it," Colonel Sterling agreed, as the jeep came to a halt next to him and the big MP officer clicked to attention, touching his gloved hand to his helmet.

"The Ph.D. candidate", as he always called Goldstein, was at the wheel, peering owlishly through his heavy spectacles, Jewish face set in what he called his "military look". "It's my war face," he would always explain to Sterling when the latter questioned about the look. "I reserve it for the Krauts. After all, General Patton's got a war face. So why can't I have one as well?"

Four years earlier, Goldstein had come to College Park from New York – "just had to get away from all those kikes!" – to study for his doctorate. But he had never made it. The war had caught up with him, just as it had with his professor, Sterling. Now they had been together in Counter-Intelligence for three years. They had been through North Africa and Italy as a team. They'd fought their way together through France and during the Battle of the Bulge, the previous December, they had been cut off by the advancing Germans for forty-eight hours. Both had been wounded and awarded the Bronze Star for Valor for braver in action. Still, after all that time Goldstein was still the "Ph.D. candidate" and Colonel Sterling "the Prof."

"Christ," Sterling would sometimes complain in moments of exasperation, "can't I ever get rid of you? We're like a goddamn man and wife!" To which Goldstein, pursing his somewhat thick lips, would simper: "But Prof, I *love* you!"

Now Goldstein was serious, as he drove the jeep down the village street. "It's the same, isn't it, Prof?"

Gravely, Colonel Sterling nodded his head. "Yes, another Kraut appointed by us murdered obviously by his fellow citizens. And again that double "V" sign." He raised his voice. "What does the Kraut radio say?" he asked Goldstein, who regularly listened to "*Radio Berlin*" as part of his job.

"Not much, Prof," Goldstein answered, neatly steering around a wrecked, rusting Sherman tank which had been knocked out in the December fighting and had not yet been hauled away for junking. "Goebbels," he meant the Nazi Minister of Propaganda, "is stating that they will soon carry the war behind enemy lines – that's our lines – and that anyone who co-operates with the enemy – will pay for it."

"Just like those three poor swine who have already paid for it with their lives," Sterling said, tugging at his big nose once more. "But does Goebbels imagine he can stop the final defeat of Germany by killing a couple of village burgomasters? It's hardly likely, is it?"

"I think it goes further than that, Prof!"

"What do you mean? And watch that goddam truck, Candidate! You know how crazy those coloured drivers are." He indicated the big truck bearing down on them at top speed, with its black driver hunched over the wheel, chewing gum as if his very life depended upon it.

Hastily, Goldstein swung the jeep off the road onto the verge and let the truck thunder by, spraying them with mud and pebbles. "Damn *swarze*," Goldstein cursed in Yiddish and then said: "There's a lot of talk in Intelligence that Hitler's moving his best troops, underground factories and the likes to the German–Austrian alpine region. The Swiss papers are already calling the area the "German National Redoubt."

"So?"

"Well, Prof," Goldstein answered, venturing out onto the road once more after a cautious look to left and right for more "damn blacks", "if it's Hitler's intention to hole out in the mountains for years, as the Swiss and some of our guys think he will, how are we gonna run krautland without the Germans? We can't run every goddam one-horse town ourselves. We simply don't have the guys."

Sterling nodded his head in agreement. "I see your point,

Candidate. Frighten the krauts into having nothing to do with us. Yes, yes, I get it. But you're forgetting one thing."

"Like what?"

"You can't frighten the whole of the populace by bumping off a couple of petty village burgomasters. You know dog bites man is no news. Man bites dog – now that really *is* news. There'll be plenty of Krauts ready to hold office under us for whatever reason. They won't be put off by these murders."

Goldstein smiled at him patiently, as if their roles had been reversed and he was the middle-aged professor in a colonel's uniform. "But don't you see, Prof? This is only the start?"

"The start – *of what*?"

"You know Goebbels? That little club-footed creep never does anything in a small way. He's going to ensure that the world will learn that any Kraut who works for us will get shafted. So what does he have to do to bring that about?" "Goldstein shrugged in that Jewish, careless manner of his, and answered his own question. "He has somebody really important bumped off. A name – and he'll ensure that the press boys get to know about it so that they can spread the good word. "He slowed down as they started to cross the temporary bridge which crossed the River Sauer, dividing Germany from the tiny principality of Luxembourg, where Colonel Sterling had his headquarters.

Automatically, Sterling raised his hand to his helmet to return the salute of the Luxembourg border guard in his tall black *kepi*, his mind racing. The "Candidate" was right of course. There was more to it than killing a few obscure Kraut civilians. He had followed the "poison dwarf's"* career right back to the '20's and he knew the little bastard never did anything by halves. He wouldn't waste his time and energy on a two-bit operation.

"Candidate," he said after a few moments, as they drove out of the Luxembourg border village of Echternach and took the road heading west, "I think we'd better go and

* Goebbels was named the "poison dwarf" on account of his vitriolic tongue and small stature. *Transl.*

23

have a word with Brigadier General Sibert at 12th Army Group HQ."

"Thought you'd decide on that, Prof," Goldstein said, changing down swiftly as they began to climb the long incline. "I've already phoned his military secretary. We've got an appointment with the general for fourteen hundred hours – on the nose."

Sterling shook his head. "Candidate, can you read my mind?"

Goldstein shrugged again. "Hell, Prof, ain't we married or something? You know what wives are? They can always read what's going on in the old man's mind."

Colonel Sterling moaned . . .

FOUR

She was walking past the shattered former Labour Exchange
when she heard the urgently hissed, "*Hierher!*" The woman,
her mind still full of memories of the perverted little girl with
whom she had been the previous night, turned, startled.

It was the Hitler Youth. He had removed his overall. Now
he was dressed in shabby civilian clothes, complete with an
oversize pair of American black felt overshoes. He looked
like any other youngster to be seen on the streets of occupied
Aachen. All of them had bits and pieces of stolen or bartered
American uniforms.

Behind him, lounging against a bullet-pocked wall, admir-
ing his nails, or so it seemed, and looking as if he had all
the time in the world, was Wenzel, the SS lieutenant. But
his right hand was dug deeply into the pocket of his shabby
jacket and the woman knew instinctively that it was gripping
the butt of his pistol.

Casually as she could, the woman walked over to the
blond-haired youth. She flung a glance to left and right,
as the two crossed to where Wenzel lounged. There was
no one within earshot. A long way off an *Ami* was turning
a jeep. All the same, she kept her voice low when she said;
"His name is Oppenhoff – Oppenhoff, Franz. And he lives
on the outskirts of the city. Way up the Eupener Strasse."

Wenzel, his scarred face revealing nothing, absorbed the
information while the other two waited impatiently for his
decision. He was the veteran. He knew about these things.
Finally he spoke. "All right, there's no use hanging around
Aachen. We've got no papers. They could pick us up at any
time – " He stopped short.

25

The jeep was pulling by them. But the driver had other things on his mind. Perhaps he was out to find a girl – "fraternizing", they called it – or do some deal on the black market. He had no eyes for them. They were simply part of the dreary, bombed-out scenery – *Krauts*!

Wenzel waited till he had gone, then he said: "So we do it tonight. Good, let's go and tell the others." They slunk away.

Half an hour later they were back in the camp the men had set up in the forest beyond the city. Over the last of their tins, containing gooey chunks of meat known as "old man", because, rumour had it, the meat was made from the bodies of old men from Berlin's workhouses, Wenzel told them how they would do it. "Just three of us will be needed. You," he pointed to the woman, "the boy – and you, will stay behind here."

The Hitler Youth opened his mouth, as if to protest, then thought better of it.

"We go in at midnight. By that time the local *Amis* will either be drunk or fast asleep. Besides, there aren't any of the fat swine within a kilometre of the Oppenhoff house – according to her," he indicated the woman, who was sitting there, face expressionless

"We ask for the burgomaster. I've got an excuse for asking to see him," Wenzel continued. "When he comes to the cellar door, we shall shoot him. Nothing fancy. Just shoot him. Got that?"

The others nodded their heads.

"If there's trouble, we split up and cross the Rhine individually. I know it might be difficult and dangerous, but one of us has got to get through to report to headquarters. This will be the organization's first big operation. Headquarters will want to know all about it to make the most of it when the enemy finds what we've done. *Klar*?"

Again they nodded their understanding.

"*Gut*. Then I think we shall make ourselves comfortable while we've got a chance. The next few days are going to be hectic, I should guess." Wenzel laughed brutally. "Besides

26

this is a religious holiday, you know. We oughtn't to work. It's Palm Sunday." He laughed again.

Afternoon came, and high overhead the killers heard the steady drone of heavy planes. It went on for hours. Twice the Hitler Youth said he was going to leave their cover to see what was going on. Wenzel sternly told him not to. In the forest it grew warmer. The woman stretched out in a patch of sunlight, her big breasts seeming to be about to explode from the thin ersatz material of her pullover. She could feel the rays of the sun penetrate it and was overcome by a feeling of lazy lust as she remembered what the teenage girl had done and wanted to have done to her the previous night. "Perverted little bitch!" she told herself, as she recalled that sticky little body writhing and moaning under her touch. "Where do the kids these days learn such things?" She swallowed hard, her eyes firmly shutting out the sun. A delicious tingling had begun between her legs. She pressed them together hard and wished she were alone.

But she wasn't. The men were all around, snoring in the sun, while the Hitler Youth prowled about on his feet, keeping guard. She sighed and told herself when things were better she'd go and see the teenage girl again. Perhaps, when they went up into the mountains, she could take her with her? She'd find some excuse – after all the kid had been in the German Maidens and was supposedly a patriotic German, though, of course, she wasn't really. For a little while she spoiled herself with memories of that delicious, cunning, pink little tongue and then she, too, drifted into an uneasy, sweaty sleep . . .

The assassins set off just before the sun was beginning to set. They shook hands with one another, all very solemn and tense now. A few words were exchanged, but not many. Each of them was wrapped up in a cocoon of his own thoughts and apprehensions. Wenzel gave his final instructions and then took the lead, with the other two men strung out behind him at regular intervals, just as they had done in training.

Swiftly, they headed for the Eupenar Strasse. The sun had gone down now and the moon was coming out, so they could see quite well in spite of the blackout which had descended on the old imperial city. They paused when they came to an open field about one hundred and fifty metres from the Oppenhoff villa. Quickly, Wenzel and the others dumped their gear. He didn't want to be encumbered with equipment during the killing and their escape. He ordered one man to stand guard over it and keep a lookout. Then, with the other man, he set off again.

Not for long. Wenzel stopped again, pulled out his wire clippers and silently cut through the telephone wire with them. Now the Oppenhoffs wouldn't be able to summon help from their friends, the American–Jewish gangsters when the trouble started, he told himself with some satisfaction.

Noiselessly, in their rubber-soled boots, the two of them approached the cellar window. Wenzel applied some pressure to the handle. With a loud click, it opened. They didn't hesitate. They crawled through the open window. Closing it behind him, Wenzel flashed on his torch. Its beam illuminated a stack of empty green wine bottles, a sack of precious coal; a bicycle without wheels.

"Up the stairs," Wenzel whispered.

Like silent timber wolves intent on finding their prey, they tip-toed up the cellar stairs and opened the door. Not a sound, save for the heavy, sombre ticking of a clock, somewhere. "They're all safely in bed," the other man said.

"We'll soon find out," Wenzel added in a whisper.

They stole down the corridor. Carefully, very carefully, Wenzel opened the door and shone his torch inside. Three children lay curled up under a heavy feather quilt, sleeping peacefully. "His kids", Wenzel said and closed the door once more. They went to the next room. It was empty. Wenzel scratched his shaven head in bewilderment. Where was Oppenhoff? Had the woman lied? Had they trained so long for nothing?

The other man put his mouth close to Wenzel's ear. "There's somebody in there," he whispered urgently, indicating the next room.

Wenzel wiped his brow. He was sweating heavily now with nervousness. Yes, his companion was right. There was someone breathing heavily in the next room.

Wenzel indicated to the other man he should draw his pistol. Then he poised himself at the door. He counted to three under his breath and opened it quickly. "Who's there?" The voice was feminine, young and frightened.

A young woman – probably the maid – was sitting up in bed, the bed clothes clutched to her chest.

"Where's the Burgomaster – Burgomaster Oppenhoff?" Wenzel asked, hardly recognizing his own voice. It was almost out of control with nervousness.

The maid stared at the two intruders, speechless. Wenzel fired his question at her again and she stammered: "He's not here."

"Where is he then?" he demanded.

"At our neighbours."

"Go and get him," Wenzel ordered.

"I can't get dressed," the maid said, "with you here."

"All right," Wenzel said, switching off the torch. "We'll wait outside until you bring him. Now hurry up." With that they were gone, leaving the maid wondering what she should do. In the end she decided it would be safer to have the Burgomaster with her than be alone with the children and two strangers wandering around long after curfew. She started to throw on her clothes . . .

Flustered and puzzled, Oppenhoff, a burly, balding man in his early forties, arrived back at his home. The two strangers came out of the bushes immediately, saying nothing for the moment, while the Burgomaster tried to make them out in the moonlight. Underneath their civilian jackets they seemed to be wearing a mixture of German and American uniforms. Both looked fit and were of military age, so why were they not in uniform?

Suddenly Wenzel snapped to attention and, thrusting up his right hand, barked: "Heil Hitler!"

Oppenhoff gasped. It had been over seven months now since he had last heard that accursed salute to the monster

29

who had brought Germany only misery, death and destruction. "Who . . . what are you?" he stuttered, while the maid held her hand to her mouth in fear.

Wenzel lowered his hand. He had seen the fear and surprise on the Burgomaster's round, plump face and he liked the look. "We are German airmen," he lied glibly. We were shot down near Brussels three days ago. We are trying to get back to our own lines. Can you get us some passes, *Herr Oberburgermeister*?

Oppenhoff found his voice again. He shook his head and said, "I can't do that. You should report to the Americans and give yourselves up. The war's nearly over anyway. It's only a matter of days."

Wenzel's face hardened threateningly, but he said nothing.

Oppenhoff said to the maid, still standing there a few metres away: "Don't be afraid. They're only German fliers who have been shot down. Go and make them a few sandwiches." As she went, he turned to the two men again. "I'll go and help her," he said. Before they could stop him he had turned and gone into the house.

The other man hissed; "Do it when he comes back again."

In the cold, silver light of the moon, Wenzel's face looked suddenly very strange. It had taken on an almost greenish hue. "Yes," he said in a strangled voice. He took out his pistol and fitted the silencer with hands which trembled violently.

"Be quick," the other man hissed urgently. "The maid has gone off to tell the *Amis*. Believe me Wenzel."

There was the sound of footsteps coming back from inside the house. Wenzel started to breathe harsh and fast. And then, there was the traitor, Oppenhoff, outlined quite clearly in the moonlight. *But Wenzel did not fire!*

"Do it!" the other man commanded.

Wenzel didn't move.

"You cowardly sow!" the other man rasped. With a grunt he snatched the silenced pistol from Wenzel's nerveless fingers.

"What – " Oppenhoff began.

He never finished the question. The other man levelled his pistol at the Burgomaster's head and pressed the trigger. Inside, the maid cutting the sandwiches heard a noise like an unoiled door creaking, but she didn't think it was important and so she continued with her work . . .

But across the way there were people moving. Wenzel saw them too, and hissed, "There's somebody over here. Let's go. *Los!*"

"Wait a minute, *du Schwein*," the other man stopped him angrily: "We've got to have proof we croaked him. HQ will need it." He looked at the body crumpled on the cellar steps. His eyes spotted the official *Ami* armband around the dead man's sleeve, proclaiming him Burgomaster. He bent and ripped it off.

A volley of shots rang out. Scarlet flame stabbed the silver darkness. "*Amis*," the other man yelled in alarm.

Next moment, the two of them were running for their lives across the open fields.

FIVE

The Headquarters of the US 12th Army Group was in chaos this Monday morning. The previous night, Montgomery's 2nd British and 9th American Armies had crossed the Rhine. There was hard fighting everywhere and the two airborne divisions, one British and one American, were reporting back thirty-five per cent casualties.

Now harassed, sweating staff officers with clipboards and messages were hurrying back and forth at the double. Telephones jingled. Typewriters clattered furiously. A general sitting on the side of a desk, was bellowing, red-faced with fury: "Of course, I want those goddamn tanks to start crossing! And I don't care Sam Hill if they take casualties. Get those tanks across!"

Colonel Sterling, threading his way through the bustling, crowded corridors of the *Hotel Alpha*, which housed the HQ, thought it a madhouse. He had seen it all before. The men at the sharp end, the soldiers who did the fighting, kept their nerve, remained cool. It was the staff that always flapped. What was it the English said? "Even generals wet their knickers." Boy, they were certainly wetting them this fine Monday morning.

He passed an unshaven, red-eyed brigadier general, who was shouting furiously at a trembling, frail-looking WAC female soldier, who was holding a mug of steaming coffee in her thin hand. 'I told you *two* sugars and *no* cream, you idiot! I've been up all night not a wink of sleep – and you can't even get my goddamn joe right. It's got cream in it!'

The WAC started to cry. Colonel Sterling saluted. The brigadier-general didn't even notice. Sterling sighed. It was a tough life being a female at HQ with all these powerful military men. "A WAC is a double-breasted soldier with a built-in foxhole," they chortled; they felt they could use and abuse them just as they wished. It was one of the privileges of rank.

He paused at General Sibert's door, straightened his tie, for the 12th Army Group's chief-of-intelligence was a West Pointer and like all the officers from the Point he attached great importance to bullshit. Sterling knocked.

"Come," a sharp voice commanded. Sterling went in, saluted in his awkward un-military fashion and said, "Colonel Sterling reporting – *sir!*"

Sibert, a sharp-featured man with dark hair and a keen eye, gave a sharp look and then said, "Morning Sterling." He didn't salute. Perhaps he thought that Sterling's salute was so un-military that it was not worthy of a return salute. Instead, he snapped: "Sit down, Sterling." He glanced at his wrist-watch and said: 'You've got exactly fifteen minutes. It's a hellishly busy morning."

"I understand, sir. I'll make it brief." It's about the murders of the Germans we appointed as burgomasters in recent months."

Sibert said nothing – and his sharp face revealed nothing.

"So far there have been three murdered and two attempted murders. So far these murders and attempted murders have been limited to unimportant Germans, burgomasters of villages, all of them. Though there has been a death threat made to the new American-occupied chief burgomaster of Bonn."

"Who committed the murders?" Sibert asked directly.

Sterling felt a trace of unease. It was his job as head of counter-intelligence to know these things. "I'm afraid I don't know, sir," he replied.

"Could it be German Army people – or those murderous kids in short pants, the Hitler Youth? As you know, we've already had cases of kids as young as twelve ambushing lone tanks and trucks and blowing them all to hell with those panzerfaust* things of theirs."

* A primitive German missile-launcher. *Transl.*

"I don't think so, sir," Sterling replied firmly." These murders have been well organized and planned. The sightings of the murderers which we have had, indicate that they were adult civilians."

Again Sibert snapped; "I see."

They fell silent as yet another convoy heading for the Rhine front rumbled through the city, shaking the walls of the room, drowning the shouts of the angry MPs directing them and the odd cheer from the civilians, though they didn't cheer the Americans much these days; they had been in Luxembourg City too long now. They had become accustomed to them.

Sterling waited till the last giant truck had rumbled past, then he said: "There's one other thing which makes us think that these murders are not isolated incidents, carried out by separate individuals."

"What's that?" Sibert demanded.

"This, sir." Sterling handed the photograph he had taken at the scene of the latest murder. "If you'll note, there is a sign smeared on the wall – next to the honey dew pile. We found a similar sign at each of the other murders. In one case the victim had it carved on his face. Very ugly."

Sibert stared hard at the grisly photo, concentrating on the strange "V". It was silent now in the office. Still Sterling could hear the hectic buzz outside and he told himself that, once again, while they were playing their little office games at the HQ, bucking for rank, complaining about the three hot meals they got a day, wondering if they could get off that night to sleep with their local "*schatzis*", young men were dying at the front by their scores, hundreds, perhaps thousands. Here all of them would die old – *and in a warm bed.*

Finally Sibert handed him back the photo. "What do you make of it, then?" he asked simply.

"It's organized. There's somebody behind it, probably on the other side of the Rhine, making the plans, finding the killers, pulling the strings, perhaps controlling some sort of agent network on *this* side of the Rhine, which fingers the people who are going to be murdered."

34

Sibert nodded slowly. "All right, I'll buy that. So what if a few tame opportunist Krauts are murdered by their own people? We'll find more. The Krauts love crawling when they're beaten."

"I don't know about that, sir. But I don't know if we're going to keep on finding Germans to run the adminstration under our control if these killings go on. They'd be too frightened for their own lives."

"Then we'll protect them. We'll send in the troops."

Sterling looked hard at the General. "But sir, that is impossible. Imagine how many troops we would need if we attempted to protect every German official. Think of Cologne alone, sir. We'd need a whole division of infantry to keep tabs on all the officials we employ there."

Sibert pursed his lips. "I see your point, Colonel. But the way General Patton is going on the other side of the Rhine, with Hodges ready to burst out of his bridgehead – with even Monty," he looked contemptuous, "moving at last, we're going to beat the Kraut soon. It's a matter of weeks, perhaps even days now, till they throw in the sponge."

Sterling listened attentively. Then he said: "But you think yourself that there is some truth in the fact that the Nazis are moving men and material into the Alps in Bavaria and Austria. There is already considerable talk of a German National Redoubt – it was in Collier's magazine last month – where fanatical SS and the like would hold out for years. If that were the case, how could we get Germany running again without the help of the Germans?"

Sibert gave a dry laugh. "We spend four years beating the bastards, now we're supposed to get them running again, as you phrase it. I don't see the Sam Hill why."

"Well, sir," Sterling said quietly, "if we don't help them to get back on their feet, their cities re-built, some kind of industry, it might drive them right into the arms of our Russian allies – and I don't think the Administration in Washington would particularly welcome a post-war Germany which was communist."

Sibert, who was one of the few "political" generals at 12th

Army Group HQ, nodded his head quickly. "I take your point, Sterling. All right, what can I do for you in this matter?"

"Allow me to drop all other counter-intelligence work on this side of the Rhine and in the Comm Z*. The MP's can take care of that for the time being. Most of the German agents they left behind after the Battle of the Bulge have been rounded up or have taken a dive, knowing that they were working for a losing side anyway."

"Agreed."

"Anything else?"

"Yessir. Once we find who's running this murder incorporated – as it were – authorize an attack on their HQ. It is probably on the other side of the Rhine and we might be able to make an armoured thrust for it, wherever it is. If not," he shrugged," "I think it is important enough to nip this thing in the bud, chop off the head and not the various arms, well, we could make a paradrop on the place."

Sibert sucked in lips at the proposal and looked worried. "Well, Sterling," he began slowly, "that's a mighty tall order. You see – "

But before he could finish his words, there came an urgent knock on the door. Without waiting for the General to cry "enter", a dishevelled, flushed Lt. Goldstein skidded through the door, stumbled to a halt, flung Sibert an awkward salute and announced, with a gulp; "Another Kraut burgomaster has been killed, gentlemen!"

"Is that any reason for bursting into my office in this manner, Lieutenant?" Sibert demanded, eyes taking in the fact that one of Goldstein's pockets was unbuttoned and that he had got his medal ribbons the wrong way round.

"No sir," Goldstein stuttered, trying to catch his breath, "But this isn't just some kind of tinpot Kraut burgomaster, sir, no siree."

"Calm yourself, Goldstein," Sterling said soothingly. He

---

* The rear area region in France and Belgium of the US Army. *Transl.*

couldn't ever remember the "Candidate" being this excited, even on that day when they had come barrelling round a corner in the jeep to find an enormous Tiger tank facing them. Fortunately, they had done a bunk before the German crew had been able to fire their great 88mm cannon. "Who *is* the murdered man then?"

"The *Oberburgermeister* of Aachen, the first one we ever appointed in Occupied Germany when we captured the city back in October last."

Sterling whistled softly, "Oppenhoff, eh. I checked his background at the time. It seemed very decent, for a German guy. Lawyer, very Catholic, with two or three kids."

"Yeah," Goldstein still couldn't contain his excitement. "The correspondents got on to it right way. The guy from *The Times* says they're reporting it tomorrow. And the BBC has already broadcast the news."

"Yes," Sterling said, "they can see the importance of this murder. It really brings it all out into the open."

"What do you mean, Sterling?" Sibert asked.

"This one is a symbolic murder. The first German appointed by us in the first city captured by the US Army, the old Imperial city of Aachen, and we could do nothing to defend him. You can guess what kind of a propaganda coup Dr Goebbels in Berlin is going to make of this once he learns from London that poor old Oppenhoff has been murdered. The Nazis and the diehards will love it. It'll frighten the pants off those Krauts who are already co-operating with us, too. To put it plainly, General, this is the *big* one."

Sibert thought for a moment. Then he nodded his head. "All right, Sterling, have it your way. Drop everything else. Let the MPs take care of the Comm Z. General Bradley – he meant the commander of the 12th Army Group – is up to his eyes with work at the moment. But the first chance I get to talk to him, I'll take up this business of trying to take out the HQ of this murder incorporated, as you call it."

"Thank you, sir." Sterling rose to go.

Sternly, Sibert raised one finger, as if in warning and said; "You've made me realize the vital importance of finding these murderers, Sterling. They must be found – and there can be no slip-ups, or there will be consequences." He bent his head over his papers. The interview was finished.

Goldstein flashed his old professor a look. The latter shrugged, then the two of them saluted and went out. General Sibert didn't look up as they did so.

SIX

The woman had been very lucky. Instead of running with the others into the fields as soon as the firing had broken out, she had kept her nerve. She had hidden in a thicket and waited for dawn and the end of the curfew. At first light, she had set off down the hill towards Aachen. For she had calculated the *Amis* would think a fugitive would not actually go back to the city. Indeed she had walked by Number 252, now surrounded by heavily armed *Ami* MPs and gawping locals. As she passed she had heard the sound of a woman sobbing heartbrokenly, but she had felt no pity. The traitor had deserved what he'd got. In vain she had looked for the sign of the *Werwolf*. But she had not been able to see it. The men had obviously fled in panic after the murder, not waiting to daub the sign as ordered back at HQ.

As she had walked down the hill with its burnt-out, shell-holed rusting trams pushed into the gutter on both sides, she had made a rough plan. She would head south-east for Euskirchen. She had friends there in the bookshop. They would put her up without questions. Thereafter, she'd go north towards the Rhine. In the confusion of the fighting up there she might well be able to cross at Cologne and get back to headquarters to report and ask for a new mission.

On the first leg of her journey she had been picked up in a jeep by a callow young Belgian soldier who had eyed those splendid breasts of hers as he had braked to a stop. She guessed he was Flemish, for he spoke some German with a strong accent. He said he'd take her as far as Schmitt where there seemed, as far as her understood his explanation, some sort of depot. But could he first – please – touch her breasts, one by one?

She had nodded and thrown back her head to hide the bored, contemptuous look in her eyes. He had looked to left and right. Then, nervously, he had put both hands on her breasts. She heard him shiver, as he started to rub them round, as if they were puddings. His breath came a little faster and she wondered idly, if he had an erection. Perhaps he'd come in his pants and then it would be all over with.

She hadn't been afraid. After all, she still had the pistol in her pocket and she'd use it if necessary. He had tweaked her nipples, not painfully, and moaned some more. Then he stiffened, gave a sharp groan and dropped his hands hurriedly from her breasts, as if they were red-hot. She waited while he went behind a bush. When he came back, he avoided looking at her, saying simply: "Please get in." They drove the rest of the way to Schmitt in complete silence.

For a while she had wandered around the shattered village at a loss. Hardly a house was still intact. There were shell-holes, wrecked tanks and rough wooden crosses, hung with German helmets everywhere. Obviously, there had been heavy fighting in and around the village. The few villagers she came across were cowed and tongue-tied, unable to give her much information. As for the enemy, they were all black: cheerful young men who swaggered rather than walked and who chewed gum with their caps at the backs of their cropped heads. But they seemed generous and readily dispensed sweets and chocolates to the few children who latched onto them, crying in their newly-learned English: "*Candy . . . chewing gum . . . cigarette for Papa!*"

Someone gave her directions to the northern end of the village, from which the road led to Euskirchen. But for a while she had let the *Ami* trucks go thundering by, for they were all driven by blacks and she was suspicious of them. Weren't they all really animals beneath that smart khaki uniform? One old crone in the village had told her, shooting a careful glance to left and right in case she was overhead, that: "they've all got tails, you know, dearie. Somebody saw them naked when their shower truck comes for them to wash in – and they all had little tails, *just like monkeys!*"

All the same, whether they had tails or not, she knew she had to get on. The *Amis* would be combing the whole countryside outside Aachen by now looking for the killers of the arch traitor.

A jeep started to slow down when its driver saw her standing there at the side of the road. It was driven by a young black, chewing gum, driving casually, as if he was hardly aware he was behind the wheel of a moving vehicle. "*Du kommen mit?*" he asked.

She looked at him closely. He was smiling and handsome in a black way. Somehow she couldn't think he had a tail. She made her decision. "*Ja . . . danke,*" she said.

He wiped his hand across the seat next to him, as if to make sure he was clean enough for her and then allowed her to sit on it. He depressed, changed gear and with his free hand proferred her a stick of gum from an open packet. "*Kaugummi?*"

She shook her head. They had not eaten chewing gum in Germany since 1933. The authorities had thought it was a symbol of American decadence.

They began to roll again down the rutted road, with shot-up tanks and burnt-out trucks littering the fields on both sides. Here and there old, bent peasants, men and women, were toiling to get their fields in order once more, but there were dirty white tapes everywhere, marking the spots which hadn't been yet cleared of mines.

"*Wo du gehen?*" the black asked in his broken German.

"Euskirchen." She hesitated. Did one use the formal German "Sie" for "you" with black men who were rumoured to have tails? She decided she could "*Und Sie?*"

"*Ja.*" he answered in that funny German of his. "That's if the MP's don't catch me." He grinned.

She looked puzzled. She had caught the word 'MPs', but that was all. He saw the puzzled look and explained the best he could." Gone over the hill, lady. Deserter. Only for a few days, mind you, Lordy, they're breaking my back in that

Quartermaster Company. I need a rest!" Neatly he dodged a shell crater in the middle of the road.

"*Deserteur*?" she queried.

He nodded his head rapidly. "*Ja . . . ja . . . Deserteur.* Say, German ain't all that difficult, is it. Lot like good ole American."

For a while they lapsed into silence as they drove slowly down the ridge-top road that led to Euskirchen. Thousands of men had fought for the road during the previous autumn and winter and it was still in poor shape. There were holes and craters everywhere and the young black driver needed all his skill to negotiate them. Then they started to come out of the hills down to the Rhenish plain and the road improved. He started to talk again. "It's the sarge. He's black like all of us. But he's a bastard, works our asses off. Night and day we've been at it, getting up the supplies for this Rhine thing. *Verstehen*?"

She shook her head.

"Sergeant – *Schweinehund . . . vile Arbeit. Ich . . . deserteur*," He pointed a finger at his skinny chest.

Now she nodded her understanding.

"Want me a place where I can lie up for a couple o' days and get me some rest, then I'll turn myself in. It'll be the stockade for a while. But so what?" he shrugged carelessly and placed his hand on the big package on the back seat of the jeep. "Got me some goodies there to pay for a place, cigarettes, candy, chocolate, coffee." He saw the look of blank bewilderment on her pale face and tried again. "*Fur Haus . . . Kaffee . . . Schokolade . . . du helfen*?"

Slowly she nodded. The black deserter wanted a house to hide in and he'd pay in goods. She thought that's what he meant and he wanted her to help to find a safe place for him in Euskirchen. "*Ja, ich helfe*," she said, though she had every intention of dumping him once he had got her there, "in *Euskirchen*."

He flashed a big white-toothed smile and said, "Swell. Gee, thanks."

But the woman and the black deserter were not fated to ever reach Euskirchen.

They had just breasted a hill, surrounded by the usual circle of shot-up, rusting tankwrecks, for on this road every hilltop had been stormed, and were rolling down to the little village below when she spotted the barricade with, next to it, a couple of smartly painted jeeps, their radio aerials sparkling like silver in the afternoon sunshine.

"*Polizei . . . Militarpolizei!*" she cried, spotting the danger before the black driver.

"Shit!" he cursed. "MP!" Instinctively, he eased his foot from the gas pedal, black face suddenly very alert. Then he made his decision. "Hold on to ya hat, lady!" he whooped and with a grunt he turned the wheel, swinging the jeep off the road, down a small embankment and into the fields beyond.

The MP's lazing around the jeeps spotted the fugitive at once. There were shouts, angry cries, whistles shrilling and a crackle of startled, wild carbine fire. Moments later, the jeep engines burst into life. The MPs were coming after them.

As the driver, his face set and intent, fighting the terrain, as the jeep jolted and bumped across the stony fields, kept on going, ignoring the wild shooting behind them, she knew instinctively that the MP patrol was not posted there to catch deserters; it was on the lookout for the escaped assassins. She was in mortal danger!

Now the two police jeeps came bumping and jolting across the fields, lower down the slope, in an attempt to cut them off. The black laughed at the sight, as if it were all great fun, and slewed his jeep to the right. He was heading straight for a thick fir forest located a hundred and fifty metres away.

"You're mad!" she cried above the roar of the engine. "The trees will stop you dead."

Of course, he didn't understand. Instead, he pressed his foot down even harder on the gas pedal. Suddenly she saw his aim. There was a trail, a kind of steep fir break cutting through the firs, heading for the top of the slope.

The jeep raced to the edge of the fir forest. The black

slammed the shift into low gear. The jeep's engine whined and howled as it took the strain. Slowly, it started to mount the very steep slope between the trees. Behind them there came a volley of shots. Slugs howled off the firs. Angry spurts of soil and pebbles erupted on both sides of them. Someone opened up with a tommy gun. She ducked down even further in her seat, praying that the sweating young driver would do it, as bullets slashed the air everywhere.

The jeep's engine howled in protest. It slowed down even more. The slope seemed too much even for that tough little vehicle. Grimly the driver fought it up the hillside, cursing fluently now, crying: "Come on, ya sonovabitch! Take it, willya . . . take it!"

Below, the frustrated MPs who had not even attempted to take the slope, had sprung out of their jeeps and were taking aimed shots at the slow-moving vehicle. But the two of them seemed to bear a charmed life. Bullets flew on all sides twice the jeep itself was hit and suddenly, she could smell the cloying stench of petrol. Their petrol tank had been hit – but still they kept on moving.

Now she could see the summit quite clearly. Once they reached it they were safe. She would dump the black straightaway. She'd play the stupid, frightened little woman and run away. The black was a marked man now; she wasn't. She'd make the rest of her way to Euskirchen on foot. It would be safer.

Now the summit was only a hundred metres away. The jeep, however, seemed to be moving at a terribly slow pace. It kept slipping on the very steep hillside and its progress wasn't helped by the patches of treacherous mud here and there. But the black fought the mud with all his strength and skill, twisting the wheel back and forth, body bent forward, as if *willing* the jeep to keep on moving. *Fifty metres!*

They were going to do it. She knew it. Below the firing had almost stopped. They were almost out of range. At not more than five miles an hour, the jeep crawled to the summit. The two of them stared at it wide eyed, full of longing to be up there, as if they had just seen the gates open to paradise.

"Come on . . . come on . . . come on," the driver cried, as if urging on a willing, but almost beaten horse. "Come on . . . *DO IT!*"

The bullet smacked into their right rear tyre without warning. There was the sudden hiss of escaping air. The jeep slumped. Out of control, it veered crazily to the right. The sudden move caught the driver off guard. He tried to correct the movement. Too late! The crippled jeep slammed into a fir tree. The black's face slapped against the wheel with the force of the impact. Blood spurted from his smashed nose and he slumped there groggily, unable to move. "*Shit!*" he muttered thickly.

She recovered in seconds. She still had a chance. The MP's were two or three hundred metres below her. The summit was only a mere fifty away. She flung herself out of the jeep, and started to scramble up the steep slope. They started firing again, but she was out of range for their pistols and tommy gun now.

Grunting and panting, her normally pale face flushed an angry red and lathered in sweat, she fought her way to the top. Only twenty metres to go. She was going to do it. Inside, despite the tension and near exhaustion of her body, she laughed, she laughed scornfully at them. They had failed, the *Amis*. She would escape them yet.

In her haste, she didn't see the pothole until it was too late. Her right foot caught in it. She slapped the ground, all wind knocked out of her. She got to her knees, gasping for breath. She tried to stand upright, those magnificent breasts heaving in and out. Next moment she went down to her knees, again, a terrible pain searing her right foot with the intensity of a red hot poker. She tried to crawl. The summit was only ten metres away. But it was no use. She couldn't make it. Suddenly, all fight went out of her sturdy body. She simply lay there, panting and crying with rage and frustration. It was thus they arrested her.

SEVEN

"They've got one of 'em," Golstein cried excitedly into Colonel Sterling's office. "The MP's nabbed her just outside Euskirchen!"

Sterling looked up from the photostat of the headline on the front page of that morning's *New York Times*. It read: "*Non-Nazi Mayor of Aachen killed by 3 German Chutists in uniform*". He had been upset by how quickly the papers had got on to the rotten business and had decided he'd leave the photostat of the London *Times* till later.

"What did you say, Candidate?" he asked, looking up startled.

"They got one of the killers, a woman," Goldstein bellowed, face red with triumph. "Prof, are you getting old?"

Sterling was about to stand on rank, then decided against it. "A woman you say?"

"Yeah," she was one of the hit squad all right. They found a pistol on her and a map of Aachen. No doubt about that."

Sterling acted. "Kay, get the local chief of the military cops up there. Tell the operator it is a priority for General Sibert. I'll take it when the shit hits the fan."

Goldstein grinned. "You didn't use that kind of language back in College Park, Prof."

"Move it!"

The Candidate "moved' it".

A few minutes later, the Colonel was talking to the captain of MP's in Euskirchen. "Yer, sir. No doubt about it. She's one of them we was looking for. At first we thought she was just some frowlein trash the nigger had picked up. But when we searched her and found the pistol and the map – "

– "Okay," Sterling interrupted the other man, who sounded very much the southern redneck, complete with prejudices and crudities. "Have you strip-searched her?"

The MP chuckled. "Sure wish we could – she's got the goddamnest pair o'tits on her. But we ain't allowed. It's agen regulations, cos we ain't go no woman to do it."

"Forget it. Do it yourself. I'll take the responsibility."

"What am I looking for, sir?" There was a note of excitement in the other man's voice now. Obviously, he could hardly wait to get the woman naked.

"L-Pill."

"What?"

Lethal pill, cyanide usually. Almost instant, if painful, death. First the mouth and any large rings. Then her hair and then the nooks and crannies – armpits and the like. Naturally, both orifices."

"Orif?" the MP stuttered. Not only couldn't he pronounce the word, he didn't know what it meant.

"*Her ass and her cunt,*" Sterling said crudely, while Goldstein, standing next to him, grinned broadly, thinking of the pre-war times back in Maryland when the "Prof" had been very prim and proper. That was before he had lost his only son in the Pacific and his wife had left him because he had thrown up a well-paid professorship with tenure to enlist in the Army as a somewhat over-age private.

"Yessir," the MP said. "I'll see to it personally right away. I'll concentrate on them orif – holes, sir."

"We shall be with you in two hours," Sterling said. "Now take good care of her. That's all."

The line went dead.

"Did you ever study *die zweite Lautverschiebung** at College Park before the war?" Colonel Sterling asked, as Goldstein drove them steadily north-west towards Euskirchen.

"Have a heart, I was a poor Jewish boy from Queens. It was tough enough trying to keep up with my old man's Yiddish."

* The Second Law of Sound Changes. *Transl.*

47

Sterling sniffed. "Well, you'll never understand the intricacies of the German dialects, if you don't comprehend how that law works. You see, an imaginary line runs from – say Berlin to – say – Cologne. Left of that line Low German is spoken; to the right High German. Why?" He answered his own question with the smartness of the professional lecturer which he had once been. "Because of certain specific changes in the sounds of the two groupings. What is the German word for 'water', for instance?"

"*Wasser*." Goldstein answered dutfilly, skilfully avoiding what looked like an abandoned mine on the left verge.

"Correct. Now in Low German, the median double 'S' of High German always becomes 'T'. So '*Wasser*' becomes 'water', which shows that English belongs to the Low German languages. '*Besser*' becomes 'beter' or 'better' in English and so on. There is a whole range of such changes."

Goldstein gave a little sigh and said. "After this war, nobody is gonna give a fuck about German, the German people or Germany. They're finished, fini, kaputt. Jesus," he exclaimed as if he had just thought about it: "I'll have to start my PH.D. all over again in something else – basket-weaving perhaps." He gave a hollow chuckle.

"Nonsense, Candidate!" Colonel Sterling snapped. "You'll go back, get your PH.D. on the G.I. Bill and within five years you'll be an assistant prof. Germany will rise again, believe you me. There's no way we can keep the Germans down. Why should we? We need the Germans as a bulwark against the Russians." He tugged the end of his big nose fiercely (Goldstein sometimes wondered whether, with a conk like that, Colonel Sterling didn't have some Jewish blood in him). "I shouldn't be surprised if, in a decade's time, we won't see another German army being formed."

Goldstein laughed. "Gee Prof, you're pulling my pisser aren't you? Another Kraut army! Why, we haven't even defeated this bunch yet."

"Well, perhaps not so soon, Candidate. But take my word for it – you'll be assistant professor of German Studies at College Park by 1950." But Colonel Sterling was wrong

48

this once. Hymen S. Goldstein would be dead long before
1950 . . .

"Je-sus, Colonel," the big, red-faced MP Captain cried after
he had swung Colonel Sterling a tremendous salute, "the
broad's a virgin!" He grinned nastily. "I never did hear tell
of a Kraut woman under the age of twelve who was a vir-gin.
But hot shit, this one is!"

Colonel Sterling's face remained stern. "She had no poi-
sons on her person then?" he asked coldly.

"No sirr-eee!" The big cop's grin broadened. "I went into
all them nooks and crannies, as you told me to, sir. And
you'd better believe it – *I took my time!*"

"Has she said anything?"

"No, sir. We've got an interpreter – some kind of Jewboy
from New York. He's tried her in Kraut but she won't parley.
Just sits there with her kisser closed."

Sterling looked hard at Goldstein and shrugged slightly.
The shrug said all. "He's a typical southern redneck. Don't
bother with him. He isn't worth it."

Goldstein nodded his understanding and Sterling said,
"All right, can we see the woman. By the way, what's her
name?"

"You can see her, sir, but the Jewboy," the cop looked
defiantly at Goldstein, "can't get her name out of her. I
could but – " He shrugged. "We can't knock 'em about like
we could in the good ole days!"

Sterling looked at him coldly and said: "Just let's see
her."

"This way." The MP swaggered in front of them down the
corridor, his fat buttocks jiggling in the too tight olive drab
trousers. He stopped at the door and unlocked it. "She's all
yours," he said. "I'll go back and get on with my paperwork.
Back home, all we had to do was to arrest them and throw
them in the slammer. But the Army insists on paperwork.
Brother, doesn't it just!" He swaggered off, leaving the two of
them to stare at the woman, who had risen from her wooden
stool in the corner of the makeshift cell.

49

She was a big sturdy woman in her mid-twenties, with enormous, proudly jutting breasts and a pale, defiant face. Her eyes were slate grey and they too were defiant, although she was now sporting a black eye. Obviously, Sterling told himself, the fat redneck MP had roughed her up a little during his examination of her body. It would be his style.

Goldstein cleared his throat and said in pretty good German: "*Was ist Ihr Name?*"

She stared back at the "Candidate", but kept her lips stubbornly closed.

Sterling studied her. Since Normandy, he had interrogated many German prisoners. They seemed to come in two types. The majority, who were only too eager to tell all they knew. Indeed, it had often seemed impossible to stop them talking. They were like those Germans he remembered from his post-graduate year in Germany in the early thirties who had set about telling you their life story within five minutes of meeting them. "A great country for spies," he had always quipped to his friends back in the States. "You don't have to work hard to get info over there."

Then, there was that other type, the minority. They were the stubborn type, often defiantly arrogant, with a kind of primitive peasant doggedness which defied threats, starvation, even blows. How many times had he been on the verge of losing his temper, something no intelligence officer should ever do, when faced with this type? If the medics ever discovered he had stomach ulcers, he'd blame it on those stubborn Krauts.

She was one of that frustrating minority. She was going to be damnably difficult to break, but break she must. It was vital to know what she knew. He spoke. "We know you're a member of the gang which murdered *Oberburgermeister* Oppenhoff of Aachen." His German was fluent, polished by a year at the University of Heidelberg. "Even if you weren't, I could have you taken out this very moment and shot because you are a German civilian carrying a loaded pistol. There's the death penalty for that, you know."

His words left her totally unmoved, he could see that

clearly. Indeed there was a look of contempt in those cold, level, slate-grey eyes. Perhaps she considered herself a heroine, ready to die for the holy cause of National Socialism. "Do you understand what I have just said?" he tried one more time.

"*Ja.*" She spoke coldly for the first time, her mouth worked, or so it seemed, by tight, rusty steel springs.

"Well?"

She kept her lips tightly pressed together.

Sterling's mind raced. Suddenly he had an idea. "Candidate," he whispered, turning Goldstein away from her with his hand, "are you prepared to help me with this one?"

"Natch, Prof."

"It'll be a little unconventional, you know."

"What's conventional any more, Prof?" Goldstein quipped. "Aren't we in the middle of a total war? Everybody's nuts now."

"Okay, Candidate. Here we go." He turned to the woman once more. He indicated Goldstein at his side. "*Mein Freund hier ist ein Jude. Verstehen Sie – ein Volljude.*

Goldstein looked puzzled. Why was the Prof telling the Kraut dame that he was a full jew, as the Nazis called those born of two Jewish parents.

The woman looked at Goldstein. There was no interest in her eyes, just contempt. Goldstein felt a sudden anger. He'd like to sock her on the jaw, but you didn't hit ladies, even if they were Kraut.

"Now the police captain tells me he thinks you are – er – a virgin," Sterling went on slowly, noting that the word "virgin" had evinced a slight reaction in her. He thought he could see a slight blush on her pale hard face.

"But you are far too old to remain a virgin much longer. After all, it was your own beloved Fuhrer, Adolf Hitler, who maintained that it was the German women's major role to produce children. You know – *Kinder, Kuche und Kochen**"

* Children, kitchen and cooking. *Transl.*

51

He let the words sink and he could see a subtle change taking place in her. A look of stubborn defiance in those hard slate-grey eyes had changed to one of wary bewilderment. She was wondering where this conversation was going.

"Now," Sterling continued in a relaxed conversational sort of manner, "my friend here is roughly of your age. I shall leave in a minute and let the two of you get to know one another more – er – intimately." He gave a little cough. "If you know what I mean, Fraulein?"

Suddenly, she started to look apprehensive.

"Now that you are our prisoner, I don't think your Fuhrer will care very much that one of his aryans is having – er – intercourse – with a full Jew. But in order that you understand what you are getting into, perhaps I can ask my friend here to show you that he really *is* a full Jew." He turned to an astonished Goldstein. "All right, Candidate, undo you flies and show it to her."

"Am I hearing right, Prof?"

"You did. Open your flies and show her your dick."

"But it's small," Goldstein protested miserably.

"I'm not interested in its size, Candidate. Only that it's Jewish – and circumcised. Now get it out."

One minute later, the woman, tears streaming down her cheeks, was talking as if she would never stop.

EIGHT

"*Werwolf!*" an astonished Goldstein exclaimed two hours later, as they sat in the room the MP's had given them, sipping bourbon and pondering the amazing information the woman had just given. "Holy mackeral, what d'ya know, Prof?"

"Quite a lot," Sterling said easily, still mulling over the information which had come pouring out of the terrified woman.

A convinced, even fanatical Nazi, she had rushed to volunteer when a secret order had arrived at the German Maidens' HQ where she had worked the previous November. It had asked for volunteers for "secret and dangerous operations behind enemy lines".

Days later, she had been ordered to report to a remote castle in the Eifel at the village of Hulchrath. Here she had been told that she was a "P-Woman". When she asked what it meant, the reply came that "P" stood for Prutzmann, an SS General, who commanded this mysterious formation, and that she "better not ask too many questions. It's wiser not to know too much – in case you fall into enemy hands."

But being a woman, she *had* asked questions of her superiors and fellow students, who were all fanatical members of the Hitler Youth or young SS volunteers, many of them decorated in battle. They had been grouped in teams of six, each team and each member of that team, to be trained under cover names, so that in the event that they were captured, they could only reveal to their interrogators what they knew of their own teams.

All that winter, she had learned a little more, as they had

studied how to sabotage railways and power lines, silently strangle sentries, fire silenced-pistols, even use strange-looking carbines which were capable of firing round corners – a hundred and one things connected with the lethal business of killing secretly, silently and treacherously.

In January 1945, the various teams had been ordered to assemble in the great echoing Gothic dinning hall of the castle to listen to a speech from none other than the mysterious *General der SS* Prutzmann himself. "We were all very excited," the woman had told her interrogators between sobs. "We jostled and fought for places in the front rows. For we were going to see our leader for the very first time."

They had had to wait for over an hour before the General did appear – there were massive enemy bombing raids all over the Eifel that January day – but when Prutzmann did finally appear, the young students were not disappointed.

He swaggered in in the black uniform of the pre-war SS, his broad chest glittering and heavy with decorations, surrounded by a bodyguard of similarly uniformed SS officers, all looking tough, suspicious and carrying sub-machine guns. He started without preamble. "You don't know me, comrades," he barked, face set and hard. "So I'll tell you a few things about myself. I have been a party member since 1925. You see I have the Blood Order." He had indicated the red semicircle on his breast pocket, which indicated he had shed his blood for the Party prior to 1933. "You know then that I fought for our Fuhrer before we took over power. In 1941 I was sent East to introduce the New Order there to that Jewish-Slavic rabble of third class citizens. We soon cleared out the Yids, I can tell you," he had declared with a sneer and they had applauded enthusiastically.

"But now, comrades, I have the greatest task of all my long career in serving the Fuhrer, one which will, I think, be of greatest service to our beloved Fatherland in its hour of need. The enemy is on our sacred soil to the East and to the West. Until our armies are ready – and I can assure you they are being prepared for that sacred task – to drive them out, we must take the fight to the enemy."

Prutzmann's face had suddenly flushed excitedly and he had raised his right forefinger to emphasize his point. "The enemy believes he has conquered us in the territory he had already conquered. But the enemy is wrong, comrades. New resistance will spring up behind their back time and time again . . . *and like werewolves, brave unto death, you volunteers will strike the enemy down!* . . . *COMRADES YOU ARE TO BE ADOLF HITLER'S WEREWOLVES!*"

According to the woman, the whole audience had sprung to attention, right arms thrust out rigidily, faces glowing with youthful fanaticism, as they had bellowed "*SIEG HEIL . . . SIEG HEIL . . . SIEG HEIL,*" until they were hoarse.

Now, as they pondered her description of that fateful meeting two months ago, Goldstein was glad of the warmth generated by the bourbon. It had grown cold outside and already darkness was seeping across the shattered town like wings of some great black bird of prey. "Werewolves, Prof. So that's who's doing the killing." He shivered dramatically, "Reminds me of all that Bela Lugosi and Boris Karloff stuff I used to see at the movie theatres when I was a kid."

Sterling was slightly amused at the younger man, but not much. The situation was too serious. "The term '*Werwolf*'," he lectured Goldstein, "is of Germanic origin. It means literally 'man-wolf'. In the opinion of psycho-analysts, the werewolf superstition is based on fear, hatred and sadism. The Freudians go so far as to maintain that the belief rests on the purely sadistic side of man's sexual nature. The desire to hurt, rape and finally, frightening, as a way of satisfying some 'men's sexual needs'."

Goldstein took another hefty swig of his drink and shivered again. Outside it was getting dark rapidly now and soon the cops would be putting up the blackouts at the windows of this lonely house at the outskirts of the ruined town. They'd be all by themselves. "Christ, Prof, I'm convinced. I'll never see another horror movie."

Sterling shrugged. "According to the old legends anyone

can become a werewolf if he has the will to do evil and the desire to exert power. It was said that it was the proclivity of the outcasts of medieval society – lonely or dissatisfied people – who hated and scorned, their fellow men. This embued them with a burning desire to exact revenge. As a result, according to the old sages, they were able to transform themselves into human wolves."

"But did it ever happen, Prof?" Goldstein had been brought up in a Yiddish-speaking family and the Yiddish tales from the old country were full of monsters and strange goulish creatures. He couldn't reject the werewolf legend out of hand.

"Yes and no," Sterling replied.

"Now what the hell kinda answer is that, Prof?" Goldstein exclaimed. "You sound like all those damned professors of philosophy I had to suffer back in graduate school."

Sterling chuckled softly. "Well, that's what professors of philosophy are paid to say, Candidate. It's supposed to make the students, birdbrains that most of them admittedly are, think. No, let me explain. At the end of the Middle Ages when the Holy Roman Empire which contained most of what is today Germany, was in decline, groups of disgruntled German knights formed secret vigilante outfits. They met underground in their castles and in a kind of court – they called it the *Femegericht*, the court of revenge – they passed sentence on those whom they felt were creating anarchy, traitors to the cause in other words."

Goldstein cuddled his drink, interested in spite of his growing unease.

"These knights swore, on pain of death, to conceal the Holy Veme from mother and child, father and mother, from fire and wind and from everything upon which the sun shines and the rain falls, from everything between earth and heaven . . . that was roughly how the oath went."

"Sounds like the masons," Goldstein commented.

"Yes, I'm afraid so. We just can't protect all the Germans who will be working for us. There might be some of our people, too, if we judge on past performance."

"What do you mean?"

"Well, as you know, after the First World War we occupied Germany as far as the Rhine, that is ourselves, the British and the French. But we also had people from what was called the Control Commission on the other side, too. It was their job to check whether the German Army was disarming as it had agreed to do at Versailles and whether the Germans had destroyed all their submarines, tanks and airplanes, as they had also agreed to do at Versailles. Well, Candidate, several of those officers disappeared mysteriously. They were never found, and the civilian German police carried out very half-hearted investigations into the disappearances. I've talked to old hands of those days and they have all said, those missing officers were killed by some sort of German underground organization because they had discovered something they shouldn't have."

Goldstein whistled softly. "But this time we're gonna occupy the whole of Germany and these – er control commission officers – will have the backing of all the Allied armies on the spot in force."

That's just what I'm worried about, Candidate. This time they might not just attempt to kill a relatively unimportant Allied officer. This time they might gun down somebody very big. General Bradley, 12th Army Group commander . . . Perhaps even General Patton."

"Holy cow, not ole Blood an' Guns?"

Sterling nodded, a faraway, thoughtful look in his eyes. "Yes. But the biggest coup of all would be to kill the Supreme Commander."

"*Ike?*"

"Yes, General Dwight D. Eisenhower!"

That night, sprawled out in their cot beds, the two counter-intelligence men slept fitfully, waking at intervals, sweating and disorientated, to be reassured by the steady pace of the sentries on the gravel outside. Their minds were full of the things they had learned this day. Goldstein's dreams were of great hairy paws, equipped with huge claws, ripping away at Patton's throat, with ole Blood an' Guts exclaiming in that high-pitched voice of his: "Watch my uniform . . . watch my uniform. I've just had it cleaned!"

Sterling's dreams were much more sombre. He dreamed of wholesale murder in Germany's shattered cities, frightened Allied troops living in sealed-off compounds, guarded by heavily armed men; a Germany without food, water, light, communications, because no German dared to take part in the administration. Horror upon horror . . .

"Colonel, suh, colonel . . . wake up, Colonel!"

Sterling awoke with a start. He blinked his eyes in the yellow light of the single naked bulb above. The room came into focus. In the next bed, Goldstein was still snoring loudly. Above him was the red, sweating face of the MP captain.

"What is it . . . what's the matter, Captain?" he asked, his voice still furred from the previous night.

"The Kraut dame!"

"What about her?"

"She's killed herself!"

"*What*!" Sterling sat up abruptly and in the other cot, Goldstein gave one last stiffled snore and opened his eyes to yawn and say resentfully, "Hey, what's going on?"

"How did she kill herself?" Sterling asked, already reaching for his shirt and pants. He had slept in his undershirt and shorts.

"Hanged herself," the cop said and added, obviously scared that he would be held to account for the important prisoner's death, "We carried out all the prescribed checks and procedures with a suicide suspect. Took away her boot laces and belt. We even unscrewed the metal plates from beneath the boots in case she attempted to use then to cut her wrists – "

"That's all right, Captain," Sterling interrupted the doeful monologue, "I'm sure you did everything right. So how *did* she do it?"

"Her drawers," the cop. said. "The lousy bitch. We thought we'd do the decent thing by her and leave her her pants, then she goes and uses them to hang herself. Bitch!"

Moments later, they were staring in at the room where she

58

hung. The red long drawers had dug deep into her neck and forced her contorted livid face to one side, with her tongue hanging out like a piece of purple leather. Somehow, those magnificent breasts of hers were now deflated and in her mortal agony, she had lost control of her bladder. A pool of yellow liquid, still steaming slightly, lay on the floor. "Poor cow," Sterling said softly, as if to himself. "Wasted her life for what?" Suddenly he stopped short. Both her hands were red with congealed blood and her nails seemed to be broken off. "What's going on?" he asked the big cop suspiciously.

"What d'ya mean, Colonel?"

"Her hands. They're all bloody and broken."

"Well, they weren't when I last looked in on her before I hit the sack last night, sir."

It was Goldstein who found the answer to the little mystery. "Look at the wall, sir," he said urgently.

Sterling turned in the direction indicated and felt the bile rise in his throat once again. Just before she had hanged herself, she had obviously rubbed her hands red-raw on the rough concrete of the floor in order to obtain some colour – her own blood. Fanatical to the end, knowing that she was soon about to die, she painted that evil red sign on the dirty plaster of the wall. There it was that obscene double "V", which he now knew meant "Werwolf". Sickened, he turned, saying to the big cop, who was obviously very puzzled at what was going on: "Cut her down and give her decent burial. Lieutenant," he snapped to Goldstein. "Get dressed. Let's get back to HQ. As our Brirish friends say – the balloon's soon about to go up – and we gotta stop it!"

NINE

General Omar Bradley, the Commander of the US 12th Army Group, looked very grim. He took off his steel-rimmed GI glasses and said to Sterling: "Colonel, talk me through that one again, please."

Quickly and briefly, Sterling told the Group Commander what the girl had told him before she had committed suicide.

Bradley listened carefully and when Sterling was finished, he said: "It jells. It ties in with my own belief – and that of the Supreme Commander, too – that the other fellow will make a last ditch stand in the mountains to the south." He nodded to Sibert and the chief-of-intelligence sprang forward like some eager second lieutenant and drew back the curtain covering the map marked "Top Secret"

The map, Sterling saw at once, was of southern-most tip of Bavaria, where it met with Austria. It was marked with the legend "Reported National Redoubt" and it was covered with a rash of red symbols.

"As you can see, Colonel," Bradley said in that slow careful manner of his, "each of those symbols represents some kind of military resource – food dumps, gas, ammunition, underground factories, troop silos and the like. Recently, every new day has brought new identifications of troop and supply movements into that twenty thousand miles of German-held mountains. So we have every reason to believe that the other fellow intends to make his last stand in those damned crags." Bradley turned to General Sibert. "Okay Sibert, read out what your people picked up this morning."

Again springing to, as if he were some freshly graduated

young officer or, better a plebe at West Point, Sibert pulled a paper from his pocket and announced: "Our radio listening people picked this up on the German radio this morning. It's call signed 'Radio Werewolf.'"

Sterling's heart sank when he heard that call-sign. Everything was fitting into place in a manner that he disliked and feared intensely. There was more to this nasty business than a few crackpots and fanatical kids. The "P-men and women" were really organized if they had their own radio station.

Sibert began to read: "There is no end to revolution. A revolution is only doomed to failure if those who make it cease to be revolutionary. Our beloved Fuhrer, Adolf Hitler, started the revolution back in the twenties. *That* revolution still continues. Our cities are in ruins. Our territory is occupied. Our armies have suffered severe defeats. But should that dishearten us? Of course not! Remember the Fuhrer still has his wonder weapons up his sleeve. But until the time comes to employ those devasting new weapons on our unsuspecting enemies, we must fight with cunning and guile and relentless savagery to their rear. Comrades in the Revolution, this is our slogan – death to turncoats, death to the enemy! Long live the National Socialist Revolution!"

Sibert read out the radio broadcast in his steady, no-nonsense West Point manner without emotion and pathos. All the same Sterling shivered. It was the true voice of Nazi nihilism. He'd heard it before in the '30s: those screaming brown-shirted fanatics shrieking death, destruction and defiance at the world in the name of the holy cause of national socialism.

"All in all, then," Bradley was saying in his slow, considered manner, "we have to take this – er – Werewolf Organization very seriously. So what are we going to do about it? They say, Colonel Sterling, the monster's head has to be chopped off so that, if I can mix a metaphor pretty badly" – he chuckled – "the tentacles can wither on the vine. But Colonel Sterling, where is that head? Where is the headquarters of the Werewolf Organization?"

Sterling pursed his lips. "Well, sir," he said carefully,

"this is basically conjecture. We know they took off from Fuhlsbuttel near the port of Hamburg up in the north of Germany. They flew out into the North Sea and then crossed into Belgium to carry out the murder of Burgomaster Oppenhoff."

Bradley nodded his understanding and waited.

"So, we can assume that their headquarters is somewhere in Hamburg or its vicinity."

"That would figure," Sibert said quickly. "Hamburg was always the centre of the German *Abwehr*." He meant the German secret service, "and its activities. They trained their people there and they also had their radio transmitter in the port to send messages to their agents throughout the world."

"We have some confirmation of this," Sterling continued, after the general had finished, "in what we found in the dead woman's possession. The Germans are notoriously careless in frisking their agents before they leave on a mission. They always allow them to go on a job with a pack of German cigarettes, razor blades, contraceptives or the like."

Bradley laughed drily. "Contraceptives, eh! What did they want the rubbers for – *to fuck the enemy to death!*"

There was dutiful laughter from the senior officers present. The Army Group Commander's feeblest of attempts at humour would always be greeted as the epitome of wit. Sterling waited patiently until it was over and then produced the battered half of a railway ticket from his pocket. "A railroad ticket from Reinbek to Hamburg *Hauptbahnhof*. It appears that she took a train from Reinbek to Hamburg's main station and then went on to the airfield."

"There's a Reinbek up in New York State," Bradley said, "nice olde worlde sort of a place. Liked it. But where's this Reinbek?"

"It's a village east of Hamburg . . . about twenty miles away from the port. I checked it out. It has two hospitals for the wounded from the Eastern Front – it's on the main railroad line from Berlin to Hamburg. Easy to offload the wounded there I guess. The flyboys regard it as a kind of hospital town so it doesn't get bombed."

"You mean the flyboys can't find it, eh?" Bradley said, with a wicked look at his air adviser.

Sterling ignored the remark. "It must be one of the few places that is not being constantly hit by our air forces. It would be a good place to train and prepare agents and there is an airfield, as we have seen, called Fuhlsbuttel, nearby."

Bradley clicked his fingers impatiently. "Let's see what kind of recon pictures we've got of this Reinbek. They might tell us something."

Minutes later, two photo transparencies were hanging in front of the light screen with Bradley peering at them through a lens, while the others crowded behind him, appearing to be impatient to find out what lay in Reinbek.

The air adviser who had been given a two minute briefing while he was waiting for the photos said, as if he had known the village for years. "About a thousand people, basically strung out along this road here, which leads to the next town, Bergedorf. There is a small stream here – the Bille. And here's the most important building in the place – the castle. You can see it quite clearly."

Bradley, peering through his lens, asked: "What's this line of huts – I guess they are huts?"

"There's a factory, further down the road – there," the air adviser answered a little uneasily. "We guess that they may house the workers for that factory."

"Hm," Bradley was thoughtful. "Nothing that looks like a military camp to me." He made up his mind. He turned to the air adviser. "I want a recon made of that place this very day."

"Wilco, sir," the air adviser responded promptly. "I'll get on to it right away." He marched out, leaving the little conference standing there in indecision.

Finally Bradley broke the silence with: "Let's assume then that the HQ of this werewolf outfit is up there in the north somewhere. It will take several weeks for our ground forces to overrun the place, especially," he grinned maliciously, "as

63

the Allied troops scheduled to take that area are commanded by Monty. And we all know how slowly that Limey fart moves."

There was a murmur of agreement among the staff officers, and Sterling told himself that these top generals acted like oversensitive prima donnas. Ever since Montgomery had been given command of three of Bradley's armies during the fighting of the previous winter, because the latter seemed to have lost control of them, Bradley had hated the little English general with a passion. Indeed Sterling sometimes thought that Bradley hated Montgomery, his ally, more than he hated his German enemies.

"So, gentlemen, this operation has got to be airborne." He turned to his chief of staff. "What have we got?"

The Chief-of-Staff cleared his throat carefully and said: "To be frank, sir – nothing."

"What do you mean?" Bradley snapped in irritation. "Nothing! Surely the US Army has one available parachute battalion?"

"I'm afraid not, sir. The 82nd and 101st Airborne Divisions are fully engaged fighting on the Rhine and the US 17th and British 6th Airborne Divisions are involved in heavy fighting on the other side of the river under Montgomery's command."

Bradley absorbed the information for a moment and then said: "What about the two Ranger battalions in this theatre? Some of those men have been airborne trained."

"No can do, sir," the Chief-of-Staff replied. "They took a beating last winter. They're only fifty per cent effective. Most of them are made up of replacements straight from the States."

"Christ on a crutch," the bespectacled General with his lantern jaw cursed in frustration. "Surely there are must be some troops somewhere who can carry out an op of this nature!."

"Well, there is, sir," the Chief-of-Staff said cautiously, looking intently at Bradley's ugly face, as if he was worried how the General might take his words.

"Go on," Bradley prompted impatiently.

"It's the First Independent SAS Troop."

"Never heard of them. What army of mine are they with?"

"None, sir. They are British – The British special forces. You know, the people who carried out the Bruneval raid and all those raids in the desert under Montgomery."

"Limeys." Bradley shook his head emphatically. "I'm not having Limeys carry out this job. It's got to be American, especially as, if it's successful, it will hit the headlines."

"The troop's second-in-command, a Captain Al Gorey, is an American, sir. I met him once – tough hombre. Volunteered for the British Army in 1940 before we entered the war. Been right through the thick of it by all accounts."

Again Bradley shook his head. "Still the rest are limeys, no, you've got to think of something else."

"There *is* nothing else, sir," the Chief-of-Staff said a little hopelessly.

"I'd volunteer to go with them, sir. That would make me – *officially* the most senior officer. In theory, that would mean an American would be in command, at least as far as the newspapers were concerned."

Bradley looked at him as if he were seeing him for the very first time. "You've never jumped out of a plane in your life, Sterling. You're too old to learn to parachute."

"It would be only the one time, sir," Sterling persisted.

A staff officer laughed and said softly: "And probably the last time as well."

Bradley remained adamant. "There's got to be – "

– "Sir," an urgent voice interrupted the Army Group Commander. "Can I speak to the General, sir. It's very important."

Bradley frowned at being interrupted and said: "All right then, but make it snappy."

The aide leaned forward and whispered something in Bradley's ear. Sterling guessed by the change in the General's expression that it was grave news.

It was. When the aide was finished, Bradley straightened up and said: "Gentlemen, something serious has happened."

They tensed.

"An hour ago," Bradley went on, "an unidentified fighter plane with English colours tried to shoot down General Patton's light plane. Fortunately he has escaped injury. But it looks to me, gentlemen, as if this is the work of these goddam werewolves again." He turned to Colonel Sterling. "Are you prepared to take the risk of jumping with these limey SAS fellahs?"

"Yessir."

"Excellent. Then we'll use them. The operation is on, even if it is to be executed by that damned Monty's limeys . . ."

TWO

To the attack

"New resistance will spring up behind their backs time and time again . . . and like werewolves, brave as death, volunteers will strike the enemy."

Himmler, 1944.

ONE

"Right marker . . . git on parade!" Sergeant Jenkin's breath fogged on the cold morning air, as he barked the commands, his chest heaving at the effort.

Smartly, swinging his arms as if he were back on some UK parade ground, the soldier in maroon-coloured beret marched to the centre of the village square. He stamped down his right foot and stood rigidly to attention.

Sergeant Jenkins nodded his cropped head in approval and then barked. "Troop – troop will get on parade."

The thirty-odd, tough-looking soldiers in the smart khaki, worn but well pressed, swinging their arms as if they were still recruits, which they certainly weren't, marched towards the marker. They stamped to attention and stood there, their bodies rigid.

Sergeant Jenkins pivoted on his heel and bellowed so loud that the rooks nesting in the skeletal trees around the village square, rose in hoarse protest. "Parade – all present and correct, *sir!*" He swung the two waiting officers a tremendous salute.

Major Rory O'Rourke, CO of the 1st Independent SAS Troop, said in that tough Belfast working class accent of his: "All right, Yank, let's get on do 'em now."

"Yank," Captain Al Gorey, who towered above the little Major, grinned. "Yessir, let's do 'em."

Smartly, stick under his right arm, striding into the square like the pre-war NCO in the Ulster Rifles in which he had been, O'Rourke's eyes took in everything: the three ranks of immaculate soldiers, most of them wearing ribbons for bravery, the village square with the frightened housewives and kids peering from behind the kitchen curtains, and the already rusting Tiger tank which they had knocked out two weeks before which had lurched to a crazy stop behind the village church.

O'Rourke stamped his foot down hard, sparks flying off the cobbles at his feet. His gimlet eyes shot to left and right. He smiled slightly at what he saw. The troop was perfect. He opened his mouth, his bantam chest swelling like that of a pigeon. "Parade . . . parade will stand at ease . . . *STAND EASY!*"

The men's feet stamped out, one arm behind their hacks. Someone farted. But it wasn't "dumb insolence." The man obviously needed to fart.

"All right lads, I'm going to make it short – and sweet," O'Rourke snapped. The last of you is gonna get their wings for three operational jumps behind enemy lines." He raised his voice. "Brown and Bookhalter, three paces forward – march!"

The two troopers clicked smartly to attention and marched forward, rigidly at attention.

O'Rourke peered at them. Bookhalter was the only man in the troop who wore glasses, but he was a daring young man, who already bore two golden wound stripes on his sleeve. Brown was taller, blond and very handsome. He was the troop's casanova. The others chortled: "Hide yer brooms ladies, Brown's here! He'll screw anything with hair on."

"At ease," O'Rourke ordered and then took the two pairs of coveted wings from his pocket. "There's not one of us in this troop," he said, "who hasn't been decorated for bravery at one stage of this bloody business. But to my way of thinking, men, this is the highest decoration of all. The wings for three operational jumps behind enemy lines!" He pinned the blue-and-white wings on Bookhalter's thin chest and shook his hand and then did the same to Brown, who was grinning all over his handsome face.

"Take that look off yer ugly mug," O'Rourke said without animosity.

70

"I'm just thinking of the piss-up to come, sir," Brown replied evenly.

"I know what you're thinking about, you handsome rogue-*beaver*! That's all you ever think of."

"No sir, I'm – "

The rest of Brown's words were drowned by the roar of motorbike hurtling down the village street, scattering the chickens pecking for seed in the gutters and setting off the peasants' dogs barking furiously, as if their very lives depended upon it.

Startled, O'Rourke swung round.

It was a dispatch rider, heavy leather bag slung across his chest, a sten gun over his shoulder. His bike splattered in mud, as he skidded to a stop. He propped up his bike and, thrusting up his goggles, strode over to the parade, then seeing O'Rourke stopped and swung the little major a tremendous salute.

O'Rourke returned it and said bluntly, in his usual no-nonsense manner, "What's up?"

"Signal for you, sir," the dispatch rider said and pulled a buff form out of his bag. He handed it, with a pad and pencil, to O'Rourke.

O'Rourke nodded to the tall American, and as his second-in-command bellowed: "Parade – parade dismissed," he signed the receipt form laboriously, tongue between his teeth, head bent to one side. He had left his Belfast council school at the age of 13 and all these years later, writing didn't come easily to him. Then, as he handed the receipt back to the dispatch rider, he shouted over his shoulder: "All – gather on me. It's a signal from the C-in-C."

"The C-in-C," Al Gorey whistled softly through his teeth. "Holy mackerel, what have we done wrong now?"

"We'll soon find out," O'Rourke said, ripping open the buff envelope, and unfolding the signal inside.

Slowly he began to read the message from the Commander-in-Chief, Field Marshal Montgomery. "*Most Urgent. To i/c 1st SAS Reconnaissance Troop. Proceed immediately to HQ 12th Army Group Luxembourg. Rations*

71

for 48 hours will be taken. Acknowledge. Signed de Guingand."

"Hell's teeth," O'Rourke exclaimed, "we're going to the frigging Yanks."

The troop grinned and Al Gorey said: "Back to real people – at last."

O'Rourke spoke hastily to the dispatch rider, "I have acknowledged receipt. Tell 'em we'll be moving off," he glanced at his looted wrist watch, "at precisely zero eleven hundred hours." He lowered his voice, back to being the old sweat other-ranker, which he had been for twenty years before he had been commissioned into the SAS: "What d'yer know, Tosh?"

"Not much, sir," the dispatch rider said, a little uneasy at being addressed this way by a major, with three rows of ribbons on his bantam's chest.

'Don't fuck about, laddie," O'Rourke said without malice. "Spit it out. You blokes at HQ allus know things we poor sods at the front don't know about."

"Well, sir. All I know is that they sent somebody from the Yank HQ by light plane this morning and the Yank was sent straight off to to see the Chief-of-Staff. Bit of a flap, I should say." He lowered his voice, and looked cautiously to left and right. "Freddie de Guigand, that's the Chief-of-Staff –

– "I know that. Get on with it."

"Well, sir, he had someone call Maastricht aerodrome, where the brass hats keep their aeroplanes, and a friend of mine who works in the office overheard them asking if there was a Dakota available. Most of the stuff we've got went for the Rhine drop . . ." He faltered to stop, for he saw that the fierce-looking little officer wasn't listening any more. I'll be off then, sir." He saluted once more and mounted his bike. Moments later he was roaring away, leaving O'Rourke still shrouded in thought. Finally he turned and said to the waiting, expectant troopers: "It looks, lads, if we've got a job coming our way. It can't be with the Brigade," he meant the SAS Brigade to which the troop was attached, "They're already over the Rhine with the British Second Army. So it's

72

something the Yanks have dreamed up for us – and you know what balls of things the Yanks allus make. What do they call it, Captain Gorey?"

The tall American smiled. "*Snafu*, sir," he replied. "Situation normal – all fucked up."

The men smiled, too, and O'Rourke, suddenly very businesslike, snapped. "All right, lads, let's not stand around like the proverbial spare penis at a wedding. Throw yer duds together. We've got a long haul and a long day in front of us."

Thirty minutes later they were on their way south-west: ten heavily laden jeeps, each one armed with a forward-pointing Vickers and twin Brownings at the rear mounted on a tripod. They were totally self-contained as always, towing their food, ammunition, petrol behind them in little trailers. As O'Rourke always maintained: "and what we ain't got, we can always loot. God looks after him, who looks after hissen."

Up in his tiny bedroom under the attic, the one-legged peasant, with the battle-scarred face, who had been watching them all week ever since they had arrived in this border village, retrieved his morse key from its hiding place under the thatch of the cottage and began working the key furiously, a look of confident malice on his ugly face . . .

"I suggest, Rory," Al Gorey had said before they had left, "we get out of Germany the quickest way possible. I think it would be safer for us to travel through Belgium and then on to Luxembourg, rather that go the length of the frontier down to Trier on the German side. There's been talk of small convoys being attacked on the back roads by fanatical teams of Hitler Youth thugs."

"Kids in short pants," Rory O'Rourke had sneered. "I'd like to see them tackle that little lot," he had pointed to his troopers, busy packing their jeeps. "They'd get more than they'd bargained for."

All the same, he had taken his second-in-command's advice. At twelve that morning, they crossed the Belgian frontier at the little hamlet of Schoenberg and began to drive along the frontier road to the shattered town of St Vith. Everywhere there was ample evidence of the great battle which had been fought in that area when Hitler had launched his last great offensive in the West the previous December.

Everywhere there were shattered, rusting tanks, broken or abandoned artillery pieces, wrecked trucks and jeeps, tyreless, even wheel-less, for obviously the locals had stolen them for their own carts.

The great battle had obviously left an impression on the local peasants, too. They were nominally Belgian, but they spoke German as their native language and most of them had been born German. They stared at the passing jeeps with resentment in their eyes, often spitting in contempt, and once a farmer driving a cart, pulled by a lumbering ox, refused to get out of the way. They had been forced to crawl behind him for ten minutes before he finally turned off, and when he did he turned and shook his fist at them.

"I don't think they particularly like us liberators," Al Gorey remarked with a grin as they started to speed up again.

Next to him in the lead jeep, O'Rourke grumbled, "Frigging liberation! I don't think they wanted us in the first place anyhow. Nor the frogs. They were sniping at us for a month after we hit the beaches. Only lot that seems to be glad we're here is the Jerries. Funny, ain't it."

Al Gorey nodded and concentrated on driving slowly over a particularly large shell hole in the road which had been filled in but not too well. Down below, he could see the battered steeple of the church at St Vith, surrounded by what seemed to be a sea of brick rubble. "Well," he said after he had managed the shell crater, "We seem to have *liberated* the hell out of St Vith – that's for sure!"

"Look around for some sign of Yankee life, Al," O'Rourke ordered. "If they're there and they've got a cookhouse, we might be able to scrounge a meal. It'll make a change from compo rations."

"Wilco," the other officer said and turned right down what was left of the *Hauptstrasse*, following the telephone wires

74

loosely strung along a line of poles, hoping the wires would lead to an American camp.

They did. It was a small tented and hutted encampment in an open field at the far edge of the shattered Belgian town. Outside a sign proclaimed – "*531st US Signal Corps Co- 'the Fighting Linesmen'*". But there was nothing bold about the half dozen pale-faced soldier, all heavily armed as if they were in front line, and wearing helmets, who came rushing out to meet them with, "*Hi, glad to see you fellas . . . Welcome. You're the first Allied soldiers we've seen in a week . . . Great!*"

O'Rourke looked at his second-in-command. His look said: "What's wrong with these blokes? They look as if they're right up the line, instead of being on a cushy number two hundred miles behing it."

It didn't take long to find out what was troubling these signals specialists, twenty of them, running this repeater radio station far away from the bulk of the US Army. As the cook fed them fried eggs, followed by waffles dripping with syrup, the signallers, who were commanded by a staff sergeant, poured out their tales of woe. "Their lines were always being deliberately cut . . . they daren't go out at night in case they were beaten up by the locals . . . who were all Krauts . . . Twice the supply truck coming up from Liege had been shot at . . . and they knew all the locals were armed, because during the battles of the previous December, arms had been abandoned everywhere in the surrounding forests . . . even the burgomaster, who had been appointed by Allied Military Government, never dare come out to see them . . . his life had been threatened if he did . . .

It was the staff sergeant, a nervous, bespectacled little man, who was hung with combat knives, grenades and two pistols, who summed up all their fears. "It's those Kraut werewolves," he said nervously, looking to left and right as he did so, "They run St Vith. They're after our hides and any other Allied soldier they can catch out on his lonesome. So take my word for it, fellas, if you don't

75

want to stop the night – and we wish you would, keep a weather eye peeled in those forest up there on the way to Lux, and get well under cover by nightfall. *They're everywhere . . .*"

TWO

"For three months this had been the ghost front where nothing ever happened," Al Gorey was saying as they bowled along the ridge road into Luxembourg, leaving Belgium behind then. "The Kraut front was over there," he pointed to the hills to their left, "on those heights, and the Americans were up here on the ridge, mostly in the villages." He grinned. "We Yanks do like our home comforts."

O'Rourke shared his grin, staring at the same time at the rugged scenery all around. It must have been hell, he told himself, fighting up here in the coldest winter in Europe in living memory.

"Yeah," Al Gorey went on, "the front last December was so thinly held that the Krauts were able to sneak whole battalions across the river down there and through the American positions before the defenders knew what had hit them – " He stopped abruptly. "What's that?" he said sharply.

"What's what?"

"Up there, Roy. It looks like some sort of barrier, perhaps a broken down truck." Instinctively he changed down and started to slow down the lead jeep, as Rory O'Rourke leaned forward and peered at the obstacle in the growing gloom.

"It looks like an American truck," he said. "Seems as if it has skidded and blocked the road." Abruptly he felt that old cold finger of fear trace its way slowly down the small of his back; he felt the way the cropped hairs at the nape of his neck stood erect. He knew what that meant. There was trouble ahead. His instincts had kept him alive during five years of total war; he always relied on them. "There's something fishy going on," he snapped." There's no ice on the road, so why should that vehicle skid like that . . . And where's the driver and his mate – "

Crump! Scarlet flame stabbed the gloom. What looked like a vase came hurtling towards the lead jeep, trailing fiery sparks behind it. "*Panzerfaust!*"* O'Rourke yelled urgently.

Al Gorey hit the brakes hard. The jeep shuddered to a stop. Behind them the others did the same, as the rocket projectile slammed into the opposite side of the road, only yards away, and exploded in a blinding flash of light which sent the jeep reeling from side to side as if buffeted by a sudden tempest.

"Bale out!" O'Rourke yelled above the roar.

His SAS troopers needed no further orders. They were the veterans. They vaulted out of their jeeps, already clicking off the safety catches of their tommy guns, doubling bent low for the drainage ditch to their left, the side from which the rocket had been fired.

Panting a little with the effort, O'Rourke stared in the direction from which the rocket had come. He could see no movement, but he knew whoever had fired it had to be within fifty or sixty yards away: that was about the maximum range for the *Panzerfaust*.

"Ten o'clock," Al Gorey snapped urgently. "That haystack."

"Christ, yes. There are no haystacks in March. He's in there."

Swiftly, the tall lean American raised his tommy gun and prepared to fire.

O'Rourke knocked it down just in time. "No, we want him alive," he snapped. "We want to know why somebody's taking potshots at us in a friendly country, nearly two hundred miles behind the fighting front." He raised his hand and waved to Sergeant Jenkins who was at the far end of the ditch.

* A one-shot, armour-piercing rocket projectile. *Transl.*

Jenkins stuck up his big thumb. He knew what to do. O'Rourke turned to the American. "Come on, Al," he ordered, "We'll go in from both flanks. And keep yer eyes peeled."

Gorey grinned. "Like the proverbial can of skinned tomatoes."

Without another word, O'Rourke clambered out of the ditch, thankful for the growing darkness, and began to crawl rapidly on his belly towards the haystack. Now, as he came closer, he could see it wasn't really a haystack, but just some straw that had been spread over the hay-frames which they used in this area to dry the grass. Whoever had shot at them was now crouched behind it.

They got closer, with Jenkins to their left, gradually working his way to the rear of the haystack. O'Rourke nodded his approval. He made his decision. He slung his tommy gun and hissed: "Al, cover me. I'm going in after him."

"Don't take any chances, Rory. You know those Kraut fanatics."

"Never fear, Al. I'm aiming to collect my army pension one of these days."

He set off, crawling more rapidly now, knowing that the sooner he came level with the haystack, the better. As he crawled, his hand felt for the commando knife tucked down the side of his boot. Swiftly he inserted his fingers in the brass knuckles which formed its hilt. He'd use that on the bugger if he had to.

To the front, from his position behind the haystack, Jenkins raised one arm. O'Rourke nodded. That meant there was only one man hiding behind the straw. Steathily he rose to his feet. Jenkins put his tommy gun to his shoulder to give covering fire if necessary. O' Rourke drew a deep breath and then dived forward. With a crash he went straight through the hay-frame, splintering and breaking the wood and landed on something which was decidedly soft – *and feminine . . .*

Fifty miles away at the 12th Army Group HQ in the hotel opposite Luxembourg City's railway station, Goldstein and

Sterling waited impatiently as the technician gave a final drying to the aerial photos. In the corner the pilot, sweating and drained, balanced on the edge of the table, drinking steaming black coffee from a canteen cup and idly picking at bacon and eggs with a fork. He had just flown six hundred miles in his Mustang over German territory. He had gone in at treetop height to fool German radar and had only risen higher when he was beyond the flak guns of the Rhine plain.

Once he had been buzzed by one of the new Me 262 jet planes, but somehow he had dodged the German, which was at least a hundred miles an hour faster than his Mustang, and had flown northwards to the area of Hamburg. Here again he had come down to treetop height to try to confuse the circle of 88mm anti-aircraft guns circling the great port. He had managed it and then flown due east to the little village of Reinbek, coming in with the sun behind him, so that everything in front of him was thrown into stark relief, the best possible situation for clear, sharp aerial photos. Now, although he ached all over and longed to hit the sack, he waited there in case the brass wanted to throw any questions at him. It was "S.O.P" – standard operating procedure.

"Okay, gentleman," the photo interpretation specialist announced, "they're dry enough now." He offered each of the two officers a lens and then held the first photo up to the light.

They peered at it. It showed a factory spread out over several acres to the rear, all the buildings painted green and surrounded by trees, presumably for camouflage purposes. It seemed the factory was of some importance because it was surrounded by triple fences of barbed wire and at the gate there were the striped wooden boxes used by German sentries. "Probably some kind of shadow factory set up for producing armaments for the *Wehrmacht*," the specialist said. "We've got no record of it in our books."

He now turned to the second photograph, which showed the huts, only vaguely outlined in the first photo, much more clearly. The pilot had obviously come in at an angle for the huts were not level in the picture. But they were clear enough, depicting little wooden shacks, with smoke curling from stone chimneys, with here and there tiny figures frozen in the instant that the photo had been taken, staring upwards at the plane.

The specialist squinted through his lens and said, "Well, you can see they're all young – both sexes – therefore of military service age. Oh, hello, bottom right of photo, gentleman. Man in uniform. Black. Uniform – peacetime SS."

"Yeah, I remember that guy," the weary pilot butted in, putting down his forkful of cold egg. "Crazy nut pulled out his revolver and started firing it at me when I came in for the last run. As if he could knock a P-5I out of the sky with a peashooter like that!" His face contorted scornfully.

For a few moments Sterling and Goldstein concentrated on the lone figure. "Officer, judging by the lapels on his greatcoat," Sterling ventured.

"Yeah," the specialist agreed. "Look at the boots. Your ordinary Kraut don't wear boots like that. Officers' stuff," he said the last words with an air of resentment.

Goldstein smiled to himself. Typical enlisted man's beef, he thought. Officers had always had it better. Caviare for the officers, they always maintained and "shit on shingle", i.e. minced beef on toast, for the enlisted men.

"So we've got this so far," Sterling interrupted his thoughts. "Unknown factory, producing nothing we know about and nothing of its production revealed by the photos. Nearby, fifty-odd wooden shacks, lived in presumably by those men and women of military service age – and one lone officer of the *Allgemeine SS*.* Interesting, a little mysterious, but it still doesn't tell us that this is the Werewolf HQ." He bit his bottom lip in exasperation.

They studied the third photograph. The pilot had done a splendid job. It had been his last sortie and he had come down, or so it seemed, almost to ground level. Now they

---

* General SS, the general SS, used in adminstration, running of the concentration camps etc. *Transl.*

could see the SS officer with his pistol raised in the air and they imagined they could detect the look of outrage on his face. They saw, too, the young men and women scattering and running for cover, believing that the enemy plane was coming down to machine gun them. To Goldstein the moment looked as dramatic and effective as a scene from any of the current Hollywood war movies, perhaps even more so. Suddenly he gasped.

"What is it, Candidate?" Sterling asked sharply and the pilot looked at the Colonel, wondering why he used that odd word to address his side-kick.

"Look at Hut Ten, sir," Goldstein replied, voice full of excitement.

Sterling peered through his lens hard. "I can't see anything."

"Just to the left of the door, sir," Goldstein urged. "I'm sure I'm not mistaken."

"*Mistaken* about *what*?" Sterling snapped in sudden annoyance.

"It's their sign, painted on the wood. It's faint. But I'm sure of it, sir. Take a closer look."

Sterling tried harder. Then he whistled softly and the look of annoyance left his face as quickly as it had come. He put the lens down and said slowly and thoughtfully." So we've got a collection of a couple of hundred young men and women who by rights, when Germany is scraping the barrel for manpower – they're even calling up sixty-year-olds – should be in the forces. We have an SS officer out there in the middle of the back of the beyond. Then we have this mysterious factory. From a quick glance I couldn't see any production. No smoke coming out of the chimneys.

"But there's something going on there, sir," the specialist interjected. "If you look at the first photograph – here – you can see some irregular shadows close to that line of buildings to the right of the picture."

Sterling nodded.

"Well, I've done some quick length evaluations, the

relationship of the lengths of the individual shadows to that of the buildings themselves.

"Go on," Sterling urged.

"Well, sir, the shape is the top canvas cover of the Kraut Army type truck. And there are fifty of them. So, if the factory ain't producing anything, what are the trucks there for?" He looked at Sterling, his face expressing a sense of achievement and self-pride.

"Good work," Sterling said enthusiastically. "Exactly." He turned to the weary pilot. "Lieutenant, do you think that when you've had a good sleep, you'd like to tackle the same job once more at dawn tomorrow. I'd like to see more of that mysterious factory?"

"O, my aching back!" the pilot groaned. "Do you know the nervous strain it takes to fly a P-5I like that for six hundred miles, Colonel, sir?" Then he gave a tired smile." Sure, Colonel. But what about three days to gay Paree as a reward? I've not been in Pig Alley" – he meant Place Pigalle – "for months now. I'd sure like to grab me some of that Frog poontang again!"

"Get me those photos, son," Sterling said, "and you can have all the French tail you can manage."

Goldstein shook his head in mock despair. "The Army has corrupted you, sir," he intoned. "What would they say at College Park if they learned that the respected former Professor of Germanic Studies was now acting as an amateur procurer?"

Sterling opened his mouth to reply, but was beaten to it by a burly MP sergeant in a white helmet leaning his head above the door hatch and crying as if he was on the parade ground: "Some limeys here to see the colonel, sir. And they've got a Kraut prisoner with them. Female, sir!"

THREE

"And this time, there'll be no slip-ups, Candidate," Sterling ordered. "Have the women strip her and put her in OD fatigues. After the examination for the L-pill, see that she is handcuffed. I know it sounds cruel, but it's got to be done. Besides if she's inclined to suicide like the other one was, we're helping to save her life."

"Wilco," Goldstein answered and sped away, leaving Sterling to look again at the two SAS officers in their camouflaged smocks, with maroon berets tucked tightly down over their foreheads.

Sterling liked what he saw. They looked tough but not in a swaggering, boastful kind of a way. Theirs was a confident, contained toughness which was reflected in the manner they held themselves, the way they spoke. The Englishman, small, red-faced and barrel-chested, looked every inch Regular Army, but not in that lordly, arrogant manner that upper class English officers affected – "like Christ walking over the water," as Goldstein had quipped more than once. The other, the American, was Harvard right down to his class ring. But he was a Harvard man who had obviously been through the kind of experiences few from that college ever did undergo. There was steely purpose in his quiet, light-blue eyes.

Swiftly he explained the problem, how at highest level it had been decided to take out the Werewolves Headquarters once it had been found, though he was growing ever more sure that the HQ was located outside Hamburg at the small village of Reinbek.

"That's why we are here, I suppose?" Rourke said.

"Yes, you are a very experienced parachute unit, I have

been told, and besides," he added with a twinkle in his eyes, "you're the only one available. Every other is tied up in combat."

O'Rourke and Gorey smiled. The latter said; "Trust us to be there when the shit hits the fan, if you'll excuse my French, sir?"

"I will," Sterling said and took the large scale map out of a folder. "I've had this specially made for you, gentlemen. It is of Reinbek and area. I'd like you to study it and suggest a quick plan. I know nothing of military matters, so I'm leaving it all in your capable hands. Of course, I shall be in nomimal command if the operation comes off."

O'Rourke's grin vanished. His eyes narrowed. "Am I to understand, sir," he said slowly and deliberately, "that you are coming along with us?"

"Yes, that is the plan. General Bradley has ordered it that way."

"But sir," Al Gorey protested, "you don't have the US parachute badge – and besides," he hesitated a moment, "you are rather old."

Sterling grinned. "I know – and I feel it more times than I'd like to admit. Listen, I've taken professional advice. And do you know from whom?"

"No."

General Ridgway, commander of the 18th US Airborne Corps. He's a man in his mid-forties now, just about my age. I asked him whether a non-jumper should jump without training. He told me that he'd jumped *into combat* in Normandy with no more than a half-hour's instruction in what position to adopt before hitting the ground and how to use the shroud lines, etc, etc. As he put it, succinctly, you can as easily kill yourself on your thousandth jump as you can on your first."

O'Rourke shrugged, unconvinced, but Al Gorey said: "I suppose you're right, sir."

"Kay, let's get on with it. So I'm just coming along as intelligence adviser and to see that things are wound up properly. You, Major O'Rourke, are in charge of the military side of it. I defer to your commands on all things military. Understood?"

"Understood, Colonel."

Sterling pointed to the map. "As of now, and if we are right, which I think we are, that's going to be your objective – that factory there and those huts just outside the perimeter wire of the factory. Now, it's in your hands."

O'Rourke nodded to Al Gorey. He started to read the map, while O'Rourke closed his eyes and listened, memorizing what his second-in-command was saying, trying to imprint the details on his mind's eye. "The area we are concerned with," the American said slowly, staring intently at the map, "lies to the west of the village which itself lies in the valley of the River Bille below."

O'Rourke nodded, eyes still closed.

"To the south, the area is bordered by a main road leading to Hamburg. To the east, by another smaller road leading to a village some three miles away called Glinde. To the west there is a large wood, called the – er – " he hesitated about the pronunciation, "*der Sachsenwald*"

"The Saxons" Wood," Sterling translated.

Al Gorey didn't seem to hear. "Along both roads there is a single straggle of houses which end altogether where there are fields to the north of the factory. In essence then, we have an area of some five square miles, with few civilian houses save those huts and the factory. All this backed by a thick wood."

O'Rourke opened his eyes. "Those fields to the north. How big do you think they are."

Hastily, Al Gorey measured the scale with his thumbnail. "About a good square mile, I'd say, offhand."

"Any anti-glider obstacles?"

"What are they?" Sterling asked sharply.

"Usually twenty foot high poles dotted all over a potential DZ – dropping zone, to you – linked together with thick hawser. They'd tear the wings off any glider coming into land. Wouldn't worry a parachutist naturally, but where there's anti-glider defences there are also anti-personnel

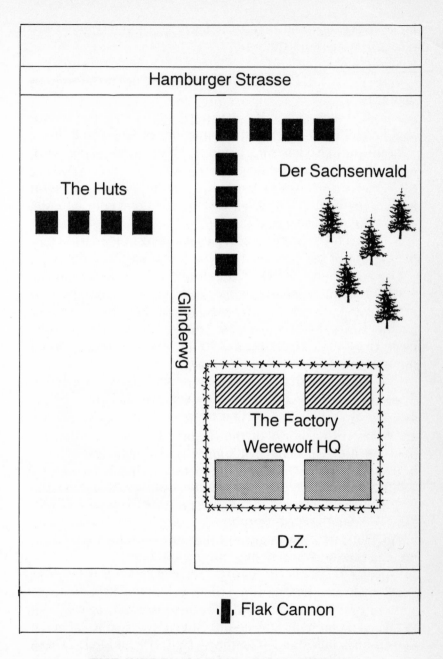

THE WEREWOLF HEADQUARTERS,
REINBEK, GERMANY, MARCH, 1945.

mines planted – and *they* would worry a parachutist. Give him a nasty pain in the ass."

"I see," Sterling said.

"No, Rory," Al Gorey continued, "there are no anti-glider defences."

"Good." He opened his eyes now and without hesitation, as if he had been looking at the map all the time, he pointed a forefinger like a hairy pork sausage at the fields to the north of the factory. "That'd be the DZ then."

"Roger," the American said. "Plenty of space, unobserved, with a direct road leading to the plant and the shacks. At the usual SAS Trot – "

– "SAS Trot?" Sterling queried, realizing that he was completely out of his depth with these tough airborne types.

Gorey smiled. "Walk a hundred yards, run a hundred yards, you can cover five miles an hour with thirty pounds of combat kit, weapon etc. etc." He addressed O'Rourke again. "Rory, if we didn't bump into any opposition we could cover the distance from the DZ to the objective in ten-fifteen minutes – easy."

O'Rourke nodded. "Yes, that would be no problem. There is one little problem, Colonel, which I don't think can be solved so easily as that of the time."

"What's that?"

"*How are we going to get back?*" O'Rourke said bluntly.

Colonel Sterling tugged his long nose, as he always did when he found himself in difficulties. "Yes," he said slowly, "that is something of a problem, I agree." He stared down at his map, as if he might find the answer to the problem, but the map was not giving out any solutions.

"I don't think the ground troops can link up with us as they've always done before when we've had to fight these sorts of ops," Al Gorey said. "They're too far away."

"We can't melt into the countryside as we used to do in the Desert back in '41 and '42 either," O'Rourke added. "There are too many villages and towns about. We might make it for a day or two, but once the Jerries started a manhunt, relying on a friendly population as they would, we wouldn't last long."

"Yes, I take your point," Colonel Sterling said slowly. "But let's put off the problem of the return journey until we find out if this place Reinbek is your objective. We'll concentrate on it then. Agreed?"

"Agreed," O'Rourke said reluctantly. "But let me say this, sir, right from the outset. I'm not going to risk my lads unnecessarily. They're a bloody fine lot. They're prepared to take risks, just like I am. But we want a fair chance of getting out again in one piece. Is that understood, sir?" He looked squarely at Colonel Sterling, his voice controlled, calm, but the American could see the determination and resolution beneath his passive expression.

"I understand that fully, Major O'Rourke," he answered. "Let's shake hands on it. Now come along to the officers' club. I'll buy you a drink and we'll see what Goldstein has found out from the girl."

The officers' club on the ground floor of the Hotel Alpha was packed, although it was only early afternoon. White jacketed black servants squeezed their way through the noisy, elegantly uniformed throng bearing silver trays heavy with drinks. At the bar staff officers were clicking their fingers for attention and crying: "Gimme a bourbon on the rocks . . . *two* gimlets I said, bartender, *two*." And everywhere there were women, elegant, well-made up, wearing clothes which obviously hadn't originated in this dowdy provincial capital.

Sipping his whisky carefully, as they sat at a table at the back of the overheated, smoke-filled club, O'Rourke said: "It must be bloody awful fighting the war like the staff. Nothing but one bleeding hardship after another. Look over there – they're not even allowed to light their own fags." He indicated a brigadier general who had summoned one of the sweating black waiters to light his cigarette.

Goldstein and Gorey grinned and Colonel Sterling smiled and said: "Yes, the velvet-lined foxhole we call it, with hot water and maid service."

Al Gorey watched as a well-built blonde in a low-cut gown bent down over her drink to reveal breasts like ripe melons. He added: "Plus a little hot momma stuff on the side." His grin broadened.

"Well, you must remember all the top brass were mere majors and colonels at the beginning of the war, getting ready for a slippered retirement somewhere where it was cheap and warm. Hell, in 1939 there was only one limousine in the whole of the US Army and that was reserved for the Chief-of-Staff." Suddenly, up comes the war and they're all generals overnight, commanding huge bodies of draftees. I guess all that sudden power went to a lot of their heads. Now then, let's change the subject. Candidate what did you find out?"

"Well, she was very co-operative," Goldstein began. "I told her she had fired on an allied vehicle and that meant she could be shot out of hand. That frightened the pants off her and she started to sing like a canary. Not that she knew much. She's basically an 18-year old kid who obeyed orders because she's always obeyed orders since she was in rompers. Anyway, her cell-leader – that's what she called the guy – told her she was to cross into Luxembourg on account of an Allied jeep convoy he had been informed was on its way. She was to knock out the last vehicle with the panzerfaust and find out what she could about the convoy – she already knew you were airborne," he added, looking at O'Rourke.

The latter whistled softly. "The bastards seem to have a pretty good organization if they can do that kind of thing," he said. "But why keep tabs on us because we're airborne?"

"Perhaps because they're suspect we're on to them and will try to use airborne troops to put them out of business?" Goldstein suggested.

"Could be," Sterling agreed.

"At all events, she panicked and hit the wrong vehicle. Hence she's here. So what could she tell me else?" Goldstein answered his own question. "That after training last month she was smuggled across the Rhine and assigned to a werewolf cell operating from Bollendorf – that's on the other side of the border in Germany. The cell has six members, all with aliases and living at different addresses, commanded by an older man called 'Egon'. Not much. But there's one interesting thing she had to tell me." Goldstein grinned impishly.

"What's that?" Sterling asked.

Goldstein broadened even more. "That she was trained at – you guess where?"

"*Reinbek*?" They cried as one.

He nodded simply. "Yeah, Reinbek."

FOUR

"Georgie," General Bradley said patiently, "you're getting almost pathological about the British. You know I'm no friend of one particular Englishman, Field Marshal Bernard Montgomery," he spelled out the rank and name bitterly.

"That little fart," General George S. Patton snarled contemptuously, showing his dingy, sawn-off teeth. "Why can't our American boys carry out this mission? They'd go through the Krauts like shit through a goose."

"There are simply not the paratroops available," Bradley said in his slow soothing manner, knowing the tall, immaculate General facing him across the desk, wearing the shining helmet with its three outsize gold stars and which Bradley often thought Patton slept in, had a very short fuse indeed. "So we've got to use the English."

"I could get you a bunch of my GI's from Third Army together who'd volunteer to jump – without training. That's the way my boys are." He slapped the side of his highly polished riding boot with his swagger stick angrily. "Hell, Brad, you're handing Monty all the glory if you let his men carry out this mission."

Quickly Bradley explained that an American, Colonel Sterling, would be nominally in charge and as 12th Army Group controlled any press releases that would be issued after the mission, the emphasis would be on an American-led operation.

Slightly mollified, Patton said; "All right then, I can understand that. I can understand, too, Brad, that we need to put an end to this outfit pretty damned quickly. I mean, that incident the other day with the plane trying to shoot me down has got my staff pissing around like a lot of old women. They've even gotten me sleeping with loaded carbine under my bed, goddammit! And now everywhere I go I ride in a lousy Staghound armoured car. Christ, it's murder!"

Bradley smiled sympathetically. "Yes, I know. My staff have put the wraps on me as well. I have to sleep in a different bedroom every night and have to come in here through the kitchen and not the main entrance. So, all in all, the sooner we deal with these guys, the better it'll be for us."

Patton nodded and shifted his left foot, because Willie, his ugly, striped bull terrier, was trying to go to sleep on his polished boot.

"Remember Georgie," Bradley went on, seeing that Patton was now slightly appeased, "last week, just after you crossed the Rhine at Oppenheim, you suggested to me that you would reinforce your beach-head on the other side with infantry ferried across by light plane."

Patton's narrow face lit up. "I thought it was a brilliant idea until you put the kybosh on it. A whole battalion of infantry carried across in perhaps ten minutes by the artillery spotter planes. I mean, there aren't many commanders who can display boldness like that, Brad."

"No, of course not, Georgie," Bradley reassured the Third Army commander quickly. Privately, he thought Patton had absolutely no modesty whatsoever whenever it came to his role as a general. In Patton's book there never had been a commander like him. "Now then, I've found a pretty sure way of getting these SAS guys in, but getting them out is going to be a problem, I can tell you."

Patton nodded. Obviously he was not very interested in the limeys' problems. "If they're so tough as they are supposed to be, they could fight their way out," he said.

"Come off it, Georgie. Thirty men fighting a whole German army, miles behind the other fellow's lines. Impossible!"

Patton shrugged and looked at his image in the mirror behind Bradley's desk. He tilted his jaw a little upwards, putting on what he called "war face number four" and was pleased by his martial look.

93

"No, George, I've mulled over your own brilliant idea."

"Brilliant idea?"

"Yeah. You know, ferrying troops across the Rhine in artillery spotter planes. Well, that would be one way to take out these SAS fellas. Those spotter planes of yours can land on a dime. They can go virtually anywhere. Fighters are not much good against them. You know how they can weave and turn, out foxing any fighter. The only way to shoot them down is if some doughboy on the ground gets lucky and pots them with his piece."

"Yes, yes," Patton agreed. "I know all that. But what's this got to do with me, Brad?"

"This, Georgie. I'd like to borrow thirty-odd light planes from your Third Army for a couple of days to carry out this mission."

Patton's thin, pale face flushed an angry red. "Impossible, Brad," he snorted and slapped his boot angrily with his swagger stick. "That'd mean I'd lose the spotters for a whole corps of artillery – and who could guarantee that they'd ever come back? Some of them could get knocked out."

"I'll ensure that any plane wrecked or damaged will be replaced, Georgie," Bradley said softly.

Patton swore and clambered to his feet. He strode over to the big map of Germany on the opposite wall. He slapped it with his cane. "Here – my Third Army . . . and here – this place Reinbek. Perhaps a distance of two hundred and fifty miles between the two. Five hundred miles the round-trip. My spotters don't have the range."

Bradley listened attentively and then said; "But they won't be flying from the Third Army zone of operations, Georgie."

"They won't?" Patton was obviously caught off guard.

"No. This morning Big Simp" – he meant General Simpson commanding the US 9th Army, currently fighting out of Montgomery's bridgehead on the Rhine much further north – "told me that he confidently expects to capture the airfield at Munster within the next forty-eight hours – "

– "Big Simp couldn't fight his way out of a paper bag, a

wet one, in forty-eight hours," Patton growled, feeling that Bradley was attempting to work a flanker on him. He didn't know how, but he could sense it.

"Well, Georgie," Bradley continued calmly, as if he hadn't heard Patton's remark, "as soon as Big Simp does capture Munster airfield, I want you to transfer your spotters to it pretty damned quick. The distance there to Hamburg as the crow flies is about two hundred or less miles. That's a round journey of four hundred, just within the spotters' range."

"But I lose my artillery spotters," Patton protested.

Bradley beamed up at him encouragingly. "But don't you see what you'd get out of it, Georgie?" He spread his hands to left and right, palms upturned. *"Patton's Third Army Takes Out Werewolf HQ in Bold Aerial Raid."*

Patton's thin face lit up immediately. "I didn't see it like that, Brad," he exclaimed enthusiastically. "Hot shit, that would be something wouldn't it! That little limey fart Monty would be as sore as hell. You know just how vain the little guy is?"

Yes, Bradley agreed, telling himself that if anyone was vain it was the tall, immaculately dressed general standing before him at that moment.

"All right then, Brad," George S. Patton said, "as soon as Big Simp takes Munster airfield, I'll send up the spotters. I only hope these SAS limeys are as tough as they are cracked up to be. I don't want them to frig up *my* raid."

Bradley said reassuringly: "No, Georgie, we don't want anyone to frig up *your* raid."

But the irony was wasted on Patton, as it always was. "Kay, Brad," he touched his cane casually to his gleaming helmet by way of salute, "watch those SAS guys for me." He tapped the ugly pooch gently in the ribs. "Come on, Willy, your master's got a war to fight. With that he swaggered out of Bradley's office, leaving the latter shaking his head, as if in wonder.

But General George S. Patton need not have feared for O'Rourke's SAS men. They could look after themselves very well. While the officers, together with the two American officers, got down to discussing the planned operation in

95

more detail, Sergeant Jenkins announced that the men were off duty till one minute before midnight, which was curfew time for the military in Luxembourg City. The men were jubilant in that quiet contained way of theirs. They had their pockets full of back pay and most of them had captured Lugers which they knew the Yanks would pay a fortune to acquire, especially the rear echelon clerks and GI office workers who made up most of Luxembourg's military population.

So, in little groups of twos and threes, they sauntered off into the evening to enjoy the pleasures of the old city, hemmed in by the ruined fortifications which had once made the capital one of the most impregnable places in Europe.

There were whores, pimps, black marketeers and drunken soldiers everywhere. *Bal musette* music, all clashing cymbals and squeaky accordions, mixed up with American swing music, came from every cafe. Sex was in the very air they breathed. And there was already a long line of relaxed-looking, if drunken, American GI's standing outside the prophylactic station to receive their treatment after sex. If they didn't, and caught VD, they were liable to a fine or even a prison sentence. Catching VD these days, with the fighting divisions crying out for men, was regarded as a self-inflicted wound.

Sergeant Jenkins wandered the steep cobbled streets of the red light area by himself. He wasn't exactly a loner, but he didn't think it good policy to go out with the other ranks. Besides, he felt himself older and more experienced than the rest, and the events of the last few years of war had made him reserved, quite content with his own company. Once, when he'd been "up the blue", as they had always called the Western Desert, on a mission, he had been captured by the Italians. They had made him dig a hole and had put him into it up to his neck in sand. When he had asked for water during the heat of the day, they had urinated on his head. He had stuck it out and that night he had managed to escape. But it was those sorts of experiences – and he had had many of them – which had made him wary of his fellow men, whatever their nationality.

He circled a crowd of drunken GIs, straight from the front, dressed in captured black German leather jackets, with combat knives stuck down the sides of their combat boots. One of them said something about "frigging limeys". He ignored the remark, avoiding eye contact, not letting them see the look of merciless determination in his hard blue eyes. He knew he could have seen off the lot of them before they'd have known what hit them. But he was out for pleasure, not trouble.

"*Tu viens, cheri?*"

Jenkins turned round. A whore was standing in a doorway to his right. A torch was pressed below the slow bulge of her belly suggestively, the thin blue light illuminating her thin face. She looked like all the other whores he had seen so far in the old city long dyed, shoulder-length hair, shaggy, hip-length rabbit skin jacket over a thin floral dress with no slip underneath. "You wanna jig-jig, GI?" she asked in an American accent with professional concupiscence, her scarlet, thick-lipped mouth opened in fake passion.

"How much?"

"Five dollars American . . . for jump. Ten for the night. French love, the works . . . I suck, GI."

Jenkins worked out what ten dollars was in pounds. She came across and squeezed his penis, a little too hard. Perhaps she was tired and didn't care much. Or perhaps she wanted to get him finished sooner. As always, Sergeant Jenkins considered all the angles.

"I'll pay five dollars," he said. Five dollars were a pound. She was cheap." But not in the doorway. On a bed," he added.

"Okay," she said quickly. Later, he realized she had jumped at it too quickly. But that was later. "Come on, GI I show you good time, fuckee-suckee . . ."

FIVE

Prutzmann waited haughtily, almost as if he was unaware that anyone else was present, as the uniformed flunky removed his greatcoat, adjusted his tunic and then held the mirror in front of the SS general so that he could ensure that he was correctly attired.

Prutzmann nodded coldly and the flunkey bowed, withdrawing backwards as if he was in the presence of royalty. Standing at the wall of the ornate, gilded private salon of Hamburg's *Hotel Vierjahrszeiten* von Witzleben grinned. Prutzmann, he told himself, was a real bourgeois *parvenu*, typical of those middle-range Party leaders who had come to fame and fortune in these last twelve years of Hitler's vaunted "1,000 Year Reich". Why else had Prutzmann ordered the briefing to take place amidst the now somewhat shabby surroundings of what had once, before the war, been Hamburg's leading hotel? Their HQ out in Reinbek would have been much better and more discreet. But, he reasoned, the Prutzmanns of this world wanted to *sehen und gesehen werden**, as the old German formula had it. Later, they would go into the great dining room overlooking the Alster, Hamburg's lake, where the *Prominenz* would nudge each other and say: "That's Prutzmann of the SS – great friend of *Reichsfuhrer* Himmler."

But the tall, lean aristocrat, with his chiselled features and his wooden arm clasped by the other, as if it hurt, kept his thoughts to himself. I was something that he had learned to do since 1933, and more especially since 1944, when his

* To see and to be seen. *Transl.*

98

uncle, Field Marshal von Witzleben, had been strangled to death by chicken wire for being a traitor to the Third Reich. Aloud he said: "*Obergruppenfuhrer*, can we begin? Dinner is to be served at seven, and by some miracle the head chef has conjured up venison ragout with wild mushrooms and cranberry sauce."

"Excellent," *Hauptmann* von Witzleben, "Prutzmann said and then, eyeing the tall aristocrat in his black panzer uniform, heavy with medals for bravery, a little suspiciously, he added; "It will be near the window with a view of the Alster."

"*Selbstverstandlich*, *Obergruppenfuhrer*," von Witzleben snapped, clicking his heels together smartly and giving a small bow, "the head waiter could not but give you the best table in the restaurant. I gave him twenty cigarettes – American – naturally."

Prutzmann looked at von Witzleben, wondering whether that last remark meant that the young, one-armed officer was making fun of him, then he decided he wasn't. Who would dare make fun of *Obergruppenfuhrer* Prutzmann, the man who dare address *Reichsfuhrer* Himmler as "thou", and by his first name "Heinrich". "Well, what is new?"

The assassination of the Burgomaster Oppenhoff in Aachen has been widely reported in the Allied press and radio. Both the American *New York Times* and the *London Times* have reported on the matter. The British BBC has also mentioned it in its news bulletins. They are now beginning to believe the National Redoubt, as they call it, to be defended by the elite of the German nation while our brave werewolves fight back in the underground. "He thought of that rabble of short-panted boy scouts up the road at Reinbek, fanatical as they were, and told himself they would be unable to stop the implacable advance of the Allied war machine.

"*Grossartig*, excellent," Prutzmann snapped. "My friend, the *Reichsfuhrer*, will be highly pleased when I tell him what you have just said."

Von Witzleben smiled to himself. "There he goes again," he thought, dropping names.

"We failed to kill the Ami cowboy General Patton, I'm afraid," von Witzleben continued with his report. "The pilot was too hasty and overexcited. But we are beginning to target General Bradley in Luxembourg City. He is very static and we have plenty of people in the capital. I think we should succeed."

"Very good. Give it priority number one, von Witzleben," Prutzmann said hurriedly, as if he were already wondering if he should not be off into the dining room before all the venison ragout was eaten up. Meat was very scarce these days.

"There is one disturbing thing, though, *Gruppenfuhrer*," von Witzleben said carefully. He enjoyed deflating Prutzmann's overwhelming ego.

"What is that?" the General asked sharphly.

"There have been several overflights at Reinbek in the last forty-eight hours – we assume that they are reconnaissance missions."

Prutzmann nodded. "So?"

"They might be connected with the movement of a small elite Tommy airborne unit." He shrugged. "Perhaps."

"Spit it out then, von Witzleben," Prutzmann said urgently. He could already smell the tantalizing odour of venison and in the dining room the string trio were beginning to scrape their way into a tune by Lehar.

"It's just conjecture, but a unit of the Tommy SAS – they were people who tried to kill Rommel two years ago in the desert and kidnapped General Kreipe on Crete in '43. Very nasty characters, by all accounts, recruited from the country's toughest jails. Twice we have tried to find out why they have been transferred from the British front to Bradley's HQ and failed. But we are making a third attempt."

"Carry on then," Prutzmann snapped, "though I think you are making a mountain out of a molehill. We have kept HQ very secret and I think we are too far behind the front for a parachute attack on the HQ, if that is what you are thinking of. *Guten Abend, Herr von Witzleben*."

The one-armed panzer soldier raised his right arm. "*Heil Hitler*", he barked as if he were back on the parade ground.

100

Prutzmann flipped up his arm weakly and then was gone – in a hurry.

Von Witzleben relaxed. He took out a gold cigarettte case adorned with the family's coat-of-arms and took out a captured American cigarette. He lit it and puffed out a little moodily. Through the door which Prutzmann had left open – Prutzmann obviously thought one of the prerogatives of the great was to let other people do such things for them – he could see the elegantly gowned women and smartly uniformed senior officers enjoying their ragout, as the trio scraped at their instruments and elderly waiters in black tailcoats creaked back and forth bearing trays of steaming food and bottles of champagne.

Von Witzleben sniffed. He imagined that this was how the first class passengers must have looked just before the *Titanic* had struck that famed iceberg: laughing flirting, drinking, eating as if life would go on for ever. Did they not see the sea of ruins outside on the other side of Alster, the "death zone" as the authorities called it, which had been sealed up after the great, week-long raid of July 1943, where no one lived and which was inhabited solely by the thousands of dead still buried beneath the ruins?

Suddenly, he stubbed out his cigarette. He couldn't bear to watch them anymore, living in their fools' paradise with their world tumbling to the earth all around them. He walked to the foyer, collected his black side cap and strode into the street. He clicked his fingers. Inge, behind the wheel, started the engine and drove the staff car round to the front portal. He got in and Inge put her free hand on his crotch and pressed gently. "Has the *Herr Hauptmann* any special wishes this evening?" she asked, a naughty look on her pretty, girlish face.

"He has. But not in front of the *Vier Jahreszeiten*, thank you kindly," he answered as she set off, driving expertly into the flow of traffic, neatly dodging an ancient car propelled by a huge gas bag in a trailer behind it which had obviously broken down.

Inge was barely sixteen, a pretty blonde with a slight figure and long legs who had once been a fanatical supporter of Hitler. But since von Witzleben had taken her virginity the month before, she was no longer so fanatical. Only the other night, lying in a rumpled damp bed, her girlish body lathered in sweat, she had gasped excitedly." Give me sex before service to the Fatherland any day. Now more, Klaus *more*," and she had writhed and bucked like a wild horse being put the saddle for the first time.

Now as they drove through the battered surburb heading for the country, he told her what he had told Prutzmann. He felt quite justified in doing so. There was no one else in whom he could confide. His two brothers were dead, killed in action in Russia, his wife had been killed in an air raid two years before and most of the rest of the family were now in* *Sippenhaft* as a result of Field Marshal von Witzleben being involved in the plot to kill Hitler in July 1944. A man, he told himself, had to have someone with whom he could share his secrets and problems.

She listened attentively as they drove through the growing darkness, though she could not quite refrain from touching his genitals every now and again. It was always the same, he told himself. At first they couldn't get enough of it and then, in the end, it was: "oh, not again tonight!"

"Do you think the Tommies will attempt an attack on HQ from the air?" she asked when he was finished.

"They are a slow people, not very well led. But they are hard and tenacious. What they set their minds to do, they *will* do. I should know. I have fought them three times – in '40 in France, in 42 in the Desert and last year in Normandy, which got me this – " he tapped his wooden arm – and finished my military career, for better or worse." He sucked his teeth thoughtfully, as they left the surburb of Lohbrugge and drove into the country heading for the Glinde Road." There's one thing which puzzles me, however."

"What's that, Klaus?"

---

* In Hitler's Germany, the kin of any suspect or political prisoner was held in prison too. *Transl.*

"They can get in by air, all right. But how would they get out?"

"What do you mean?"

"It would be virtually impossible for a force of airborne men to escape after an airborne attack. Their lines are too far away and the whole area around Reinbek is pretty well built up. There'd be no hiding places."

"Perhaps they could be towed off in gliders. We did that when I learned to fly gliders in the Hitler Maidens. There's a large hook and the towplane comes in low with a hawser – "

"No," he stopped her short. "They couldn't use that method. Gliders crossing our part of Germany would be easy meat for the flak – they are too slow. They'd never reach Reinbek."

"The Elbe?" she suggested. It's only a few kilometres from Reinbek. They could send in a naval craft . . ."

He laughed and she ceased speaking. "My dear little girl. A Tommy naval craft wouldn't even get as far as the entrance to the Baltic, never mind right across the Kaiser Wilhelm Kanal and into the River Elbe."

"You're laughing at me because I'm silly. But I'm not. I'm a mature woman."

He laughed again at her schoolgirlish outrage. "You're young enough to be my daughter."

"Then what we did last night was incest, oh?" Suddenly, she applied the brakes – hard. Von Witzleben shot forward as the big staff car skidded to a halt in the verge, next to thickly packed firs which ran the length of the lonely cobbled road. "I'll show you the little trick you taught me then, you pig."

"Not *here*, Inge," he exclaimed.

"Oh, so the big war hero with the Knight's Cross and all the other tin", she meant the medals for bravery, "is afraid, eh – afraid of a silly little girl." Her hand went out and started to fumble with his flies.

"Inge!"

She wasn't listening. Her little hand, already hot and damp with perspiration was inside his trousers, caressing him. He started to stiffen at once. The heat of her attack made him excited. She began to stroke him more quickly, muttering to herself under her breath, but he noted she was starting to breathe faster as well.

Abruptly she stopped her excited stroking. She bent down and took him in her mouth. It felt shockingly hot, as if his member had been thrust into a furnace. She began to work her head up and down, her tongue curling the length of his penis, licking here, sucking there. He began to groan. Suddenly he could contain himself no more. His whole body shook. His face contorted as if with pain. A spasm of unutterable joy coursed through his lean body. He fell back against the car seat, gasping as if he had just run a great race.

After a moment she said cheekily; "Daddy, will you teach me another trick tomorrow?"

He hadn't the strength for checking her. All he could manage was a weak: "Drive on, you little devil. You'll be the death of me." And she would.

SIX

The whore opened the door of her bedroom. It smelt of cheap scent and stale cigarette smoke. Jenkins' keen eye noted the still smoking tab-end of her last visitor in the ashtray on the battered bedside table next to the brass bedstead. She flung off her coat, kicked off her shoes and flung herself on the bed, which squeaked in protest.

She hitched up her skirt and spread her plump, black-stockinged legs. She wasn't wearing any underclothes and her pubes were shaven. Jenkins thought she looked vaguely obscene. She ran her red-tipped finger the length of her vagina. "Come on then, honey," she urged.

Sergeant Jenkins reached for his flies. Then something caught his attention on the glass-fronted picture of the Holy Virgin, which lay beneath the crucifix above her bed. Something was reflected in the glass – and that thing, which was behind him, had moved!

Jenkins reacted instinctively, as he had been trained to do. He stepped one pace to his left and jabbed his right elbow smartly behind him. There was a howl of pain as the sharp elbow connected with a stomach. There was a gasp. In a flash, Jenkins spun round. An evil-looking little runt stood there, gasping for air and slightly bent, but the knife with which he had been about to stab the unsuspecting sergeant was still firmly clasped in his right hand. Jenkins moved. Speed, he had always been taught was of vital importance. His hard right fist lashed out. In the same instant that his attacker raised his knife, the fist slammed into his jaw. There was a click. The little man's head snapped backwards. He flew against the wall, unconscious before he hit it, and began to slither slowly down it to the floor.

On the bed the whore rolled over. Her hand sought something under the dirty, stained pillow. Jenkins dived onto the bed. It squeaked in protest at his weight. He grabbed the girl's thumb and pulled hard. She screamed in pain. His left hand beat her to it. Under the pillow there was a whore's pistol – a little .22 with an ivory butt.

Now the whore started to scream hysterically, rolling from side to side as if in mortal agony. "Shut up!" Jenkins commanded, a little breathlessly.

She kept on screaming.

Jenkins didn't hesitate. He hauled back his fist, muscles rippling beneath his tunic. His fist slammed into her face. Her screaming stopped abruptly and he felt the warmth of her blood on his fingers. Her head lolled to one side and he knew she was out for a little while.

With the heel of his boot, Sergeant Jenkins kicked the door behind him closed. All thoughts of sex had vanished now. He realized the whore had deliberately selected him. It hadn't been difficult. He stuck out with his maroon beret among the helmeted Yanks. He had been lured to this room deliberately. Now, he considered the matter; you couldn't get a wank in Hyde Park for the equivalent of five dollars, a pound. But she'd offered him the works for the same price. Yes, he told himself, it had been a put up job.

But why?

He remembered the incident of the girl with the panzerfaust on their way to Luxembourg City and Major O'Rourke's talk of the Jerry werewolves. Had that something to do with it? After all, the two of them wouldn't roll him for his money. He didn't have more than a couple of quid to his name.

Sergeant Jenkins made his decision. He couldn't take the two of them. But the girl possibly knew more and besides she was lighter and easier to control. He turned and opened the door. Somewhere down the dimly lit corridor rusty bedsprings were squeaking noisily. "Like a ruddy fiddler's elbow," he whispered to himself. And a drunk Yank was declaring unmusically that he was "dreaming of a white Christmas," though Christmas was long gone. Otherwise there was nobody in sight.

He pulled the key and put it into his pocket. Then he turned to the girl. He pocketed the little whore's pistol, then pulled down her skirt to cover the shaven vagina. Lightly, he slapped her across the cheek. She moaned softly. He did it again and she opened her eyes, closed them and then opened them again. Suddenly everything came into focus for her and she whimpered – in German – "*nicht schlagen.*"*

Sergeant Jenkins didn't know what the words meant, but he guessed their meaning from the look of fear on her mean, cheap face. "I won't hurt you," he said quietly. "As long as you behave yourself." He indicated her cheap rabbit skin coat. "Put that on."

She got off the bed carelessly, legs spread apart. But Sergeant Jenkins was no longer interested in her body. His concern now was to get her back to Major O'Rourke. He waited until she had got the coat on, then he ordered: "Come with me. Put your arm through mine and no monkey tricks, understand?"

Weakly, she nodded her agreement and did as he commanded.

Jenkins stepped over the unconscious man, telling himself that he should have searched him. But there was no time for that now. He opened the door, thrust her into the corridor and locked the door behind them. "All right, off we go – for a nice walkee."

Outside the street was still crowded with drunken GI's and laughing and screaming whores, most of whom seemed drunk, too. Carefully, keeping the whore to inner side of the pavement, Jenkins threaded his way through the drunken crowd. He wanted no trouble. He just wanted to get the whore back for interrogation. He passed a group of GI's bargaining with a black marketeer. The Luxembourger was saying: "You get me a truck with gas, I give you much money

* Don't hit me. *Transl.*

107

– a fortune." The GIs were unimpressed. "Sure," they were saying, "we get you truck – a decue-and-half full o' gas. But we wants greenbacks, US money, not this European latrine paper."

Inspite his inner tension, Jenkins smiled softly. The Yanks stole like magpies. If it wasn't nailed down, they'd take it.

They walked on. Up front in the dim light, for the blackout was in full force now, he spotted two GI's lounging in a doorway. It was a typical GI pose, hands in pockets, garrison caps tilted to the back of the head, jaws moving mechanically back and forth as they chewed gum, and surveyed the scene, waiting for something to happen. It seemed to him he had seen Yanks lounging in doorways like this for ever now, from Algiers, through Bari, Normandy and here in Luxembourg. Perhaps they drill 'em in it back in their training depots, he told himself.

He came level with them. They were both tall men and powerfully built, both a head taller than Jenkins, who was lean but of medium height. "Hey, you," the taller of the two drawled.

Jenkins pretended not to hear.

"I'm talking to you, buddy," the American said menacingly. "Where you going with that dame?"

"Not your business," Jenkins answered quietly but firmly.

Now the other man spoke and Jenkins could suddenly see the dull silver glint of a knife. "We can make it our business, *limey*," he emphasized the name with a sneer. "Ya see, we're poor soldjer boys with no greenbacks to pay for the whores. We kinda thought you'd sort of lend us your whore – for free." He grinned at the taller man and the taller one grinned back.

Jenkins told himself that the two Yanks thought they were in complete charge of the situation. What bloody fools they were! Still, he didn't want to lose the girl in any fight. Could he reason with them, tell them that the whore was probably a spy; that she was badly needed hack at HQ for questioning?

But even as he deliberated with himself the whore dropped

him in the shit. She had understood enough of the conversation and saw what it might lead to for her. She said, licking her lips suggestively: "You like a good time, American boys? Fuckee-suckee?"

"You betcha, baby," the bigger of the two said and straighened, eyes gleaming in anticipation. "Okay, Limey – beat it." He edged forward, obviously thinking the Englishman, intimidated by his size, would move back.

But Jenkins had long been trained into doing exactly the opposite. He took a pace forward, still keeping his grip on the girl's arm. The move caught the GI off balance. But before he could recover Jenkins struck. There was no mercy about the punch and it caught the American completely off-guard. Jenkin's fist struck him a tremendous blow in the genitals. The American gasped with the shock of it. An intense pain surged through his big body. He bent double, gasping, choking, retching with pain. As he went down, Jenkins clubbed his fist and brought it down – hard-on the back of his neck. He went out like a light, a mess of tangled arms and legs on the pavement.

"You bastard!" the other one yelled. "You didn't have to do that to Hy." He lunged with the knife. Jenkins dodged to one side, the vicious swipe missing his guts by inches. Desperately he hung on to the screaming girl, as the GI with knife lunged again.

He yelped with pain as the keen blade slashed the knuckles of his right hand. Blood started to arc out of the deep wound in a scarlet jet. "Christ Almighty," Jenkins cursed in sudden anger, "you silly American cunt!" He had to let go of her now.

The GI lunged at him again. This time Jenkins was ready for him. He side-stepped. As he did so his foot shot out. The American stumbled and almost fell. Jenkins didn't give him a second chance. The girl was already recovering from her hysterics. She'd be off in a minute. He swung round behind the rattled American. He grabbed the little finger of the hand that held the knife, prising it from the hilt with all his strength. The American wriggled desperately, trying to boot him in the groin, but Jenkins had his legs spread well apart. "All right, you sod," he grunted through gritted teeth, "you frigging well asked for it." He exerted one final pressure. The American's little finger snapped neatly. He howled with pain, as the knife tumbled with a clatter to the cobbles.

The girl was already running as people started to move in the direction of the fight. "Christ," Jenkins thought, "I'm going to lose her. Old O'Rourke will have my guts for garters if I do." Angrily he pushed through the whores and the GI's. A soldier tried to stop him. Jenkins kneed him in the groin and his false teeth shot out of his mouth foolishly.

The girl was almost gone, disappearing round the corner. If she did she'd vanish into the welter of narrow alleys and lanes that made up the medieval old town. Jenkins pelted after her, arms working like pistons, blood flying in bright red gobs from his wounded hand.

Suddenly, completely out of nowhere, the motorbike came roaring down the narrow street. Men and women scattered, shouting in alarm. Curses rang out as the driver wobbled from side to side, bouncing up and down in the saddle whenever the bike hit a cobble larger than the rest. "The guy's drunk as a skunk!" someone shouted. "Stop the bastard before he kills somebody."

The whore, in her fear, did not hear the roar of the bike as it raced towards her. Jenkins, his chest heaving with the effort of running all out, yelled: "*Look out. Look out –* "

His cry was drowned by the impact the bike made as it crashed into the running girl. She screamed in agony as she went under the flying wheels and the rider flew over the top of his bike and slammed into the opposite wall, his head bent at an unnatural angle, body shattered.

Jenkins bent beside the girl, on one knee. In this war he had seen enough dead to know that there was no hope for her. But he went through the routine. He felt her neck lightly. There was no pulse. He bent and opened her blouse to reveal skinny fallen breasts. He bent his head close to them. Nothing. She was dead all right.

He rose slowly, deep in thought. Should he search her?

He decided against it. The drunken Yanks might think he was robbing the dead whore's body. Besides, he didn't think she'd have known much anyway. She had been just a cheap tart to lure him into the trap. Probably, ever since she had been old enough to fuck, she had sold her skinny body for a couple of quid. Now she'd sold it for the same sum – for good. He looked down at the pathetic piece of human garbage, a cheap, wasted life, for one more time. Then he faded into the awed, suddenly silent, crowd. He still had the would be killer locked in the knocking shop. Perhaps they'd get something out of him?

"Poor bitch," someone was saying as he walked away, "it oughtn't to have happened, even to a cheap cunt like her . . ."

SEVEN

"All right," Colonel Sterling announced as they gathered in the Army Group Commander's private dining room for the briefing. "This town is obviously unsafe. The little guy who tried to knife you, Sergeant Jenkins" he indicated Jenkins, whose hand was now swathed in a thick bandage, "unfortunately got away. The door was probably made of plywood. It would be in that run down, cheap whorehouse. But he broke it open and fled. But he was one of them – that was for sure."

There was a mumble of agreement from the assembled SAS men.

"So I've got General Bradley's permission to have you moved to a little hotel in the border village of Echternach. It's the most secure place we could find at short notice – hill to the back, the River Sauer to the front, open fields to either side. Good fields of fire." He raised his voice, "In addition the General has allotted a company of infantry and four tanks to guard you."

There were gasps, a few surprised whistles, and Gormless George Ramsbotham, the troop's self-appointed funny man, said in his thick West Riding accent: "Ruddy hell – Yanks guarding us! What a ruddy cheek. We're the SAS ain't we?"

"Shut up, Gormless," Rory O'Rourke commanded sharply.

"Yessir," Gormless said, looking offended in the hangdog manner which he affected whenever a superior spoke to him sharply, which was often.

"You will stay there until we've worked out the airborne

part of the deal, something which is almost completed, I might say. Indeed, it is being taken care of at the highest level between Generals Bradly and no less a person than ole Blood an' Guts Patton." He smiled.

There were low whistles of surprise and Al Gorey exclaimed: "Not Patton!"

"Yes indeedee," Sterling said. "But while you're there, Major O'Rourke, it will be up to you to work out the plan of attack on this place in Reinbek. I might be nominally in charge of this operation, but you are the real leader."

O'Rourke nodded, his hard Irish face revealing little, though, in fact, his mind was racing electrically as he figured out the odds against him – and they were pretty large, he told himself.

"Now before you go," Sterling said, "I want to show you a photo, one I think will interest. you. Goldstein!"

The Lieuetnant stepped forward smartly, large portfolio under his arm. Swiftly, he untied the strings at each end and handed it to the Colonel.

Colonel Sterling opened it and removed the large photograph which lay there. He held it up.

O'Rourke recognized the plane immediately. He had seen enough of the clumsy-looking, three-engined planes with their corrugated metal sides back in '41. Then, on the beleagured island of Crete, he had watched in awe and impotent fury as seemingly hundreds of them had sailed over their heads, dropping paratroopers everywhere. "It's old Junkers 52 of the German *Luftwaffe*," he said, a little surprised. "I thought they were obsolete and that Jerry wasn't using them anymore."

"I don't know about that," Colonel Sterling said, "but I do know that this one exists and it's presently located in a hangar, not more than five or six klicks from here. Tell 'em, Goldstein."

Smartly, he stepped to the centre of the group and explained. "When we took over the Kraut airfield just outside Lux City, we took it to have been a *Luftwaffe* fighter base. It wasn't big enough for anything larger than a fighter.

113

Besides, we found wrecks of Kraut fighters everywhere. But during the Battle of the Bulge last December, the field and the city came under long-range Kraut artillery fire from the other side of the river. One of their heavy shells opened up the side of a hangar at the far end of the field which for some reason the Army Air Corps boys, who were using the field then, hadn't bothered to search. God knows why – those flyboys'll loot anything that's not nailed down." He shook his dark head, as if in mock wonder. "Any hows, when the flyboys went to examine it they found this." He indicated the photo of the Junkers 52. "Perfect condition. They checked out the engines – all great stuff." He looked at Sterling.

Sterling took over again. "Now our intention is to have the pilot to fly you out into the North Sea; you'll avoid the great anti-aircraft belts around the Ruhr industrial area. 'Flak Valley', as the flyboys call it."

The SAS troopers nodded their agreement. Jumping out of a plane was bad enough, but jumping through flak was ten times worse. All of them had done it at one time or another; they knew.

"Then it is our intention to have the pilot to bring us in low over the coast of Schleswig-Holstein, north of Bremen, away from the flak belts then, coming in very low so that we're under their radar. At the same time, if we are spotted by visual observers on the ground, they'll take us for one of their own aircraft."

"We're going in at daylight?" O'Rourke snapped swiftly, frowning hard at the thought.

"No, not exactly. The aim is to be above the objective while it's still quite dark, probably about zero six hundred hours, jumping immediately at first light, perhaps zero six ten."

O'Rourke relaxed. "That's fine," he said shortly. "Thank you."

"So let me sum up," Sterling said in the businesslike manner which had always made his lectures back at College Park so attractive to students. With Professor Sterling they

114

had always known exactly where they stood. "It is obvious that the Krauts are on to us. They have targeted us because you fellows are airborne. So that must mean they expect an attack. So far, they don't know where –

– "But they'll obviously conclude sooner or later that it's their HQ at Reinbek," Al Gorey cut in sharply.

"Exactly, and we are now running daily overflights to check if there are any kind of airborne defences being erected. I'll keep you in the picture. Two, I think we shall be able to get to the DZ without too much difficulty. That Junkers 52 should do the trick. Three, the plan of attack and the supplies needed, which incidentally will have priority number one here at 12th Army Group HQ, will be your problem, Major O'Rourke."

The Irishman nodded his understanding.

"Four," Sterling went on, "the problem of getting you out has still not been one hundred per cent resolved. But I am confident that it will be in the next twenty-four hours. It needs only the approval of the Supreme Commander, General Eisenhower, and I am sure he will give it without fail. As soon as you know what it is, Major, you make the necessary adjustments to your overall plan."

"I can tell you what it will be right now, Colonel," O'Rourke said, trying to lower the sense of tension he felt rising all around him among his troopers. "In like Flynn and then damn well out again – just like Flynn."

There was a burst of amused laughter from the troopers, while Sterling stared at them, a little puzzled at the reference.

At his side Goldstein enlightened him. "It's a reference to Errol Flynn, the actor, Prof," he whispered into his former professor's ear. "He's reputed to be pretty snappy with the ladies."

"Oh, I see, it's a reference to copulation then."

"Exactly, sir."

"Cor-pulation," Gormless George said aloud, "does that mean fooking?"

This time O'Rourke didn't tell the big Yorkshireman to

shut up. The tension had vanished as soon as it had arisen and he was glad of Gormless George's help.

"Well," Colonel Sterling said, "that's about it." He flashed a glance at his watch. "I suggest you'll all get an early chow and then pack your duds and be off. I don't want to expose you too much on these lonely country roads leading to the German border, especially after dark."

Gormless George gave one of his fake falsetto laughs and simpered in what he thought was a famale voice (difficult with his West Riding bass) "Oh, I am frightfully scared. I think I'm going to have my monthlies . . ."

Two hours later, the jeep convoy came rolling down out of the hills into the ruined border village of Echternach, with Germany just on the other side of the River Sauer, the frontier river. "They say," Goldstein commented with a certain amount of irony, "that it was an Englishman – a certain St Willibrod – who converted the heathen Kraut from his base here." He indicated the ruined abbey to their right. "That was back in the eleventh century."

"Didn't do too much of a job of it, did he?" O'Rourke said sourly, as he sat in the back of the lead jeep together with the American. "But what can yer expect of a Roman Candle?" he meant a Catholic. "They allus make a ballsup of things. Typical, thick-headed Mick."

Goldstein laughed shortly and told himself he had always thought New Yorkers were prejudiced, but it seemed the limeys were just as bad.

They took the narrow road to their left, running along the length of the river, with Goldstein giving the directions as they rolled a little way out of the shelled village, ruined by the fighting of the previous December, when a German general had been killed taking part in the assault on the local shoe factory where a handful of Americans had held out against all odds for a week.

"That's it," he said suddenly, pointing to a poorly repaired white-stucco building to their left. "*Hotel des Sources*", that'll be the place where you can hole up – in peace and quiet, we hope."

O'Rourke looked at him sourly. The Yank was a Jew and he didn't like Jews, but there again, he didn't like most races and creeds, starting with the hated "Roman Candles" of his youth in Belfast. "Don't worry, Lieutenant," he said coldly, "We'll see there is peace and quiet – with this." He tapped the .45 Colt at his hip.

Looking at the two of them in the rearview mirror of the jeep, Gorley grinned: the CO was living up to form. He always knew how to put everyone in place.

Once O'Rourke had told him how he had been captured by – of all people – the Bulgarians, back in '42 when he had been caught raiding with the SAS on a stretch of the Greek coast, then occupied by the Bulgarians, who were at the time Germany's allies.

"The greasy buggers put me a pit below ground level. Perhaps ten to twelve square. I knew what they were about. They were going to try to break my spirit, but they had another fucking think coming. I decided to hate them and by God, Al, when I hate somebody, I friggingly well *hate* them!"

For ten days he had lived in this hole, living off a quart of water a day plus hunks of stale black bread. It was an unreal existence, just a patch of sky overhead and the dry brown walls of the pit. But O'Rourke had clung to some form of normalcy. He had began by assigning a separate function for each of the four corners of the hole.

"One corner I shat and pissed in – there was no other way. The other corner opposite was where I kipped, with a handkerchief around my mouth and nose to keep out the pong. In the third, I ate my grub and drank my water, but not all of it. I kept a thimbleful to wash my hands and face and around my balls and arse once a day. That kept me clean, and in the other corner, I'd sit during the day, keeping my eyes skinned and doing secret exercises, cos I had to keep fit for what was to come – you know, flexing yer muscles, keeping yer guts in tight while counting up to two minutes and the like. The most important thing of all, Al, was to keep my dignity. I was living like Paddy's pig in shit, but I wasn't going to let myself fall into that shit."

On the eleventh day, or rather the night of that day, he reached up from the step he had secretly dug with his fingers half way up the pit, pulled in the one sentry and had strangled him with his own helmet chin-strap. "Then I was out and by God, didn't I see them buggers off!"

That he had. Using the dead sentry's bayonet, he had crept from one sleeping Bulgarian to the next, slitting their throats noiselessly, thereafter, he had taken whatever food and water he could find and had set off for the coast and rescue. But before he had left, he had taken off his winged dagger cap badge, the badge of the SAS. "I pinned it to the breast of their sergeant with a bayonet. It was a good badge – silver, I think. But I wanted to let the fuckers know who they were dealing with – *the best!*"

Now, staring at the back of O'Rourke's cropped head, Al Gorley told himself that they were the best. But could even the best tackle a German HQ some two hundred miles behind enemy lines and get back safely? At the back of his mind a harsh cynical little voice rasped: "*Of course, you goddam can't!*" But for the time being, Captain Al Gorley studiously ignored that voice of warning.

A minute later they were drawing up in front of the hotel, which had obviously suffered in the recent fighting and had boarded-up windows and a stucco facade badly pitted with shellfire and rifle bullets. A fat sergeant, with a worried look in his eyes, was waiting at the once imposing entrance. Even before they had returned his sloppy salute, he blurted out "Gentlemen, the infantry hasn't turned up and there's only me and two darkie cooks in the whole place."

"Don't worry," Goldstein said soothingly, "We're here in strength now. The infantry'll be along in due course I'm sure."

The fat sergeant forced a nervous smile and then said, as if he were the manager of some grand hotel: "I would appreciate very much, gentlemen, if you would instruct your men to wipe their shoes when they enter. We're trying to raise the standards of the place, you see."

O'Rourke and Al Gorley looked at each other and behind them Gormless George said, "I bet it's one o' them places where the waiters give each other tips – it's that posh!"

Then they went in, as the night shadows started to descend from the surrounding hills like sinister, black, silent hawks . . .

EIGHT

The three officers and Sergeant Jenkins started planning the operation after "chow", which consisted of the customary US Army "Shit on shingle" – chipped meat on toast – followed by coffee, which raised a storm of protest from the SAS troopers. "Only tarts and nancy boys drink coffee," the exclaimed in disgust. "Why can't we have a brew?"

"The obvious DZ is these fields outside the factory of whatever it is," O'Rourke explained, pointing to the sketch map of the area with his bayonet. "Pity we don't have any vehicles. So we'll hoof it. Ten minutes at the most."

The others, slowly sipping coffee or smoking the rich, satisfying Camels nodded their understanding, as the faint sound of someone playing the mouth organ and those of the men losing their backpay over poker filtered into the "*salon*", which was now O'Rourke's command post.

"We'll split into two parties," O'Rourke went on. "You'll take a third of the Troop, Al, and deal with these huts – *there*."

"Wilco," Al Gorley said. "And I'll take Lieutenant Goldstein with me. He speaks German."

"Yes, and I'll take Colonel Sterling, who does the same, with me. In the bigger of the two parties, I think he'll be safer."

Sergeant Jenkins tugged his nose and told himself, no one was bloody safe when Major O'Rourke was around. He was a mad bugger in action.

"Now," O'Rourke continued. "The situation there is uncertain. We guess that this is the Werewolf HQ, but it's only a guess. So – A – we don't know how many of

120

them there are. B – what kind of armament they are equipped with. And – C – what exactly we are there to destroy."

"What about offices, head guys – those are the sort of things and people we should be taking out, Major?" Goldstein suggested.

O'Rourke shot him glance. "Oh are they now?" he said, his tone seamingly modest. Suddenly his voice rose to a roar; "And how the ruddy hell are *we* to know who their top people are, answer me that?"

Goldstein's sallow face flushed and Al Gorey felt for the young officer as he mumbled: "Well, I guess we don't know, Major."

O'Rourke wasted no more time on Goldstein. "So, this is what we do," he continued. "As far as it is possible, we go in prepared for every possible emergency. Every man in the troop will carry a length of plastic explosive in case we have to start blowing things up." He smiled suddenly at the thought.

Al Gorey smiled, too. O'Rourke dearly loved blowing things up.

"Every trooper will carry four bandoliers – that's 200 rounds of ammo." He looked sharply at Goldstein. "Do you think we could get some of your Yank bazookas? Our own Piats are too bloody clumsy and don't have the range against tanks.*"

"Yessir," Goldstein answered, glad to be out of the doghouse so soon. "Colonel Sterling says you can write your own ticket for this one."

"All right, six bazookas with – say – ten rounds apiece." O'Rourke snapped. "We'll dismount the Brownings from the jeeps and take four with us. Each man will take a belt of ammo for them."

Al Gorey whistled softly and said in mild protest: "But Major, we'll be loaded down like mules."

"Better that than running out of ammo in an emergency, and if it comes to that we'll soon lighten our load, don't you think."

* Both are anti-tank missile launchers. *Transl.*

Al Gorey shrugged and left it at that.

"Now then here comes the crunch," O'Rourke said grimly, staring around the circle of earnest faces in the hissing white, incandescent light of a Coleman lantern. "Where do we rendezvous for the withdrawal?"

No one answered. How could they? They didn't know how they were to be taken out.

O'Rourke waited for a minute, then he said: "Well, until we know what the drill is going to be, I'm planning to rendezvous at the DZ. It's too obvious, I know, but it's the only place I can suggest at this moment."

"That about the River Elbe?" Goldstein suggested out of the blue.

O'Rourke shook his head in mock wonder. "Lieutenant, are you plain crackers?" he snorted.

Goldstein didn't know the English usage "crackers", but he guessed the meaning of the phrase. It's only a good mile away as the crow flies from Reinbek. We could escape by water."

O'Rourke didn't deign to reply. Instead he said, "That about winds it up for the time being. There's only the question of rations. I suggest a tin of bully per man and some hardtack." He sniffed. "If they don't get us that same day, we won't be needing any grub – we'll be among the daisies – or eating shitty frigging German black bread, providing we've still got the choppers to do so. All right, that's it. Let's have a drink." He nodded to Sergeant Jenkins and the NCO got up and poured three hofty tots of whisky into enamel cups. O'Rourke nodded, and he poured one for himself.

O'Rourke waited until they all had theirs and then he raised his mug in toast: "Gentlemen, let's drink a toast. To Operation Dare and Win." He grinned. "The pun on our regimental motto is pretty obvious. But I think it's what we're aiming at – *Dare and Win!*"

"*Dare and Win!*" they shouted, keen young faces bold and smiling, filled with the confidence of young men who had diced with death before and had come through unscathed.

"Bottoms up!" O'Rourke commanded and started pouring the fiery liquid down his throat greedily, as if it might well be the last drink of spirits he ever took.

The plane came thundering down at the valley of the River Sauer opposite at four hundred miles hour. Soaring in out of nowhere, flying in at treetop height, its prop wash lashing the grass below, it headed straight for the hotel. "Duck!" Al Gorey yelled above the ear-splitting racket, *"it's a Jerry!"*

O'Rourke flung a last glance through the window. The American was right. He could see the black-and-white cross painted on the plane's fuselage quite clearly. He dropped to the floor just as the pilot opened fire. Brilliant white tracer shells zipped through the air. Windows shattered. A length of holes was ripped violently along the wall behind them. They were showered with plaster and shattered woodwork. Somewhere a Browning machine gun opened up. But it did not deter the plane.

Risking another glance through the window, now a gleaming spiderweb of shattered glass, O'Rourke saw it tearing round in a tight curve, white smoke coming from its exhausts, as the fighter-bomber positioned itself for another attack, the tracer surging skywards, trailing way behind it. "Here she comes again," he sang out and then dropped his head beneath the cover of the wall.

Again the German fighter-bomber came into the attack. This time, knowing that there was no danger from below, the unseen pilot lowered his undercarriage to slow the plane. Now, it came in like a great, sinister metal bird, the pilot aiming right for the centre of the hotel. Suddenly, startlingly, the length of its wings crackled with angry violet lights. Once more eight streams of 20mm cannon shells sped in sudden white fury towards the building. Shells slammed into the masonry. More windows shattered. Abruptly the air was full of the stench of burned cordite. With a great roar, the plane soared just over the roof, little black eggs tumbling from its blue belly in crazy profusion.

The hotel was rocked time and time again, as they exploded all around. It rocked and swayed like a ship at sea suddenly caught in a great storm. Someone screamed, high and hysterical, like a woman. The chattering of the lone machine gun ceased. Abruptly, everything was chaos and confusion.

Then the lone plane was gone, hurtling high into the darkening sky, heading eastwards, going all-out before the fighters at their fields in Belgium and Luxembourg were scrambled.

Five minutes later Jenkins reported. "One jeep a total write-off sir, one damaged. Gormless George got a scratch. Nothing worth mentioning. It'd take more than a scratch to get through that tough Yorkshire hide of his. But that Yank, the sergeant, he's got a nasty wound in the guts. The lads have patched him the best they could with a shell dressing. We're taking him back to Luxembourg to the dock now."

"Thanks, Jenkins." O'Rourke said, and handed him his mug. "Best fill that up, Jenkins and have a another one. I think we all need another one after this."

In silence, broken only by the sound of a jeep being started up, they sipped their whisky, each man wrapped up in a cocoon of his own thoughts and apprehensions. Somewhere outside in the hall, a grandfather clock ticked away the seconds of their lives with metallic inexoriability.

Finally O'Rourke broke the heavy silence, with: 'It's pretty obvious that these werewolf blokes have got us spotted again. Why else would that plane pick out this place in the middle of nowhere?"

There was a murmur of agreement from the others.

"For all we know, they might have somebody over there," he indicated the hills on the German side of the river-frontier, "watching us even now. No," he said, face, set and determined, "right from the start they've been onto us."

"So what do we do?" Al Gorey asked, taking his lips from his mug, and telling himself the CO was right.

"We disappear."

"*Disappear?*" the others asked, as one.

"Yes, we stick out like a sore thumb, here right in middle of the Yank army dressed in camouflage smocks and our red berets. To find us in these outfits is as easy as falling off a log."

"So what can you do?" Lieutenant Goldstein asked, knowing what the red-haired Irishman with his ugly, tough face said made sense. They did stick out like a sore thumb.

By way of an answer, O'Rourke asked: "How long would it take you, Lieutenant, to get us say three Yank trucks and uniforms to clothe my chaps?"

"Not long. You've got the highest priority. So if necessary we could even get those lazy bastards of quartermasters to get out of their cots and start issuing stuff. That is, if they've got anything left," he added cynically. "Most of their wares go on the black market.

"Good. Then I want my men kitted out as Yanks," O'Rourke said.

"We're going back to Lux City?" Goldstein asked surprised.

"No, you're going to bring the trucks and uniforms here. This night the 1st SAS Recce Troop is going to disappear. Before it's light tomorrow morning, we'll be on our way again, dressed as Yanks."

"But if they've got watchers out there," Goldstein protested, "won't they tumble to it when they see no activity here after first light?"

O'Rourke shook his head. "No, because there *will* be activity here at daybreak."

"How?"

"Because you'll be bringing back a dozen or so Yanks, volunteers or pressed – makes no difference – who'll move about the hotel pretending to be us in our uniforms."

Al Gorey's face lit up at the idea. "You're a devious bugger – if you'll excuse my French. Didn't think you had it in you, Rory."

Rory O'Rourke winked solemnly and said in a throaty

gravel, imitating the popular comedian Jimmy Durante: "You ain't seen nuthin yet."

The imitation was poor and the American accent was atrocious. But they laughed. The tension was relieved. They had a plan . . .

NINE

It was nearly midnight.

In the great former factory, which now housed the Were-wolf HQ, all was silent save for the steady tread of the sentries on the gravel paths which linked the units. The young trainee werewolves, boys and girls, had long gone to bed, exhausted from another hard day of dawn-to-dusk training. There was a kind of canteen for them where they could buy weak wartime beer and eat ration-free sausage. But most of them were too young to drink beer anyway and the sausage was ersatz, containing more soya bean flour than meat.

But in von Witzleben's quarters the lights still burned behind the blackout shutters, though they were subdued, with a red silk scarf thrown over the lamp on the table so that it cast a subdued, sensual hue over the room.

They had been drinking – as always at night. She didn't like to drink really, and the captured English whisky tended to make her cough and splutter at first. But after several glasses, she took to it all right. "It makes me relaxed," she had said tipsily more than once this evening, "and *so-o* sexy." She had looked at him through half-closed eyes in what she obviously thought was a come-hither, seductive gaze. He could have laughed, but he didn't. She wanted to be treated like a mature woman, and indeed she did have the sexual appetite of a woman much older, always wanting to try new tricks, new positions.

How often had she questioned him about his past sexual experiences? What was it like with French women? Are they really better than German women? What about the

Russians? Surely you've had those? They say they are enormously strong and insatiable . . . On and on she often went, until he was forced to shut her up with: "What are you, Inge? *The damned Gestapo or something?* Whereupon she would pout her bottom lip and sulk. But not for long. She had the quick-change of moods of a teenager, which, of course, she was: a beautiful, utterly depraved teenager.

Once in a serious moment he had asked gently: "Inge, why the haste? You've got a lifetime in front of you. Why do you want me to teach you all these things – decadent and depraved as they are?"

She had looked back at him, equally serious. "But do I?"

"Do you – what?"

"Have a long life in front of me?"

He had not answered. He had seen the look of near despair in her blue eyes. There was pain there, too, as if she could not really come to terms with the fact that she thought she was going to die before this war ended. He had changed the subject, but at that moment, he resolved that if anyone survived, it would be Fraulein Inge Petersen of Reinbek.

Now she was completely naked, save for the short white socks the Hitler Maidens wore. Her slim white body was glazed with sweat, as if oiled, from the love-play they had been indulging in for the last half hour. Time and time again she had writhed in passion, climaxing in a frenzy of twisting lips and fervent little fluttering cries which came from deep down inside her. But she wanted more. "Something new," she had cried and he had been forced to put his hand over her mouth gently, to stuffle her cries in case the sentries outside heard. "I must try everything. The other way – I want to do that."

"But it will hurt – hurt a little too much," he had objected.

"I don't care," she had dug her nails into his lean naked back fervently till the blood came. "I want that. I want to be hurt."

Now as she crouched over the side of the couch, her body raised even higher by the cushion he had placed under her stomach, he looked down at her, as if in wonder. At the same time, he rubbed the vaseline on his stiffened member in an odd sort of lazy way. The sensation was pleasant, but he was much too concerned about her desires to be aware of his own.

She wriggled her pert little bottom and said throatily: "Come on. Don't waste time. I want it hard and deep. Oh, come on, Klaus stick it in *please!*" Her buttocks trembled even more.

He felt his breath come more sharply. She really was excited. Her excitement fuelled his. His heart began to beat rapidly. He placed his good hand against her pert buttocks. They trembled, as if they had a life of their own. Slowly he approached her, jockeying for position, his penis throbbing with the sexual tension. Slowly, very slowly, he slipped the tip between her legs. She bucked wildly. A low moan came from her lips.

"Are you all right?" he asked, hardly recognizing his own voice.

She shook her head from side to side, her blonde locks flying. "*More*," she hissed hoarsely.

He thrust a little deeper, trying to control himself; attempting not to let it get out of hand. Otherwise he would have plunged in with all his strength.

She moaned even more. Her buttocks thrust upwards, trying to get more of him inside her. "Please," she cried in a strangled voice, her mouth open and gasping. "Oh God in Heaven – *more!*"

He could contain himself no longer. Savagely, he thrust the whole length of his penis inside her. She screamed shrilly and reared up with the burning pain. He clapped his hand over her mouth. Then he was riding her hard, brutishly, ignoring her whimpers and cries, his only thought his own pleasure . . .

It was one o'clock. They lay on the couch, close to each other, still naked and damp with sweat. He cradled her little body with his good arm. They said little to each other. Now and again they smoked, watching the blue smoke ascend lazily to the ceiling in the dusky-red light. Sometimes they

129

kissed, not passionately, just little, loving pecks, as if to reasure themselves that the other one was still there.

Von Witzleben wondered. How would it end? He knew Germany was lost. Hitler's vaunted wonder weapons wouldn't materialize, even if the werewolves did de-stablize Allied Occupied Germany. He had heard this very morning that the *Amis* and Tommies had taken the airfield at Munster. That meant the enemy already had a flying base on the other side of the Rhine. How long would it take before they reached the Elbe, the last natural barrier in the whole of Western Germany?

He pressed her a little. She was a perverted little darling, but she was all that he had left. Everything else had gone – the family treasure, the family estate in the East, and since the abortive generals' rising the previous July, even the family honour. Three hundred years of Witzlebens who had fought and killed and had died for the German state, whatever its form.

Should he run for it? Try to make a new start with her? But how and where? He was still a serving officer, though he supposed with his one arm he could easily get himself discharged. Could he live in a defeated Germany, where he and all Germans would be lorded over by the conquerors – even with her? And even if he could, wouldn't she tire of him in the end: a brokendown ex-cavalry officer, with no money and no prospects, who was twice her age

Suddenly, startlingly, the phone at the side of the couch rang. She clutched him, as if she felt they were in sudden danger. He gave her a quick peck on her damp cheek and picked up the receiver: "Von Witzleben," he barked, one hundred per cent the professional officer.

"Prutzmann here," the voice at the other end said, with no attempt at an apology for ringing at this late hour. "Berlin Air has just reported the plane we sent to deal with them has reported that the mission was not totally successful. It seems the Tommies are still in business."

As he listened, von Witzleben put his hand over the mouthpiece and whispered, "Prutzmann."

The girl reacted at once. She placed her hand across her breasts and over her lap, as if Prutzmann might be able to see her nakedness through the phone.

Von Witzleben grinned at the instinctive girlish reaction and listened again. Prutzmann was saying: "I don't know what the Tommies' game is exactly, but I do think it is something to do with us. What do you think, von Witzleben?"

"I'm sure you're right, *Obergruppenfuhrer*. But, if I may ask, sir, why the call at this time of the night?"

"For this reason. I have other pots on the fire, *mein Lieber*. My friend *der Reichsfuhrer SS*, Heinrich Himmler, has asked me to help him in some – er – delicate negotiations, which at this moment are no concern of yours. Hence this urgent call. For the time being you are, as my deputy, in control of the werewolf movement. Is it up to you to ensure that the tightest degree of security is maintained at Reinbek. Is that clear?"

"Clear, *Obergruppenfuhrer*," he replied dutifully.

"Good, then I shall wish you good night or – er is it perhaps good morning? *Auf wiederhoren. Heil Hitler.*"

"*Heil Hitler*," von Witzleben said without enthusiasm.

The line went dead.

She took her hands away from her body. "What was that about?" she asked, lighting a cigarette from the cigarette butt still smouldering in the ashtray.

"Not another coffin nail," he remonstrated with her.

She shrugged, "*So oder so kaput*. I'm going to die one way or the other."

"Don't be so damned fatalistic," he remonstrated with her, his mind suddenly full awake and racing with the *Obergruppenfuhrer*'s news. You know, I think the Tommies are going to attack this place. It'll be an airborne attack, I'm damn sure of that."

"What will you do? How are you going to defend this place?" She sat up, interested.

"Not with that rabble of boy scouts in short pants," he answered scornfully. "They're just half-trained sneak killers and saboteurs."

"Can you get regular troops – infantry – from Hamburg garrison?"

"Doubt it. The Army's fighting for its life on both fronts. I'm sure they're not going to tie up troops here in the expectation of an attack which we're only guessing might come." He tugged at the end of his nose thoughtfully, trying to reason out the problem as he had done in the old days in Russia just before a panzer attack. What was it always? One way in – and another way out. In that manner you avoided having the enemy waiting for you at a given spot when you'd completed your attack.

"'They' could drop anywhere. The fields behind us," he mused, thinking aloud. "Even in the forest, if they were well trained enough to know how to deal with trees when they hit the deck. It would be just too much terrain to cover, even with a full infantry battalion, and I think it was Frederick the Great who said – "he who attempts to defend everything, defends nothing". So you'd have your troops spread out in twos and threes all over the place." He shook his head. "No, that would be it." He fell silent for a moment or two and there was no sound save that of the night breeze in the trees outside. She waited expectantly and lit yet another "coffin nail".

Suddenly he spoke, voice full of suppressed excitement. "But, no matter where they parachute in, they've got to depart in *one definite spot!*"

"Where?"

"Those fields behind us. It's the only place where planes could land to pick them up, and that's the only way they're going to get the Tommies out." He walked briskly to the chair where his uniform was piled up. He started to pull on his black uniform trousers.

"What are you going to do?" she asked, surprised. "It's nearly two o'clock in the morning."

"There's no time to be lost," he said, pulling his belt tight and reaching for his black tunic, heavy with decorations for bravery in battle. "The attack could start at any time. Look in that box behind the couch. There's heaps of captured *Ami* Hershey chocolate bars."

132

"Chocolate bars, what in three devils' name do you want chocolate for at this time of night? "She stared at him in complete bewilderment.

He grinned at her, as he put on his cap at a rakish angle, as if he were still that cocky young lieutenant of 1939, going to war for the first time, full of what he used to call "piss and vinegar." He said: "Because, my little cheetah, I'm going out to bribe a lot of teenage flak gunners with a sweet tooth to do something elicit with their popgun." He blew her a kiss. "Off you, go, into the bed. I won't be back till morning." A moment later he was gone, clattering down the stairs as if he couldn't get wherever he was going soon enough . . .

TEN

"Well, I suppose that's about it," Colonel Sterling said, a little hesitantly. He looked at the pile of chutes at his feet, as if he wondered if he had done the right thing after all.

"Yes, it is," O'Rourke snapped, all businesslike and professional, his sharp gaze taking in all the activity in the shattered hangar, where the SAS troopers were busy checking their equipment, slapping their chutes hard to check for last minute faults, buckling on equipment, slinging khaki-coloured bandoliers of ammunition around their shoulders. "The pilots tell me we should be over the DZ just before first light. As soon as it's dawn, we jump. You'll be in my stick, Colonel," he addressed Colonel Sterling, whose middle-aged face seemed dwarfed by the huge US helmet he was wearing, "and Lieutenant Goldstein will jump with Captain Gorley's stick over there."

Goldstein raised his thumb in acknowledgement as he had seen the SAS troopers do, but his heart wasn't in it. His face showed that. "Hell's teeth," O'Rourke said to himself, "I hope he doesn't freeze. The op is dicey enough as it is."

Aloud he said, "The light planes which will pick us up will start exactly one and a half hours after us. That means we'll will have one and half hours to carry out the op and get back to the DZ. It'll be very nip and tuck, but I think if we keep our heads and don't do anything ruddy foolish, we'll pull it off."

"Rory, are you still sure we shouldn't leave a couple of men to cover the DZ?" Al Gorey asked.

O'Rourke shook his head. "We'll need every man in the troop, Al, if we're going to do it in time. But I have decided to make some arrangement to have the DZ defended by other means."

"What do you mean?" Colonel Sterling asked in a puzzled manner," By other means?"

"This," O'Rourke snapped, "and strode over to a large ammuniton case which one of their American helpers had brought into the ruined hangar a few minutes before. He snapped off the catches and brought out what looked like a large calibre bullet with a prong set at its tip. "The debollocker," he announced.

"The debollocker?" Colonel Sterling echoed in bewilderment.

"Yes, an anti-personnel mine, usually made by the PBI – the bloody infantry to you, Colonel – themselves. Step on one of these Colonel and it explodes at the level of your crotch. You can imagine, without me drawing a picture, why it's called a debollocker."

"Oh my God," Sterling groaned and behind him Goldstein instinctively held his hand to his groin, as if he already feared for the safety of his testicles.

"Every man, on his way in, will plant three of them before he leaves the DZ site. That'll cause just some gnashing of teeth and wailing, if the Jerry infantry stumbles onto those," O'Rourke added with a nasty smirk on his, tough red face.

Outside, on the glowing darkness, the twin pilots of the big lumbering Junkers 52, had started to warm up their engines. Elsewhere on the newly captured airfield, just outside the shattered cathedral city of Munster, the jeeps were taking out the ground crews of the long line of artillery spotter planes from Patton's Third Army, which would follow them in ninety minutes after they had taken off.

O'Rourke nodded his approval. So far, everything had gone to plan. They had left the *Hotel des Sources* under the cover of darkness in American uniforms and in American trucks, their place being taken by GIs who would wear their uniforms until the operation was over. By dawn, they had been on their way to the Rhine, fighting the huge traffic jams heading to and from the great river. They had crossed the

Rhine over a Bailey bridge in Cologne. Two hours later they had arrived at the Munster, many of the shattered airfield buildings still smoking from the recent infantry assault on the place, just as the Junkers which would fly them into battle came swooping down from the clouds.

Now it was only a matter of an hour till take-off and instead of the last minute panics, which always seemed to take place on ops like this, everything was running perfectly smoothly. O'Rourke didn't think much of the Americans' fighting ability, but this time, he told himself; "The Yanks are spot-on." They were handling everything in a tremendously efficient manner. He turned to a waiting Sergeant Jenkins and snapped; "All right, Sergeant. Get the men fell in."

Jenkins nodded and, raising his voice above the racket coming from the bomb-cratered field, with wrecked German aircraft scattered everywhere, he barked: "All right, you heard the CO. Get fell in!"

Purposefully, the men moved forward and, under Jenkin's eagle eye, formed up in three ranks. Sergeant Jenkins barked: "Attention – attenshun!"

They stamped smartly to attention, for they knew the CO. Although he commanded an unorthox unit, O'Rourke was still very much the regular soldier, who was a passionate believer in smart turnout and drill.

O'Rourke acknowledged Jenkins salute, then running his eyes down their ranks, as if trying to etch the troopers' faces on his mind for ever, he commanded: "Stand at ease – stand easy!"

Thirty odd pairs of feet moved as one and a watching Colonel Sterling grinned slightly. He told himself he still loved their centuries' old drill. What was it O'Rourke's troopers said about the bullshit of the British Army? "If it moves, salute it. If it don't, paint it white."

"All right, lads," O'Rourke said. "You know the mission. You know what to do and you know how and where we're going to be picked up by those light planes over there. It's all perfectly straightforward but naturally, as there always is, there's bound to be a ballsup somewhere along the line. But remember this one word – *speed*!" He emphasized the word, with a hardening of his jaw. "If you move fast enough, the shit won't hit you. All right, enough said. You can march 'em off, Sergeant Jenkins and feed 'em. The Yanks are laying on bacon and eggs – as many eggs as you want."

He gave the men a wintry smile and said: "It ain't one egg per man, per week, *perhaps*."

They gave a little laugh at the hoary old wartime joke and Gormless George said in a sinking voice: "The condemned man ate a hearty breakfast."

This time nobody laughed.

Fifty minutes later, replete with eggs and bacon and awash with strong American coffee, which most of the troopers didn't like, laden like pack animals and with two parachutes, American style, strapped to their fronts and their backs, they clambered and struggled aboard the old-fashioned German transport. Outside, the GIs who had been guarding it, cried: "You'll be sorry, guys." To which Gormless George shouted above the roar of the engines: "Of course, I'll be frigging sorry! I've been frigging sorry ever since I joined the frigging Kate Karney," – he meant the Army. It was an outburst which occasioned Sergeant Jenkins to cry sharply; "Watch your fucking language. It ain't decent."

Slowly, the crowded plane started to taxi down the runway, the little emergency lights on both sides whizzing by at an ever-increasing speed. A shudder. A shriek of protesting rubber and abruptly, they were airborne and climbing, the metal at their backs getting steadily colder as they rose.

O'Rourke winked at Al Gorey.

The tall, lanky American winked back. Then he closed his eyes, as if he were going to sleep. They were the veterans. They had done it often before. They knew there was nothing they could do. The operation had taken over. They had become the victims . . .

Two hundred miles away, von Witzleben wiped the sweat off his brow with his good hand and was glad that the back-breaking work of getting the weapon into position was over.

137

The 17-year-old gun crew chief, in charge of the mixed team of schoolboy and schoolgirl flak gunners, said in a worried voice: "I hope there won't be trouble, *Herr Hauptmann*. My CO is a bit of a tartar, sir."

Von Witzleben laughed easily. "Don't worry, I'll square it with your CO as soon as it gets light." He took yet another Hershey bar from his leather satchel and handed it to the kid. "Here have some more *Ami* choc."

The kid took it from him greedily and said, resisting the temptation to bite into the bar immediately – for these kids, von Witzleben knew, hadn't seen chocolate for years–: "Thank you, sir. I hope you will deal with it promptly in the morning."

"Have no fear, I'll take care of it." Doing the best he could in the darkness, von Witzleben peered at the four barrelled, high-speed flak cannon which they had camouflaged among the trees at the side of the Glinde road, after having pushed and pulled it along that road for the last hour. The cannon, he knew, could fire 20mm shells at a rate of a thousand a minute. On the Eastern Front, they had called them the "meat choppers". For when they had been used in a ground defence role they had chopped the Russian infantry attacks into steaming piles of what looked like the offal pre-war butchers had placed outside the doors of their shops to be carted away.

"Remember," he warned, satisfied that the gun was well camouflaged from the air, "when they do come, and I think they will in the none too distance future, I want you in position and waiting for them, when they re-assemble in those fields over there. We shall do our best to deal with them at HQ. But those who succeed in getting away are to be dealt with by you. Do you understand that?"

"I understand, *Herr Hauptmann*," the boy said in a thin, high-pitched voice.

"Good." Von Witzleben took one last look at his thin, pale face and then switched off his torch. "I'm off," he said.

The boy clicked to attention and saluted.

Casually, von Witzleben returned the salute and then

started to walk across the road to where his motorbike was propped up. Even as he strode across the damp cobbles, he could hear the boy tearing greedily at the paper around the chocolate bar.

He shook his head. "Cripples and children," he said, half aloud, "cripples and children."

A moment later he was speeding back up the road.

The stage was set, the actors were in place, the final act of the drama could commence . . .

THREE

Operation Dare and Win

"He who dares, wins."

Motto of the SAS.

ONE

"The front," the American dispatcher said. "You can see it down there."

O'Rourke peered through the little porthole from the darkened interior of the slow, lumbering Junkers. Down below, the inky darkness was split by repeated bursts of cherry red flame of hursting shells. Here and there a fire burned and all the time red and white tracer hissed back and forth like flights of angry red hornets.

O'Rourke's face took on a pensive look, one that was unusual for a man of his experience and temperament. Three Allied armies were fighting all-out down there. There'd be boys among them who had been in short pants at the beginning of the war and others who had been with him at Dunkirk when the British Army had been run out of Europe so ignomiously. But, all of them had thought, now that the Rhine had been crossed, the war would be over sooner and they could go home to their kin and loved ones.

Slowly, the pensive look was replaced by the old, angry determined one. He and the lads wouldn't let the PBI down. They'd sort out these werewolves, come what may, and put an end to the whole bloody awful business of killing and being killed.

Surprisingly similar thoughts were going through Colonel Sterling's mind. He was afraid of what was soon to come. He hoped he wouldn't make a fool of himself. But he wasn't afraid of death, if it helped to end this damned war. There was little to live for anyway. His family was gone and he felt he had seen too much and experienced too much over these last years of the war, so that he couldn't simply go back to the middle-class boredom of Collge Park. He'd not have the patience any more to deal with university politics, committee meetings, "football heroes" and "college Joe".

"A penny for them, Prof?" Goldstein, seated next to him on the hard canvas and steel seat, asked.

"What . . . what, Candidate?" he stuttered, torn from his reverie.

"A penny for them, I said."

He shrugged. "Oh, not much. I was just thinking about what is to come. I hope I don't chicken out when it comes my time to jump."

Goldstein grinned. "You won't with that mad Irishman in charge, Prof. He'll kick you – "

Suddenly, his words were drowned by the voice of the senior pilot over the intercom. "Pay attention," he said with metallic urgency. "We're about to take evasive action. We've been twigged. There's a Jerry fighter on our tail!."

Behind the two Americans, Smith and Bookhalter, who were as always, inseparable, looked at each other and Bookhalter said in a plummy accent: "Here we go again. Once more into the frigging breach, dear friends." He giggled and ducked instinctively next moment, as the first burst of cannon shells ripped the length of the fuselage. Suddenly ice cold air came flooding in. The pilot reacted immediately. He let the Junkers go into a shallow dive to port, all three engines working flat out.

O'Rourke flung a glance through the little window, as kit came tumbling to the floor. He could make out a dark shape and twin scarlet flames from exhausts some five hundred feet away. He cursed. Next moment, he shouted, knowing that there was no real need to do so: "All right, no panic. The flyboy's got everything under control. Remember – you're British!"

"Ay, but does that frigging Jerry know it?" Gormless George said in his broad Yorkshire accent, determined to be the Troop's comedian to the very end.

O'Rourke ignored the comment as the pilot started to

throw the old three-engined plane all over the place, as if it were a fighter and not a cumbersome transport.

But the German fighter pilot who kept overshooting the Junkers, persisted. He was determined to shoot the plane out of the sky. Desperately. the co-pilot slid open the side window of the cockpit and, levelling his bulbous flare pistol, fired off recognition flares, using the known German sequence in an attempt to fool the enemy fighter pilot into believing that this was a German plane.

He wasn't fooled. Instead, he came in again, cannon chattering furiously, determined to knock the Junkers out of the sky.

"Holy sweet Jesus," Buokhalter exclaimed in mock horror, "what's wrong with that Jerry? He must be mad keen. Do you think he's out for a frigging gong – " The rest of his words were drowned by another burst of 20mm shell punching a row of holes the length of the front of the plane. At the controls, the co-pilot screamed shrilly and buried his face in his hands, as if he were about to sob, blood already seeping in a bright scarlet through his clenched fingers.

The pilot, face glazed with sweat, gave him a shove and forced him from the wheel, as the big Junkers went into a sudden dive and the fighter shot above their heads, making the transport shake with the effect of its prop wash. Now the US pilot was throwing the Junkers from left to right, as he headed straight towards the earth, seemingly intent on smashing the Junkers into the ground.

Grimly, O'Rourke held on to his seat, as his ears popped and red and black dots started to explode in front of his eyes. He hoped that the Yank knew what he was doing. The tactic was to force the enemy pilot off by taking the plane close to the ground. It was a matter of who turned yellow first and broke off the attack. But if it went wrong, the pilot wouldn't be able to bring the plane out of its death-defying dive. For the first time since he had left his council school, Rory O'Rourke started to pray.

Down and down they went, the troopers holding on to their seats like grim death. Time and time again, the pursuing fighter fired bursts at the Junkers – they could see the lethal morse of the tracer shells buzzing by the windows – and missed. Now both planes were hurtling earthwards, as if out of control; as if intent on self-destruction.

Next to O'Rourke, Al Gorey felt the pain as his nails dug into his palms till the blood came. "Hot shit," he cursed to himself, "bring the fucker out of the dive! *NOW!*"

Suddenly, startlingly, the pilot jerked back the joystick. Next to him, the dying co-pilot fell out of his seat, scattering a big gob of scarlet-red blood everywhere, splattering the pilot's face with it. The Junkers shuddered. Every rivet creaked under that awesome strain. Al Gorey could see how the veins stood out on the pilot's face as he hauled back the stick. For what seemed an age nothing happened. Then the plane started to rise gain He had done it!

But not the enemy fighter pilot. As the Junkers started to rise, the German plane still shot downwards. O'Rourke craned his neck as the dark shape hurtled past them. Next instant, there was a great roar, which set the Junkers rocking from side to side. Then, there was a blinding flash of scarlet flame, as the fighter's petrol tanks exploded. They had done it!"

In a shaky voice, which he hardly recognized as his own, O'Rourke cried: "All right Sam Smith, you fancy yersen as a bit of a crooner. Give's a song. Cheer us all up."

"Righto, Major," Smith yelled back, the relief obvious in his voice. "All right, lads here we go." He raised his voice. "*Little Miss Muffet sat on tuffit, eating her curds and whey. Up came a spider, sat down besides her, whipped his old bazooka out and this what he said –* "

"*Get hold o' this,*" they joined in in sudden heartfelt relief. "*Get hold o' that. I've got a lovely bunch o' coconuts. I've got a lovely bunch o' balls. Big balls, small balls, balls as big as yer head. Give 'em a twist around yer wrist and sling 'em right over yer head . . .*"

They sang lustily, young men who had escaped death yet again, as the Junkers hurried towards the North Sea and the last stage of their journey

Five minutes before, a flak ship had spotted them as they started to descend, heading for the coast of Schleswig-Holstein. It had fired off a few rounds, but stopped firing when the harassed pilot, with the dead co-pilot still slumped in the seat next to him, fired the German recognition flares. Now they were crossing the coastline flying over what O'Rourke knew from the briefing was farming villages and open spaces, where there was no flak because there were no towns to defend. It was something that encouraged O'Rourke. He didn't want the men upset by enemy fire at this stage of the operation. In a few minutes they were going to take their lives into their hands by jumping out of a plane. He didn't want matters made even more difficult through enemy flak.

Awkwardly, he worked his way up the narrow corridor to where the pilot was. He took his handkerchief out and put it across the co-pilot's bloody face, which looked as if someone had thrown a handful of strawberry jam at it, and said; "How are we for time?"

"Dead on time. Ten minutes to the DZ," the American pilot answered, without taking his gaze off the green-glowing dials and controls. "I'm bringing the ship down gradually. Guess you'll jump at four hundred."

"Make it three hundred feet," O'Rourke snapped. "I know it's risky and we could end up with a few broken bones. Better though, than being in the air too long and being spotted."

"I guess you'll be okay on that score," the pilot replied. "I just picked up a Kraut signal. Your Royal Air Force guys are raiding Hamburg tonight – at this very moment in fact. The Krauts'll be concentrating on them – I hope, I hope." He grinned in spite of the tension.

O'Rourke grinned back. The pilot was only a kid, but he had kept his head, even though he had lost his co-pilot. "Good. But watch you don't bump into the brylcreem boys," he meant the RAF. "They're trigger happy lunch o' bastards."

"Will do," the pilot said, as O'Rourke began to work his way back into the compartment, nodding to the dispatcher, and snapping above the roar of the engines; "All right, on your feet. Check your kit. Snap to it now, lads."

The men, laden with kits so that they appeared to waddle, got to their feet, checking their ammunition, grenades and weapons, slapping the two parachutes which were strapped to their backs and front. That done, they paired off checking their mates' gear and parachutes too, with Bookhalter remarking, as he always did just before a jump: "Why Smithie, you've got a very fine bosom there," to which Smith invariably replied without rancour: "Get off me tits."

Colonel Sterling, his nerves jingling electrically now that the jump was close, carried out the same routine, then inspected Goldstein, who was also looking very pale at the thought of what was soon to come." Well, Candidate, to my unprofessional eye, you seem to be all right," he said finally. "The parachute appears to be on in the right way."

Goldstein forced a grin. "Famous last words, Prof, famous last words." Suddenly he felt a surge of emotion for Sterling. He thrust out his hand at the surprised ex-professor, and said: "Stick it there, sir. The best of luck."

"Why, Candidate, thanks . . . thank you very much," Colonel Sterling stuttered, surprised by his former student's sudden emotionalism. "And all the best to you, too."

Then, at the door, the light changed from green to an urgent red, blinking on and off rapidly. "Stand to. Move to the door," Major O'Rourke barked above the roar of the engines. The time for talking was over. It was time to go.

TWO

"*Go!*" the dispatcher yelled above the roar of the wind at the open door. He struck Major O'Rourke on the shoulder.

O'Rourke flung himself out of the transport. The tail wind caught him and dragged him to the rear of the plane. He caught one last glimpse of the dark outline of the Junkers and then he was falling at one hundred miles per hour. He counted to three. By then he was sure he was clear of the plane. He tugged at the ripcord. Once again he felt a great sense of relief as, with a sharp crack, the canopy opened. A bounce upwards and then he was descending gently to the earth.

Hastily, he squinted between his feet. There was the wood to his right as it should be. Directly below him, where the fields should be, there were no lights and no movements. It appeared that DZ was empty.

For a moment or two he occupied himself with getting his shroud lines right, tugging hard at the webbing until he was satisfied. Now the ground was racing up to meet him. He prepared himself for the usual shock, knees tightly together, but bent. He gave one last pull at the shroud lines. He hit the ground with a bang, falling backwards, with his helmet hitting a rock or stone or something hard.

For one long second he lay there, a little winded, trying to collect himself, watching as the others came floating down, automatically noting that they were coming down in a tight stick, which was good. Now he threw off his chute and unbuckled the one unopened on his chest. He made no attempt to conceal them. The Jerries would know soon enough, he told himself, that they were there. All around him the others were struggling to free themselves, as well. He heard the safety catches being clicked off. That meant his troopers were getting organized already. He nodded his head in approval.

A minute later he had located Colonel Sterling and the younger American. "How did it go?" he asked swiftly, mind on other things.

"Quite exhilerating," Sterling exclaimed a little breathlessly. "I didn't think I'd like it, but I did."

"Ought to do it more often, Colonel," O'Rourke said with a hurried attempt at humour, eyes searching the stark outline of the buildings at the other end of the field for any sign of movement. But there was none.

"No, I think that will be the first and last parachute jump, I shall ever make, Major," Sterling said and finally freed himself from his chute.

O'Rourke nodded and said; "All right, come with me." He nodded to Goldstein. "Off you go to Al Gorey."

Goldstein doubled away, while the two groups formed up rapidly. No orders were given. They weren't needed. The troopers had been through this often enough before. They took up their positions, each man quite certain of the role he was soon going to play.

O'Rourke looked at the green-glowing dial of his watch. It hadn't been damaged in the fall. He beckoned to Gorey. "All right, Al," he said, holding up his watch."

"Circumcize your watch," Al Gorey beat him to it with a grin.

They checked the times and then O'Rourke said: I'll give you a one minute start." He stuck out his hand. "Good luck, Al, and watch your arse."

Al took it and said in a fair imitation of O'Rourke's tough Belfast accent. "My arse, skipper, will remain viriginal and inviolate to the end." Then he was off.

Behind him, in single file, his men slipped into the night and were gone.

O'Rourke counted off his sixty seconds and then set off,

too, waving at his men to follow, making sure that Colonel Sterling was just behind him.

The fields were damp and soggy. They made for slower going, but he dare not risk the cobbled road which ran parallel to the fields. Besides, the road would lead straight to the main entrance, to the cluster of sheds and buildings to his front. And the gate, he was certain, would be guarded.

Five minutes later they reached the perimeter fence which surrounded the camp. It consisted of two separate, barbed wire fences, with a distance of two yards between them. Both fences were about ten foot high and a panting Colonel Sterling, crouching with the SAS troopers, eyed them with apprehension. He felt he would incapable of scaling anything like that.

He need not have worried. After eyeing the fences for a moment and testing them gingerly to check if they were wired up to some sort of alarm system – they weren't – O'Rourke hissed: "Bookhalter and Smith – up here."

Swiftly, the two young troopers went into action without any further orders. They bent slightly to take the strain and crossed their rifles. O'Rourke didn't hesitate. He sprang onto the rifles and with a jump, threw himself to the top of the concrete pillar holding the wire. There was a loud twang and he waited there for a moment, head cocked to one side, but there was no sound save that of the wind in the trees. He nodded. "All right, Colonel, you next."

Hesitantly, Colonel Sterling stepped onto the rifles, knowing he'd never be able to jump the intervening distance. But O'Rourke helped him. He held out his hand. "Come on," he grunted and taking Sterling's weight, he hauled him to the post on which he balanced himself. "Right," he breathed, "I'm going to lower you as far as I can. Let go and keep your legs straight when you land. This would be a helluva time to break an ankle. Okay, here you go."

He lowered the ex-professor, saying: "All right. Now!"

Sterling let go, and remembering O'Rourke's warning, landed on his knees between the two fences.

Now the remaining SAS troopers cleared the fence in

style, until finally there were just Smith and Bookhalter to be hauled up and over.

For a few moments they crouched there between the fences, taking their bearings and staring at the stark silhouettes of the buildings to their front. "Looks okay," O'Rourke said finally. "Old Jerry doesn't seem much cop at patrolling at night." He sniffed. "Right, follow me, we'll keep inside the fences for the time being. We'll have a shufti, Colonel, at the lie of the land before we decide where we'll cross the other fence."

Feeling quite proud of himself now, Colonel Sterling whispered: "Yes, let's have – er shufti," he agreed though he didn't have the slightest idea what "shufti" meant.

Stalking forward on the balls of their feet, every man tense and alert, ready to spring into action at the first sign of discovery, the twenty-odd troopers behind Sterling and O'Rourke followed the line of the fence.

Inside the wire everything remained silent. Once they passed the back of the two-storey-high camouflaged buildings some twenty feet away from the inner fence and heard the sound of someone snoring heavily. Gormless George whispered: "Snore on, sweet prince", while O'Rourke hissed: "Shut your damn big trap." A little later they heard the steady tread of steel-shod boots on gravel and froze instantly, but the steps went by and finally vanished.

Now O'Rourke was sure he could take the camp by surprise. But he had to act soon. The dirty white light of the false dawn was already beginning to flush the sky to the east. It would be properly light in a quarter of an hour's time. By then he would have to have the plastic explosive in place, with the time pencil detonators set to explode them ten minutes' later, by which time he hoped to be pulling back to the recovery site where the American spotter planes would land.

Suddenly O'Rourke stiffened. He held up his hand. The men behind him froze immediately, nerves tingling electrically, wondering what the skipper had just spotted.

A dark, low shape moved out of the shadows cast by

the buildings to the left. It raised its long sloping head and sniffed the pre-dawn air. "Christ," O'Rourke cursed to himself bitterly. It was something he hadn't envisaged: damned guard dog!

For a moment the Alsatian poised there motionlessly. It was as if it were trying to reassure itself it had been mistaken; that it hadn't smelled a strange human smell. O'Rourke knew how they trained them like that. They were schooled to attack anyone who didn't smell the same as their handlers. Had their smell registered?

He felt a cold trickle of sweat seeping down the small of his back. If the beast barked now, they were lost. What the hell was it going to do? "*Piss or get off the pot*", he cursed angrily to himself.

Suddenly the dog moved. It lowered his head and trotted away in the opposite direction. O'Rourke let out a sigh of heartfelt relief. Now he knew they wouldn't go any further in the lane between the two fences. It was time to get into the inner compound. "Smith and Bookhalter," he commanded in a whisper. "We're going in here."

The two friends nodded.

"Below . . . check for alarms."

As one they bent, and side by side, they ran their hands underneath the second fence for about two feet to left and right. "Nothing," they reported. That meant there were no linking wires or unground sensors to trigger off an alarm.

"Good," O'Rourke snapped. "Get cracking."

They needed no urging. Both of them knew that time was running out fast. The light planes coming to pick them up after the op, would soon be crossing the Elbe and it was growing lighter by the minute. Swiftly, they started to snip through the strands of barbed wire at the bottom of the fence. "Clear," Bookhalter reported, after a minute.

"Okay," O'Rourke hissed. "I'll go through first. You follow me, Colonel."

Sterling nodded his understanding. He had seen the dog, too, and knew how close they had come to disaster almost before the mission had started.

Hurriedly, O'Rourke slithered through. In a flash, he was up at the other side, sten gun at the ready, as Sterling followed more slowly. One after another, the others, spread out automatically in a defensive half circle, weapons at their hips.

Sergeant Jenkins, bringing up the rear, was halfway through, when he was stopped in his tracks by a low growl. He froze. But this time the Alsatian didn't go away. He could hear the soft pad-pad of its paws coming down the track.

Jenkins reacted. He levered himself back noiselessly. He turned to face the guard dog. Behind him O'Rourke who had heard, too, swallowed hard. They had all been trained to fight dogs, but he wondered if Jenkins could do so without the dog barking and sounding the alarm. He hoped so.

The dog came closer. It stopped. It sniffed the air, ugly snout raised. It started to come on once more, more purposefully now. It had detected something strange, that was for certain.

Jenkins tensed, dropping his weapon and clenching his big hands. The Alsatian was an ugly-looking brute, long-haired, with yellow teeth that seemed too big for its snout.

Suddenly it stopped. It had seen Jenkins lying there motionless in the grass. It let out a low, menacing growl. Its ears sloped back against its skull. It bared its upper teeth aggressively. Its upper lip curled back. It would attack in a moment!

Jenkins beat him to it. He lunged forward from the lying position. The sudden move caught the Alsatian completely by surprise. Before the dog could react, Jenkin's big paws had clamped themselves on its long jaw. The bark was stiffled in its throat.

The Alsatian wriggled crazily, trying to shake off that vice – like grip. Grimly, for all he was worth, Jenkins hung on. The dog lashed out with one of its paws. It ripped the length of Jenkins' white, strained face. Gobs of blood splattered everywhere.

Now the Alsatian, which must have weighed at least eighty pounds, dug its hindpaws into the gravel. Grunting and fighting wildly for breath, it started to drag Jenkins along on his belly, whipping its jaw madly from side to side.

"Fuck this for a tale", O'Rourke cried, angry that the beast was holding up the whole operation. He dropped his sten, wriggled through the hole and with one hand grabbed the Alsatian's penis. With all his strength he pressed hard on it.

The Alsatian yelped. Suddenly it went limp and prostrate with the excruciating agony of that hellish hold. O'Rourke didn't give it a chance to recover. With his free hand he felt for his fighting knife. "Force the bastard's head back, Jenkins," he ordered.

"Yessir."

Jenkins exerted all his strength, forcing the head upwards to expose the throat. He knew what the CO was going to do.

O'Rourke did it. He slashed through the dog's vocal chords. "Let'go!" he ordered.

Jenkins did so gratefully. Next moment O'Rourke plunged the knife deep into the animal's heart, still holding on to its penis. Its spine arched like taut bowstring. O'Rourke plunged his knife in once more. It came out with a dreadful sucking sound. His hand ran red with blood. Undeterred, he loosened his grip. Nothing happened. The beast was dead.

"With my luck, the bastard's got rabies," Jenkins mumbled.

"Come on," O'Rourke hissed.

Next minute the two of them were through and advancing on the nearest buidling. Behind them the dog stiffened in the dawn cold.

THREE

Cautiously, very cautiously, Al Gorey started to open the door of the first of the little cottages. Opposite him, on the other side of the doorway, Goldstein tensed, big Colt .45 in his right hand. He looked pale and nervous.

The door squeaked open to reveal a room dominated by a large bed. Otherwise the only furniture was a rickety wooden chair. On the bed, which was rumpled and creased, lay two girls, totally naked and clasped in each other's arms. Judging by their small breasts and delicate pubic fuzz, neither could have been a day older than fourteen. "Start early in Germany," Al Gorey mouthed at Goldstein.

The latter nodded, but didn't speak; he didn't trust himself to to do so.

Gently, almost noiselessly, Al Gorey closed the door. Together with Goldstein, covered by the rest of the troopers, crouched low, weapons at the ready as it started to grow lighter and lighter, they went down the line of the little white-washed cottages, which might in former times have been used by farm labourers. They were all occupied – and all by girls, most of them in their teens.

At the end of the inspection, Al Gorey looked grim. "Don't like it," he whispered to Goldstein, "don't like it one bit."

"Why?"

"They're only kids, and girls to boot."

"They're Krauts and very deadly kids, aren't they," Goldstein objected, "being trained to murder, stab people in the back, shoot innocent civilians just like this Chief Burgomaster Oppenhoff."

Al Gorey shook his head, obviously not convinced.

"They've been brainwashed, indoctrinated by a crazy system. It's the only kind of life they've known – the Nazi system. You can't blame them for it, can you."

Goldstein didn't answer.

Al Gorey made his decision. "I'm not going to have those kids, however perverted sexually and politically, killed. Okay lads, set the incendiaries, not the plastic. Once they smell smoke and hear the bombs going off, they'll have time to beat it before the flames get too high."

Swiftly, efficiently, the SAS troopers started laying the incendiaries, tiny little bombs, which were set to go off by pulling the cord of the time pencil at the base of the contraption.

Goldstein watched, pistol in hand, knowing that Gorey was right, but that he was risking the whole mission by giving the Kraut kids a chance to live. If one of them raised the alarm before they cleared the area, all hell could be let loose.

"Someone coming,!" Goldstein, she was standing lookout, hissed urgently. "Two men!"

As one the SAS troopers dropped what they were doing and hit the ground between the huts. Two middle-aged soldiers, with carbines slung across their shoulders, were coming leisurely down the little track, talking loudly to one another. If they were sentries, Al Gorey told himself, they were damned careless about it.

"*All diese Kleinen ficken vie verruckt,*" the taller of the two men was saying. "*Vorgestern hatte ich eine. Kaum mehr als vierzehn. Aber, Mensch, war die geil!*"

"The big Kraut says that all these little girls fuck like rabbits," Goldstein whispered into Gorey's ear. "The day before yesterday, he had one of them, not more than fourteen. Horny as hell."

Gorey nodded, mind on other things than the middle-aged Kraut's sexual boasting. The bastards couldn't have turned up at a worse time. Now they had to be taken out, but silently.

"*Sollen wir die jetzt wecken?* the smaller of the two asked.

"*Nee*," the other one answered. "*Wir gucken mal erst durch die Tur. Die meisten schlafen splitternackt.*" he winked. "*Vielleicht haben qir Gluck – ein paar nackte Fotzen ware mir angenehm.*" He chuckled.

"The little guy wants to wake them," Goldstein translated hurriedly. "But the other guy says no. They mostly sleep naked and he wants to see a couple of cunts."

"Shit!" Al Gorey cursed. He waited no longer. Like a shadow, he darted behind the hut, ran doubled to the end of the line and waited, gasping as the two middle-aged soldiers approached the hut, walking on their tip-toes in an exaggerated fashion like awkward schoolboys. The bigger one put his hand on the door handle and was about to turn when Gorey was on to him.

"*Was*" – the man's cry of surprise was stiffled immediately, as Gorey tugged at his helmet and pulled it backwards so that the chinstrap fell just around his prominent Adam's apple. His companion turned, startled, as Gorey thrust his knee into the small of the German sentry's back and exerted pressure. The nearest SAS trooper, realizing the danger, sprung up from his hiding place. He lashed out with the cruel brass knuckles of his fighting knife. The German dodged and yelled as the blow landed, not on his chin, but on his shoulder. He staggered back, as Gorey, face grim, determined and sweat-lathered, continued to garrotte the other sentry. "Don't let him get away!" he hissed through gritted teeth.

The SAS trooper raised his knife. The German's face was abject with terror. "*Nein*," he screamed . . . "*bitte nicht –* " His words ended in a shrill shriek, as the knife struck him in the chest and he went down on his knees trying to pluck the blade from his breast. He failed. He fell face forward, dead before he hit the ground . . .

Hauptmann von Witzleben awoke with a start. He had slept in a chair since he had returned from the anti-aircraft position. He hadn't wanted to get into bed with the girl in case his batman had found them together. That, he thought, would have been bad form. It had been his intention to wake at dawn, clean the mud off his boots – the position he had found for the teenage gunners had been very muddy – have a shave (something which was very time-consuming with one hand) and then set about organizing the camp's defences.

Now he rubbed his eyes, looked at his watch, which told him it was time to be up and about, and wondered what had startled him from his sleep. It had been a sort of a cry. Hadn't it been the girl? She moaned and groaned a lot in her sleep, grinding her teeth and offering little cries as if in sexual ectasy, which perhaps was what it was. No, he decided, it hadn't been the girl. It had been a base tone – more masculine.

Frowning, he rose to his feet, adjusted the springs of his wooden arm – it had a tendency to turn back to front, which von Witzleben always thought was a little disconcerting for ordinary mortals, and walked over to the blackout in his stockinged feet. He took down the shutter and stared outside.

The compound was empty except for one sentry whom he could see was having a quiet smoke among the trees, his hand cupped around his cigarette, just in case the orderly sergeant came to inspect. He looked around. Nothing there that could have occasioned the sound which had awakened him. Suddenly he stopped. Lying between the two barbed wire fence was one of the guard dogs! It was stretched full length as if it was enjoying a hearty sleep. But he knew that the fierce Alsatians never slept whilst on duty. They would have received a severe beating from their handlers if they had. *No, there was something the matter with the dog*!

All thoughts of a shave and clean-up gone now, he tugged on his muddy boots. As an afterthought, he buckled on his pistol belt. Seizing his cap, he went outside. At the double he crossed over to the fence. "Get up," he commanded the lying dog. But even as he spoke, he could see that the animal wasn't breathing. It was dead.

In that same instant, he took in the fact, too, that the wire had been cut. Right at the base of the inner fence the barbed wire was curled inwards, the ends gleaming brightly where they had been cut. And the cutting had taken place recently; there was no sign of rusting. For a moment he was rooted there, wondering what it all signified: the dead dog and the cut wire. Suddenly, it all came to him in a flash.

He turned. As quickly as he could, he ran back to the building. "Get up!" he cried. "Get up at once."

She opened her eyes, smiled vaguely at him and began rubbing her eyes like a small child does when it finds it hard to wake up properly. Then she threw back the feather bed and spread her naked legs so that he could glimpse the delicate pink flesh there in the little fuzz of black hairs. "Come then," she breathed.

"No, not that!" he snapped almost angrily. He grabbed her by the arm and pulled her to her feet. "Get dressed – get dressed quickly!"

"*Was ist los?*" she cried, puzzled, allowing herself to be jerked upright.

"*Der Teufel ist los*," he cried back. "The devil is up." With all his strength he jerked the steel-framed bed upright. "As soon as you're dressed, stay behind that," he commanded. "It should be effective protection."

"Against what?" she asked stupidly, pulling on the white cotton knickers she always wore, as if she were still the virginal schoolgirl she had been when she had first seduced him.

"Don't know. But there's something," he answered her, looking at her worried, puzzled, degenerate but innocent little face, as if he were seeing it for the very first time. "No time for any more questions," he rapped. "I'm going to sound the alarm."

"Kiss me – *please*," she begged, suddenly very serious.

"Oh, all right," he relented.

She pressed herself against him fervently and for the very last time he felt those upward-tilted little breasts of hers press against him as she opened her mouth to swallow his tongue. Then he was pushing his way out of the door, leaving her standing there, holding her bra in

160

her hand, as if she didn't quite know what to do with it.

Still the compound was empty. That pre-reveille calm that he had known for years as a soldier reigned. From the cookhouse there came the first signs of smoke, as the cooks prepared the morning soup, and there was the muted rattle of a dixie being scoured out with sand. Otherwise, nothing stirred. For a moment or two he wondered if he was making a fool of himself. Was he imagining things?

He shook his head. How often on the battlefield had he relied on his own hunches that the balloon was soon to go up. What was it his comrades, now dead, all of them in Russia, had used to say: "Klaus, hell, he can smell the shit's going to start, even before it's been shat!" Something told him that the "shit" was about to start now.

He doubled over to the orderly office. He burst through the door. The Hitler Youth group leader who was that night's orderly officer sat at his desk reading the werewolves manual: "*Werewolf: Hints for Hunting Units.*" He saw von Witzleben's agitated face and jumped to attention immediately. Hands slapped rigid to the side of his short black pants, he cried: "*Gaufuhrer Filbinger meldet sich z –* "

– "Cut out the crap," von Witzleben interrupted him brutally. "Anything suspicious to report?"

The blond youth looked at him in bewilderment. "Why no, *Herr Hauptmann*. It's been a – "

From the other side of the road where the girls slept in the farmworkers' cottages, there was a sudden series of faint explosions.

Von Witzleben thrust the surprised youth to one side and bolted for the window. Thick white smoke was rising from the line of huts. Girls, most of them undressed, were running from them screaming and shouting, though through the closed window he couldn't make out what they were shouting. He didn't need to. He knew instinctively, although he couldn't see any of the enemy, that this was the attack that Prutzmann had been expecting. He swung round on the startled Hitler Youth. "Sound the alarm!" He shouted.

161

"Sound the alarm?" the youth echoed stupidly.

"Yes, that's what I said. Are you deaf, boy?"

The Hitler Youth acted. He jumped to where the hand-cranked siren, used to sound the air raid warnings, was bolted to the orderly officer's desk and began to turn the handle energetically.

Slowly at first, but rising in power by the instant, the siren started to shrill its warning . . .

FOUR

Major Lee Rogers, the commander of the spotter plane force, pressed his throat mike, eyes fixed firmly on the river line ahead. "To all," he barked in his tough New York accent. "That's the Elbe ahead. The Krauts have got flak down there. So we're going down to zero feet. Now guys, we're going to do a little hedge-hopping. Roger and out." He took his hand away from the mike and concentrated now on flying.

Veteran that he was of nine months of combat with the artillery spotter planes, he knew "hedge-hopping" was not a manoeuvre to be treated lightly. A pilot had to concetrate totally when flying at zero feet, for not only had he to contend with the changing terrain, flat country suddenly becoming hills, fields abruptly turning into woods, and the like, but there were also enemy soldiers taking potshots at low-flying planes. And the spotter planes were easy targets at zero feet, constructed as they were of wood and canvas.

So now Major Rogers made his decision as he brought the plane down lower and lower. He had the map of the area in his head. To his right there was the small inland harbour of Geesthacht. To his left, there was the ribbon development of villages running into one another on the road that led to Hamburg some twenty miles away. He reasoned that there'd be flak guns on the heights around Geesthacht to protect the little harbour itself and also to provide the first line of defence for the great city of Hamburg. So he'd go in to the left of the Geesthacht heights.

Now he was almost down. The fields, muddy and water-logged, were clearly visible, flashing by at 100 mph. Here and there men on cycles, probably working men going to

163

the early shift at the factories in Lauenburg further up the road, got off and stared upwards at the strange sight: thirty odd light planes spread out in a long extended V zooming over the countryside at not more than tree-top height. Some shook their fists when they spotted the star of the US Army Air Corps on the planes and Rogers laughed tensely. As long as they only threatened, they were safe.

Now the Elbe loomed up in front of them – a silver snake of water beyond the dyke that ran the length of this side of the great northern river. Barges, mostly heavily laden – because they were deep in the water, puffed and chugged their way up and down the river. Rogers flung a glance to left and right. None of the bargees seemed armed. Again he was grateful.

Up ahead now came the bluffs on the northern bank of the Elbe, white in places and well wooded. He tugged back the stick. The plane rose dutifully. Now he could see the cobbled road that led to Hamburg. There were a few cars on it, lugging behind the trailers, complete with the fuel balloons that held the coal gas which powered them. There were men, too – men in helmets, running.

"Christ on a crutch," he cursed to himself, "flak gunners!"

He was right. Almost instantly, white tracer shells started streaming up at the planes in a lethal morse. He recognized the shells immediately. 20mm quadruple light cannon, used against low-flying planes. He felt the sweat break out underneath his leather flying helmet.

Face grim, he weaved from side to side, praying he was going to get through to the empty fields beyond the Hamburg road. Behind him his pilots did the same. For all the world they looked like those performing planes he remembered from before the war, when he had earned his keep barnstorming and performing for country hicks right across the States.

A burst of shellfire to his right, which sent the plane reeling wildly until he caught it again, told him that this wasn't peacetime. Those bastards down there were aiming to kill him if they could.

He flung a look behind him. Most of his planes were over the bluffs now. He nodded his approval and then concentrated on his own safety, as another burst of shellfire sent the light plane scudding wildly to the right.

Now the dawn sky was full of shellbursts. It was peppered with ugly brown patches of smoke, through which the line of light planes flew, defying death every second. Behind Rogers, one of his planes was hit in his rear view mirror. Rogers could see the pilot trying to control his machine. Rogers grimaced. "Come on, boy, pull her up. For fuck's sake, pull her up and jump!"

But, already, thick black smoke was pouring from the plane's ruptured engine. In vain the pilot fought the controls, trying to make the crippled plane rise so that he had sufficient height to jump by parachute. It wasn't to be. Suddenly, startlingly, the plane went completely out of control. It fell out of the sky like a stone. Next moment it slammed on its nose on the Hamburg road, its wings breaking off as it did so. Cherry red flames started to lick the shattered fuselage immediately. No one got out.

"Shit, shit, shit!" Rogers cursed furiously, the tears streaming down his face unhindered. For he was an emotional man, who felt his responsibility to his pilots, most of whom were barely out of their teens. He had made the wrong decision to go in low over the Elbe. One of his kids had "bought the farm," as they said, as a result.

He forgot the dead pilot and concentrated on his navigation. None of his pilots were trained in navigation. They simply flew by the seat of their pants, as they phrased it. It was up to him to get them to the landing zone. He had to make it simple for them.

Now he skidded across the wet fields beyond the roadside villages heading for the little hamlet of Buchen. There, the main railway line from Berlin to Hamburg ran through the place, heading west and running through Reinbek. He intended to follow the railway line as the easiest means of navigating to the scene of the action.

A few minutes later he found Buchen, a collection of low

red-brick houses and outflying farms clustered around the railway station. He pressed the throat mike: "All right, guys," he commanded, "We're following the railroad on a due west bearing. Keep spread out. The Krauts tend to have flak guns on important trains these days. Roger and out." He looked back in his mirror. His kids were following him all right. Everything seemed to be going well again. He flew on.

They flew across the station's shunting yards. A couple of locomotives were being turned on the turntables, belching thick black smoke from their stacks. In his mirror he saw one of the pilots lob one of the grenades which they all carried over the side of the cockpit.

Rogers grinned suddenly. He knew who that pilot was. It was Red O'Hara, whose Irish temper was notorious. He hated everything and anything German. He always took any opportunity to kill or hurt Germans. Now Rogers watched as the grenade sailed down to disappear right down the stack of the bigger locomotive. There was muffled, hollow boom. Suddenly, startlingly, the locomotive's boiler burst with a great roar and the heavy engine lifted itself clean off the turntable and slammed on its side in a great cloud of dust.

Everywhere on the platforms, the crowds waiting for trains to Hamburg and other stations along the route, scattered wildly, shoving and jostling angrily with each other to escape these strange little "terror bombers". "Swell job, Red," Rogers said, pressing his throat mike, "but save your ammo. We might need it where we're going. Kay?"

They flew on, dragging their shadows behind them over the fields cast in the blood red light of the rising sun. They overtook a slow, heavy train chugging westwards. It bore red crosses on its sides and roof. But Rogers had seen the Germans use that trick before, hauling ammunition or troops under the cover of the red cross. He came lower. The leather-masked gunner, peering out of his tower at the end of one of the carriages, spotted the approaching planes. But he didn't fire. Instead he must have pulled the brake. For the train skidded to a halt and in an instant bandaged men, some on crutches and sticks, were streaming out of the stalled train, hopping and limping to the cover of the fields on both sides.

Rogers sniffed. This time he had been wrong. It had been a genuine hospital transport.

Five minutes passed. Now Rogers concentrated on finding the lake and the castle, which, as he had been briefed, were the landmarks by which he would recognize Reinbek. He reduced speed. Obediently the others to left and right did the same. Somewhere a machine gun was spitting tracer at the aerial armada. But they were out of range and, like glowing pingpong balls, the bullets were falling short of them.

Suddenly he had it. "That's the lake;" he called over the radio. "It's Reinbek. All right, fellas, close up now. I don't want any of you missing the landing strip."

He waited till they had done so, then he came down even lower.

People were stopping in the cobbled streets below and, shading their eyes against the blood-red glare of the March sun, were staring upwards as if they couldn't believe the evidence of their own eyes. On impulse, Rogers zoomed under two linked telegraph poles and the crowd scattered immediately, screaming and crying in panic. He smiled, pleased with himself.

Now, to his front, on the hilly ridge above the town, he could see the red flames of fire and a mushroom of bright white smoke of the kind made by incendiary bombs, rising to the sky. "This is it, fellas," he cried and headed in that direction.

An instant later they were flying over a line of burning huts, heading straight for a compound surrounded by low dark-green buildings. Men were running all over the place, some were firing, others were ducking and taking cover in the ditches that ran on both sides of the cobbled road.

Rogers bit his bottom lip, worried. Now everything depended upon his making the right decision. Beyond the dark-green buildings he could see the open fields, with, to left and front, thick woods. The fields were empty and looked pretty good for landing – there were no obstacles that he could spot and they were meadows, not ploughed fields. But what about the woods? Whole armies could be concealed in them.

He did a slow turn. The others followed . . . Nothing moved. All the action was taking place half a mile away, where the Limeys presumably were carrying out their sabotage mission. "To all," he announced over the radio, "keep your height for the time being. I'm gonna have a look-see at those woods. Keep circling. Out."

Now he played the bait. He had done it often enough before, baiting hidden German guns to take a potshot at him so that he could radio back his own artillery for a counter-shoot. All the same, it was a chancy, nerve-racking business. He came very low at tree top height, his prop-wash lashing the top branches of the firs into a wild green fury. His speed was just above stalling so that anyone hiding below with a weapon couldn't have missed him; they couldn't have had a bigger target.

Nothing happened.

Still Rogers wasn't satisfied. The fate of thirty other kid pilots lay in his hands. He couldn't afford to take chances that might cost them their lives.

While the others circled the site slowly above him, he did another length of the woods. This time he decided if there was a hornets' nest hidden down there somewhere, he'd stir it up. Leaning over the side of the cockpit, he pulled the pin out of a grenade with his teeth and tossed it deep into the trees.

"*rump!*" There was a sharp explosion. Two firs broke off, snapping like matchwood, scattering branches everywhere in a sudden green rain. Nothing happened. He tried again with a second grenade. Once more there was no reaction from below. The woods were empty.

He flashed a glance to his front, where the smoke of battle was rising ever higher, and told himself that time must be running out fast for the Limeys. They'd be dropping back to the DZ soon.

He pressed his throatmike. "Kay, fellas," he snapped, very professional and businesslike now, "I'm going in . . ."

FIVE

Gorey's team were now backing off down the cobbled road that led to the factory and the DZ beyond. Every few yards they stopped and snapped off quick bursts to left and right at the houses on both sides of the road from which enemy fire was coming. It had been very weak at first. Now it was increasing in intensity by the second. Twice Gorey had glimpsed an old face, surmounted by a pre-war type of coal scuttle helmet, and guessed the houses were occupied by the *Volkssturm*.* Perhaps it was they who had the task of guarding the werewolf camp. He didn't know or care much. All he wanted was his men cleared of the street before the regular *Wehrmacht* troops arrived from the nearby town of Bergedorf not more than a couple of miles away.

Covering him as he fired another burst from his sten, a sweating, wild-eyed Goldstein yelled above the angry snap-and-crackle of the small arms fight: "The shit's hit the fan behind us, Gorey! O'Rourke must have run into trouble."

Gorey forced a grin and said to Goldstein, who was bleeding from a wound at his temple: "O'Rourke *always* run into trouble." He raised his sten and fired a burst at a German, who was attempting to snipe the SAS troopers below.

The old man shrieked, threw up his arms and came pitching down from the roof screaming. He slammed into the road and lay still, every bone in his body broken. They moved back another half dozen yards.

Now the fire was intense and, although so far only

* The German Home Guard, *transl.*

169

Goldstein had been wounded by it, Gorey knew their luck wouldn't hold out much longer. Old as they were the *Volkssturm* men could hardly miss at that range. "Follow me," he yelled and, grabbing a surprised Goldstein by the tunic, added: "Stick close to me – or you'll get hurt again."

"Roger," Goldstein gasped, as Gorey aimed a terrific kick at the door of the nearest house. It gave immediately and they went inside. Routinely Gorey sprayed the stairs and the ceiling above with fire. Lath and plaster fell in a white rain. Someone yelped with the pain and there was the sound of something heavy falling. "Through the back door," Gorey bellowed and smashed it open.

Hurriedly, he and the rest blundered through it, down a garden path and onto the narrow track which ran parallel to the house at the back. Gorey had guessed there'd be a track running the length of the houses and he gambled the *Volkssturm* would have set themselves in the front of them. He was right and he told himself that it would take the old boys a little while to react to the little trick.

"At the double now," he yelled. "And keep yer eyes skinned!"

"Like a tin of peeled tomatoes, sir," one of the troopers said and laughed heartily, as if he were really enjoying this confused, bloody business.

A panting Goldstein told himself that he had always thought the English were slightly mad. Now he knew he was wrong – *they were totally loco!*

They doubled down the track, with hardly a shot being fired at them now. Up ahead, one of the factory buildings was burning and the sound of the battle coming from that direction was intensifying. A girl in the white skirt of the Hitler Maidens lay sprawled in the ditch at the side of the track, her head a mess of blood, with the blue-bottles already beginning to buzz greedily around it. Al Gorey shook his head. She didn't look older than fourteen or fifteen. Now she was dead. What a world!

A *Volkssturm* man came panting up the trail towards them, a long old-fashioned rifle slung over his shoulder.

"*Die Tommies greifen an*," he kept panting in some kind of terrified litany. He didn't see the SAS troopers till too late. Goldstein raised his Colt. Gorey knocked it down before he could fire. "Poor old fart – let him live," he gasped.

As the old man staggered to a bewildered stop, still mouthing: "The Tommies are attacking," as if he were back in the trenches in the Old War, Gorey lashed out with his clenched fist. The old man was lifted off his feet and slammed into the ditch, unconscious before he bit the earth. "At least he'll survive to go back to his old woman," Gorey commented. They ran on.

Now, Gorey in the lead, could see that there was one hell of a connemara going on in the factory. Fire was coming from the upper storeys of the buildings and further off he could hear the characteristic high-pitched hysterical blurr-blurr of a spandau machine gun firing 1,000 rounds per minute.

Another building went up in flames and Gorey told himself that O'Rourke would soon be getting ready to disengage; his luck couldn't hold out for ever. Regular troops would be on their way to Reinbek already. The Krauts always reacted quickly to an attack.

"*Sir – ten o'clock!*" an urgent call cut into his thoughts.

He swung his head to the left. Next to him Goldstein croaked, "Oh, Holy Christ – *not that*!

An armoured car was coming round the corner of the factory's perimeter fence, its long overhanging gun twitching from side to side like the snout of some primeval monster seeking out his prey.

Al Gorey reacted. "Get that bazooka up front her," he yelled. He saw that the armoured car had not yet seen them. Once it did, it would make hamburger meat out of them with that great gun. A trooper slapped the bazooka into his arm. Another one shoved the projectile up the back of the long tube. Hurriedly Gorey balanced it on his right shoulder and peered through the sight. It neatly dissected the armoured car's turret with its black and white iron cross emblem. He squeezed the trigger. The bazooka erupted on his shoulder. A flash. A puff of smoke. Next instant, the projectile was streaking towards the unsuspecting armoured car.

Thump! There was the hollow boom of metal striking metal. Suddenly, the turret armour flushed an angry pink. The armoured car staggered and stopped abruptly, as if it had just run into an invisible wall.

The turret hatch was flung out. A mushroom of dark smoke erupted from it. A soldier, uniform torn and smoking, his face black, tried to pull himself out groggily. The SAS troopers showed no mercy. They riddled him with fire. He slumped over the edge of the turret, body leaking blood like a sieve.

"Come on," Gorey yelled. "Let's get the hell outa here!"

They ran on. As they passed the smoking armoured car, one of them clambered up the side, shoved the dead soldier back inside, followed that with a grenade and flung the hatch shut. "That's should give 'em a nasty headache," he yelled triumphantly as he dropped off hurriedly.

There was a muffled explosion. Next moment the armoured car was burning furiously from end to end.

Al Gorey spotted a door in the outer perimeter. "Over here," he cried, running towards it, as to the left yet another of the factory buildings went up in flames. The men needed no urging. They could hear from the volume of fire from within that the O'Rourke party was in trouble.

A vicious burst of machine gun sliced the air. A trooper flung up his arms with shock, a puzzled look on his suddenly ashen face, a row of red buttonholes abruptly stitched across his chest. Next moment, he fell to the ground, dead.

"It's over there – top window," Goldstein yelled above the racket. Carried away by the unreasoning bloodlust and anger of war, he started blazing away at the upper window, from which the fire was coming, with his pistol. Frantically, Al Gorey pushed him to one side. "Another rocket," he bellowed.

Behind him a trooper slapped a missile into the rear of the bazooka. Al Gorey aimed and fired as one. The missile slammed into the window area. Glass spintered. Bricks rained down. When the smoke cleared, there was nothing to be seen of the German gunner. They ran, heading for the firing.

O'Rourke said to Sterling, shouting above the firing: "I think we've about done all we can." He raised his pistol and snapped off a shot. A kid in short pants who had come running the corner of the building opposite with a stick grenade in his hand screamed and let the grenade drop. It exploded. When the smoke cleared, it revealed a headless body. The head itself was rolling towards the gutter like a football abandoned by a careless boy, "Silly young sod," O'Rourke said without emotion.

Sterling was shocked, but said nothing. He knew that these men were fighting for their lives. They had no time for sentiment or emotion. Instead he shouted: "Which way shall we pull back? To the gap in the fence?"

O'Rourke shook his head. Across the way another of the factory buildings had erupted in flames. Screaming girls came running from it, their uniforms on fire. "No, never go out the way you came in. S.O.P.* We're going out through the gate. They won't expect that. Come on." Again his pistol cracked and an old man who had been attempting to take a shot at them from an upper window, collapsed over the sill, rifle tumbling to the ground.

Together the two officers ran into the compound. All was chaos. Flames were on all sides. Little groups of SAS troopers pelted down the row, sticking plastic explosive to the sides of the remaining undamaged buildings and thrusting home the time pencils. Tracer zipped back and forth lethally. Dead and dying lay everywhere in the gutters. To their right, a girl with her left leg blown off at the knee was dragging herself to cover, tears streaming down her face. Sterling shook his head. It was like a picture out of hell.

O'Rourke paused in the centre of the compound, while Sterling crouched apprehensively next to him. He felt very vunerable. O'Rourke swung the hunting horn round from

* Standard Operating Procedure. *transl.*

his back. He raised it to his lips and sounded a swift blast on it. Sterling knew it was the Troop's rallying cry. In that confusion it carried – and it worked.

The SAS troopers swung round. They started back to the centre of the compound, firing to left and right as they went. Some were wounded, Sterling could see that. But they were still moving, even the one who had a blood-stained yellow shell dressing crudely wound around a shattered knee.

O'Rourke shook his head in admiration. "A good bunch o' boys," he said, as if to himself.

"All right, Colonel," he turned to Sterling. "Stick close to me. We're backing off now. Once we're through the guardroom, we're heading straight down the road to the DZ where the planes are. No one's gonna stop. Clear?"

"Clear."

Now the SAS troopers started to move purposefully towards the big gate, which was closed. Next to it on the right there was the guardroom from which fire was already coming, though it was erratic and wild.

O'Rourke told himself as soon as whoever was in charge realized they were coming out that way, the defenders would put up a tougher show. But he'd deal with that hurdle when he came to it. First, they had to get there. For fire was coming in from both sides and he had already taken another casualty – young Bookhalter shot in the arm – though he was still capable of using his sten gun.

To the right, a group of men burst out of the smoke. O'Rourke groaned. The Jerries were attacking in force. Then he recognized Al Gorey, helmetless and with blood streaming down the side of his face, but grinning like a Cheshire cat when he saw that the rest of the troop was intact. "Bloody Yanks," he grumbled, but he didn't mean it.

Hurriedly, he signalled his intention of attacking the guardroom and indicated that Gorey's party should tackle the place from the right, while his own group would give them covering fire from the left.

Gorey signalled that he understood. He snapped something to his men. They reached for their grenades, as Gorey slammed the bazooka to his shoulder, and when he saw his men were ready, grenades in hand, fired a round right at the brick guardroom. It slammed right into the wall next to the door. Bricks flew everywhere and then they were charging forward, screaming and yelling obscenities, hurling grenades as they ran.

"*Fire . . . give them covering fire!*" O'Rourke yelled in sudden fury and anger, as he saw one of the Gorey party clutch his stomach, and spin round, with what looked like a steaming purple-blue snake, which was his intestines, already escaping from his stomach. Next moment, he sank to the cobbles, choking out the last moments of his young life.

Willingly, O'Rourke's men poured a hail of fire at the opposite side of the guardhouse. The windows shattered instantly and kept the defenders lying low.

Then they, too, were up and running for the gate. A couple of men went down, but SAS troopers were not leaving their wounded behind. They were scooped up and supported by their comrade as they hobbled on to the smashed gate and the road to freedom and rescue beyond. They had done it!

SIX

Hauptmann von Witzleben heard the great clang as the gate was ripped open; he heard, too, the firing at the guardroom ceasing and realized the Tommies had done it. He slumped down on the bullet-riddled chair and let his weapon drop. In the fighting, a bullet had shattered his wooden arm. Now it lay in splinters on the littered floor all around him, though the hand in its black leather glove was still intact. He stared at it as if he could not make out what it was.

He heard, too, the massive drone of engines and told himself that it was the planes which had come to pick up the Tommies. What a surprise they were in for! But the knowledge gave him no sense of triumph. He felt too hollow, too drained of energy. The Tommies had done what they had come to do – wreck the werewolf HQ. In the process a lot of old farts of the Volkssturm and those silly fanatical kids, boys and girls, had been killed or wounded.

Suddenly the phone on the debris-covered desk jingled. It startled him. He looked at it, as if in surprise. It was so normal, the ringing of an office phone, that it seemed bizarre, so totally out of place in this scene of death and mass destruction.

Reluctantly, he reached for it, his thin face hollowed out to a glowing death's head by the reflected light of the burning building opposite. "Von Witzleben," he said a little wearily.

"Prutzmann". There was no mistaking that arrogant sharp voice, full of what the German called "*Schneid*", the harsh cutting edge favoured by the military.

"*Gruppenfuhrer?*"

176

"You are alone?"

Von Witzleben could have laughed. Yes, he was alone, surrounded by scores of bodies. But he said, "Yes, I am *Gruppernfuhrer*."

"Good, then listen carefully, and remember what I am to say to you now is absolutely secret. It will cost you your head, if you reveal it to any other person."

The threat left von Witzleben totally unmoved. What else could happen to him now?

"This afternoon I am setting off with Heinrich – er – *Reichsfuhrer* Heinrich Himmler for Lubeck. The *Reichsfuhrer SS* has made a very important decision, one which will decide the end of the war."

Von Witzleven listened, but he couldn't seem able to take in the words.

"He is to meet this very night Count Folke Bernadotte of the Swedish royal family, who is prepared to act as an intermediary between him and the American General Eisenhower, chief of the Allied armies."

Von Witzleben gasped.

Prutzmann heard the gasp and said: "Yes, you're right. Herr Himmler has realized that Germany has lost the war. Now it must end without further losses to our beloved country. We must save as much of the country as possible from those Russian swine in the east. As Heinrich said only an hour ago to me; "I am willing to surrender to Eisenhower unconditionally. Between men of the world I could offer my hand to Eisenhower."

"Surrender . . . men of the world," von Witzleben gasped. "What what are you talking about?"

Outside, the flames had begun to consume the dead body of a naked teenage girl. Before his eyes she started to shrivel and char a flaky black in the gremendous heat. He shifted his gaze hurriedly.

"Himmler wants an immediate end to the war, that's what I mean," Prutzmann said sharply. "Can't you understand that, von Witzleben? And in order to facilitate these delicate negotiations, I am ordering you as my second-in-command to disband the werewolf organization immediately. *Immediately*, is that clear? We want no further murders which might provoke the Americans. Who knows, within the week they might be our allies and be fighting at our side against the bolsheviks in the east."

There was silence and after a moment, Prutzmann asked sharply: "Are you listening to me, von Witzleben?"

"Listening to you," von Witzleben exclaimed, a note of madness in his voice. "You're mad, man!"

"How dare you speak to me like that?" Prutzmann shouted angrily.

"Disband the organization!" von Witzleben yelled into the phone, his eyes bulging like those of a man demented. "It is already disbanded. There are scores of dead kids outside to prove that it's disbanded. Teenaged kids, who people like you seduced into believing they should give their young lives for Folk, Fatherland and Fuhrer – and have done so now, dead before they had begun to live. And you," he shouted, face red with fury, "what do you and the precious *Reichsfuhrer* do? I'll tell you what you do."

– "I forbid you to speak to me like this."

Von Witzleben ignored the remark. In fact, he never even heard it. "What you do now when all is lost, is to abandon the sinking ships like rats. You'll try to curry favour with our conquerors in order, so you think, to retain your positions – the fawning adjutants, the big cars, the titled mistresses, lining your own pockets at the expense of the poor long-suffering German people – "

– "I shall have you court-martialled for this," Prutzmann bellowed at the other end. "This is gross insubordination. I have never been talked to like – "

In a sudden paroxysm of overwhelming rage and sense of outraged injustice, von Witzleben pulled the phone out by the wire and flung it against the wall with all his strength, where it exploded into its component parts.

Now, outside, the noise was beginning to die down, though to the rear there still came the roar of many aeroplane engines. People were shouting the names of their lost

178

comrades. Wounded were whimpering and in young thin voices, calling "Sanitater . . . stretcher-bearer . . . Over here, please!"

He remembered the girl. God, he told himself, pray to all heaven, she hasn't been hurt – *for nothing*. He picked up his automatic and stuck it in his belt and went out.

Hurriedly, he went down the stairs, stepping over the dead who littered them, and through the door. Outside, a body blown up in the trees, hung there dripping blood like some obscene sort of human fruit. He cursed and looked away. A *Feldwebel*, his head bandaged, machine pistol in his hand, came running up. "*Herr Hauptmann*," he cried, face flushed with excitement, "enemy planes . . . enemy planes landing everywhere down the road."

"They'll be taken care of," von Witzleben said, mind racing electrically, knowing now that he was finished with the damned war. "Help to look after the wounded." He indicated a boy in short pants zig-zagging wildly across the battle-littered compound, hands held to his eyes, crying weakly; "Please help me . . . I think I've been blinded . . . Please help me.."

"*Jawohl Herr Hauptmann*," the NCO clicked his heels and ran off to help the blinded boy.

Von Witzleben pushed his way through the shattered door and brick rubble that blocked the entrance to the building where he had left her. "Inge," he called.

There was no answer.

He called her name again. Still no answer. His fear mounted. He pushed aside a dead Tommy, who leaned against the wall, as if he had just closed his eyes and had leaned there for a few moments' rest. The man pitched forward to reveal a great gaping hole in the small of his back through which the bones glittered like polished ivory against the mess of red gore. He mounted the steps two at a time.

He swung into the room. The windows were shattered and there was broken glass everywhere on the floor. But the bad he had overturned was still in position. Nothing had been moved there. "Inge!" he called urgently.

Still no answer.

Madly, he seized the bed with his hand and tugged hard, using all the last of his remaining strength. The bed came clattering down. He jumped back and saw Inge. She slumped there as if asleep. There was no mark, no blemish on her thin girlish body. She just slumped there, eyes closed, as if she were in a very deep sleep. Surely, he told himself with an ever-increasing sense of foreboding, she couldn't have slept through all that racket?

"Inge," he called, "wake up! It's all over". "He reached out to touch her shoulder. She tilted to one side and remained thus. He gasped. Hastily, he ripped open the front of her blouse to reveal those delicate, pink-tipped childish breasts of hers. He put his hand on the one and felt for her heart.

Nothing.

His fingers trembling violently now, he rubbed his silver cap badge against the front of his tunic until it shone. He held it to Inge's lips carefully. The silver badge remained unfogged. She wasn't breathing. *Inge was dead*!

For what seemed a long time he knelt there, staring down at her. Then slowly, very slowly, as if he were an old man whose joints ached, he lowered her to her side. He took off his tunic and draped it over her dead face, blotting it out for ever. He supposed he should have said a prayer for her, but his mind was abruptly blank. He knew no more prayers. What use were prayers anyway – they couldn't bring back the dead?

Slowly, as if sleep-walking, he moved down the stairs again into the open once more. Flames still flickered and the smoke drifted by in black-and-grey patches, blotting out the sun. It was the landscape of war a devil's landscape. Numbly he stared down at the dead, sprawled out in the careless, unreal postures of those done violently to death.

He paused once and rubbed his jaw, as if he might be thinking, but any casual observer now could see he was past thinking; that there was no more purpose to his life. Klaus von Witzleben was finished with life, or perhaps life was finished with him.

He went on a little further. Then he faltered as if his legs were going to give way beneath him. There were tears in his eyes at the thought of the girl and all those comrades of his who had gone before in France, North Africa, Russia. For a moment whole regiments of ghosts, dead comrades, marched before his mind's eye. He knew he couldn't go on.

He sat down on a pile of brick rubble. Here and there groups of harassed soldiers and werewolves were picking up the wounded, lugging them away on doors or coats which leaked blood. He didn't see them. As if in a trance, he pulled out his pistol and looked at its muzzle dully, as if he couldn't comprehend what it signified.

Slowly he clicked off the safety catch. His first intention was to place the muzzle against his temple and pull the trigger. He decided against it. If the weapon slipped he might not kill himself, perhaps just blind himself condemned to wander eyeless through this wrecked, corrupt country for years. "No," he croaked to no one in particular, "not that!"

Instead he put the muzzle slowly between his lips. He could taste the sickly oil used to clean it and the coldness rigidity, unyielding, unfeeling, of the metal. He paused.

Not for long. Suddenly, startlingly, he ripped back the trigger. A terrible pain. It was as if a red-hot poker had been thrust into the soft flesh of his mouth. The back of his skull heaved and bubbled. Abruptly it disintegrated, scattering shards of gleaming white bone on all sides in a slurry of red gore. *Hauptmann* von Witzleben was dead. With him, the Werewolf Organization died too . . .

SEVEN

The tall boy in charge of the gun was scared. As he stared at the fields on the other side of the road, his prominent Adam's apple worked its way up and down his skinny throat as if it were in an express lift.

"Heaven, arse and cloudburst," one of the girl gunners exclaimed as the light planes came ever lower, "there's scores of them. What can we do against that lot?"

The tall boy found his voice at last. He licked suddenly parched lips and said: "Shut up. We'll tackle 'em. Just got to make sure we do it right. See that one," he said slapping the gun-layer over the shoulder, "the one coming down on the road?"

The boy gun-layer, who looked no more than fourteen and wore the black shorts of the Hitler Youth, nodded, not trusting himself to speak. "We'll knock him out first," the boy in charge then said. "He'll block the road for us. I guess he's the boss too. Knock him out and we'll confuse the others. You know how the *Amis* panic when they come under fire." He said the words without conviction, but he thought they might encourage the others.

Now the light planes were coming in from all quarters. The morning air was made hideous with their noise, as they jostled for position, trying to avoid the others as they headed for the muddy fields, trying to keep away from the woods to the right.

The boy in charge said, "All right – lay on him."

The gunner squinted through his sight. Behind him the others tensed, holding packs of 20mm shells to be slid into the racks, once the gun was firing. A little further behind, they had stacked more cases; hidden by branches and a camouflage net. There were perhaps three thousand rounds, enough to keep the gun firing for three minutes going all out. Nothing, however, would survive that long when the quadruple flak began its song of death.

Effortlessly, the gunner spun the four-barrelled gun, following the descent of Major Rogers' light plane as it came down to land on the cobbled road to Glinde. Now it was almost down, its prop wash whipping the bushes on either side of the road into a green fury. It hit the cobbles, bounced and came down again; its engine thundered as Rogers braked to a stop.

"*Feuer!*" The boy in charge yelled, releasing all his pent-up tension with that command.

The four barrels thundered into frenetic life. White tracer shells streamed towards Roger's plane. The Major hadn't a chance. The fuselage was riddled, fire breaking out immediately. Rogers shrieked with pain, as his face was torn off by that cruel salvo, dripping down to his chest like molten red wax. Then he slumped over his shattered controls, dead. Next moment his plane disintegrated in a blinding flash.

Now the gun-layer swung the well-oiled mechanism round. White tracer shells spat from the four barrels. Another plane was hit as it was coming to land on the field. Desperately the pilot tried to keep control. To no avail. A wing dropped off. The plane went into a spin. At 100 mph it slammed into another plane already landed. Both went up in a spectacular ball of fire.

What happened next wasn't war; it was a massacre. The deadly gun raked the field. Plane after plane was hit. Everywhere there were shattered bodies and burning, wrecked planes. One pilot tried to take off again. He didn't get far. The shells slammed into the plane just as it was setting off across the woods. It dropped out of the sky and impaled itself on the tops of the trees.

Now, here and there, the terrified, trapped pilots were waving white handkerchiefs in a token of surrender. The battle-crazed kids behind the gun, boys and girls, took no notice of the appeal. They continued firing ruthlessly, relentlessly, carried away by a primeval blood-lust and joy in destruction.

Pilots dropped from their machines or crawled from the wrecked ones, vainly trying to get to the safety of the woods, away to any cover from that white wall of flying death. Few of them made it. The gun-layer pressed his sights as low as they would go. Now the 20mm tracer shells hissed right across the field at barely two feet from the earth, the gun being swung effortlessly from side to side like a gunslinger in a western, firing to left and right with his Colt revolver. His eyes wild, white and staring, the sweat trickling down his face set in a grimace of crazily smiling brutality, he gave the Americans no chance; while around him the others, cursing and cheering wildly at the great slaughter, thrust shell after shell into the greedy maws of the machine.

Then it was all over. Suddenly the breech clicked. The gun, steam and smoke streaming from the air-conditioned barrels, came to a stop. They had run out of shells. For a moment there was a loud echoing silence, ringing back and forth across those killing fields, broken only by the moans and weak pleas for help from the dying.

Abruptly, the kids realized what they had done. Before them lay the charnel house, filled with the dead and the blazing wrecked machines. They had destroyed, just five of them, a whole wing of corps artillery spotter planes!

"My God," the boy commander breathed in awe. "Have you seen anything like it? . . ." Suddenly his triumph turned into bewildered fear. "What have we done? *Himmelherrje, was haben wir bloss gemacht?* "He wrung his hands piteously, tears suddenly streaming down his contorted face.

"Comrades," one of the girls shrieked. "We'll have to run . . . they're coming for us!" She pointed with a hand that trembled violently.

A line of men were coming steadily across the field, advancing on the gun position with grim determination.

"We must run," she screamed. "Quick!" She burst from their hiding place among the trees. A machine gun chattered.

She went down shrieking and gorgling, her back shattered, choking on her own blood.

Another burst ripped the length of the position. Then the line of men were running, crying hoarsely, fighting their way through that smoking bloody shambles to take their revenge.

Five minutes later it was all over. All five of the teen-age gunners were dead, slaughtered ruthlessly and without mercy, for even the most unthinking of the SAS troopers knew that their fate was sealed. They were two hundred miles behind the German lines, hampered by two seriously wounded men, with the Germans bound to take a terrible revenge for the destruction of the werewolf HQ. And all of them knew previous SAS men captured by the enemy had been slaughtered out of hand.

O'Rourke, his face haggard but looking fiercer than ever, seemed to read their gloomy thoughts, for he said; "I know, I know. We're in the shit without even a shovel to dig ourselves out of it."

A weary Sterling smiled at the Irishman's choice of words. All the same he knew he was right. There were going to be no flaming headlines in the *"New York Times"* now, proclaiming: "Tank-Led Raid Takes Out Nazi HQ".

"All right, we've been up the creek before and managed to get out of it. I think we're going to do it again, or at least we're going to try. "He looked sharply around the weary, bloodstained faces of his young troopers, as if challenging them to say something to the contrary. None of them did.

"So this is what we do. All of you have got an escape map of the region. He pulled out the piece of khaki-coloured cloth which looked like an Army issue handkerchief, but which on the other side had a printed map of Northern Germany on it. 'You've got your button compass.' He meant the top button of their tunics which was a concealed compass, 'and you've got your iron ration of chocolate for grub and what you can nick. The possibilities are there, aren't they?"

Wearily, his men assented. Two hundred miles on a bar of bitter chocolate didn't seem very feasible to Colonel Sterling, but again he said nothing. From far away there came the sound of angry shouts and commands being given. Whistles were shrilled, and Colonel Sterling guessed the Krauts were getting themselves organized over at the ruined, burning werewolf HQ.

"So we're going to split into threes, Jenkins."

"Sir?"

"You'll take the fittest men."

"Sir."

"I and Captain Gorey will take the rest in two groups, splitting up the lightly wounded between the two of us. You'll stay with me Colonel Sterling and you, Lieutenant Goldstein, will go with Gorey."

The two Americans nodded their understanding.

"You two Americans stand a chance if you're taken prisoner. They'll soon know that you're not in the SAS. You're too old."

That raised a weary laugh.

"But if I were you Goldstein, I'd throw our identity discs away."

"Because my dogtags show I'm Jewish?"

"Yes."

"Well, I'm proud of it," Goldstein said defiantly.

O'Rourke shrugged." It's your baby. But I'd certainly prefer to be a *live* Jew than a dead 'un,' he growled.

Goldstein grunted and then pulled the metal dogtags from his neck, dropped them to ground and stamped them under with his heel.

Behind them, signal flares were hissing into the air and explosing in a profusion of green and red bursts in the sky over the depot. The SAS troopers knew what that meant. The Germans were rallying for an attack. It was time to be going.

O'Rourke suddenly looked very worried. He stared hard at the two seriously wounded. Bookhalter, who had had his knee shattered, was ashen with pain but conscious. Next to him in the grass lay Gormless George. His foot had been shattered by one of their own debellockers. Now it was wrapped in a swathe of yellow shell dressing, but the blood was still flowing freely. To O'Rourke, it was obvious that neither of the two was capable of moving at any speed. He hated to do it, but he knew it had to be done. But before he could speak, Bookhalter said quietly: "I know, sir. We'd only be a damned nuisance." That was all.

It was typical of the slight young man from somewhere down in the south of England. He never spoke much, save when he was carried away with the subject of his beloved cricket. Then it would be: "Do you remember when Hedley Verity was playing at Lords?" Or, "it was typical of Jack Hobbs to do something like that." It was a subject totally foreign to O'Rourke, born in the slums of Belfast.

Next to him, Gormless George forced a grin and grunted: "I'd rather fook than fight, but it looks as if I'll be fighting this time. Yon Jerries are coming this way."

O'Rourke flung look over his shoulder. A thin line of German skirmishers had emerged from the smoke, each man moving forward intently, slowly, as if deep in thought. Time was running out *fast*.

He bent and shook each man by the hand. O'Rourke was not given to emotion. He said simply: "I'm proud of you."

"Thank you, sir," they said, equally without emotion, as the first of the groups started to drift into the woods.

Brown waved to Bookhalter. "Bye, Eddie, I'll tell your people when I get back. "He turned his head sharply, as if he could not bear to see his old comrade any more.

Gormless George guffawed and called after them "Don't forget to sup a pint of John Smith's Yorkshire Ale when you get back and think of old Gormless George." Then the happy light went from his round, bluff West Riding face and he pulled back the bolt of his sten gun.

O'Rourke took one last look at them and then he, too, was vanishing into the trees.

Five minutes later, sneaking carefully through the thick firs like grey ghosts, they heard it: the quick high-pitched stutter of sten guns followed a little while later by the tight chesty bark of the German Schmeissers. For a few moments the firefight continued. Finally it was ended by two distinctive pistol shots – and one last piercing scream of absolute agony.

O'Rourke paused momentarily and bit his bottom lip. He knew what those two last shots meant. Someone had administered the *coup de grâce* – a pistol shot to the base of the skull – to poor Bookhalter and Gormless George. The hunt was on. Then he was moving fast, penetrating deeper into the woods.

EIGHT

They had been on the run for four hours now. Time and time again they had just avoided capture at the very last moment. The whole countryside north of the River Elbe had been alerted, it seemed, and Fiesler Storch spotter planes were everywhere, flying at treetop height, trying to spot the fleeing men.

In each of the three groups of fugitives, there had been some hurried talk of trying to trick the Germans by going north instead of south, as they supposed the Germans expected them to do. If they went north, they might reach Occupied Denmark, where there would be a resistance movement that could help them. But the thought of the trek through a hundred miles of flat countryside with little cover until they reached the Danish border turned them against the idea. They all continued to go south.

As Al Gorey explained to Goldstein while they had a five minute break, hidden behind an abandoned barn that stank of cow urine; "The key to the whole business is getting across the Elbe. The bridges will be guarded, I guess, but we can solve that problem when we come to it. But once we're across, then I think we have a good chance of linking up with our own guys."

"*If*", Goldstein said to himself, "*if*". But he kept his doubts to himself. Instead he said aloud. "What's the plan?"

"Hamburg," Gorey answered. "It's easier to pass unnoticed in the big city than it is in the sticks, like here. Here we stick out like a sore thumb. In the city, you're just another one of the jerks."

"But these uniforms?" Goldberg protested.

"We'll get civvies somewhere or another. The next farm perhaps – " He stopped short. The was the drone of a plane coming in to their rear. It was another of the Fiesoer Storch spotter planes looking for them. "Come on," Gorey said urgently, "into the trees again before the bastard spots us . . ." By now Sergeant Jenkins' party, made up of the fittest of the SAS troopers, ten in all, were in the lead. Indeed, luck had been on their side ever since they had split. Jenkins reasoned by being so quick they had slipped through the cordon that the enemy had tried to slap on the fugitives before it had been probably set up. Now, spread out in a cautious file, every man's finger on the trigger of his weapon, they were approaching the Elbe. To their left there was a small collection of farm buildings, the typical one storey, half-timbered farms of the area where the animals and their human owners all lived under the same straw roof. There were a couple of barges chugging lazily downstream. Otherwise the area seemed empty. They crossed the towpath and were faced with the grass wall of the flood dyke, which ran along the length of this stretch of the great German river. "Down," Jenkins ordered.

As one, the troopers dropped into the drainage ditch which lay at the foot of the dyke.

"I'm going up to have a dekko," Jenkins whispered and wondered why he did so. There was no one about to hear. "Keep yer eyes skinned."

Shouldering his sten gun, the tough little sergeant scrambled up the grassy bank, threw himself flat on top of it to present the smallest possible silhouette to anyone who might be watching, and surveyed the river more closely. There was a bridge a mile or so further downstream. It was a metal girder type of structure and he guessed that it was railway bridge. Those, he knew, from experience, were always guarded at both ends. So it was out.

He studied the bank to his immediate left and right. Then spotted it. Two boats tied to a sort of primitive wooden jetty, a small one and next to it another, large enough to ship all of the ten men under his command.

Although he knew time was running out Sergeant Jenkins took his time. All of his men had been trained to handle boats, but the Elbe was a broad river and he knew nothing of its currents. Which direction would they take a boat, he wondered. Towards the bridge, perhaps? That would be suicidal. The guards would spot them and that would be that.

He sucked his teeth. Then he crawled to a clump of bushes, broke off a branch and with all his strength, threw as far as he could towards the centre of the Elbe.

The current, running about a couple of miles an hour, caught it immediately and began bearing the little piece of wood *away* from the bridge.

Jenkins nodded his head with approval. It was what he had hoped for. He scurried down the bank, explained hurriedly what he intended to do and a moment later he and his troopers were running softly down the towpath, hidden from the bridge by the dyke, towards the spot where the two boats were moored.

Expertly, hugging the ground, one trooper after another rolled down the dyke towards the boats. In an instant Jenkins had satisfied himself the boat he had selected was not holed. Its owner had taken away the oars, but he had left the rudder, which was priceless, because they'd find some replacement for the missing oars, but without a rudder they would be at the mercy of the current.

"All right lads", he hissed urgently, not taking his eyes off the railway bridge for an instant. "Nip out the seats from that other boat. They'll do as oars. Then in we go. At the double now."

As the troopers scrambled away to carry out their task, Jenkins pulled out his trench-knife and started to saw through the stout hawser tethering the larger boat to the bank, his nerves tingling electrically, his mind already planning what they would do once they'd reached the other side of the Elbe.

"In yer go," he ordered, as the troopers returned bearing

the seats they had broken out of the other boat. "Smartish now. Look lively!"

He cast one last look at the bridge. Nothing stirred there. They hadn't been spotted. He turned his attention to the river. At the moment it was empty of barges to their immediate front. There was one, tugging several other barges behind it, about a mile away. But it was going downstream in the direction of Hamburg. It could cause no problems for them, even if the bargees did spot them. He hesitated no longer. With one last blow, he severed the hawser and jumped deftly into the boat to seize the rudder. "All right, shipmates," he said in a hearty Devonian voice, "take her away."

"Ay, ay admiral," one of the troopers answered, happy that they seemed to be escaping the death trap.

With a will, despite their exhaustion, they started to paddle the boat towards the centre of the river, while Jenkins steered the best he could to keep the craft on a straight course.

It was hard work, but the troopers were tough. With the rough spars they propelled the boat forward. Now they could see the other side quite clearly. Beyond the customary bank there was the straw roof of a fisherman's cottage – they could see his nets drying on the dyke wall – and Jenkins told himself that the cottage might just be the ideal place to lie up for the rest of the day before moving off south towards the advancing allies as soon as darkness fell. There might even be some grub there, too. His mouth began to salivate at the – thought. For now it was over thirty hours since they had last eaten at the American air base.

"Put yer backs into it, lads," he urged, new confidence and hope surging through his tired body. "I'm aiming at that cottage over there – "

The high-powered speed boat caught them completely by surprise. It came surging in at top speed out of nowhere. The man behind the bow quick-firer began firing at once. He obviously knew who they were. There was no challenge. No, "*wer da?*" Just a hiss of tracer speeding across the surface of the river directly at them. As one they dived overboard, abandoning their boat.

The first trooper was hit. He yelled piteously and tried to tread water. The man at the quick-firer let rip another burst. It ran in a series of frantic splashes directly towards the wounded man. He hadn't a chance. The second burst zipped the length of his chest. Suddenly the brown water all around was transformed to a bright red. The trooper's head sank on his chest. He floated away, dead.

Jenkins raged. But in the water he couldn't fight back. What was he to do? He knew that there was no hope for them. He thrust up one arm as high as he could and cried at the top of his voice: "*Kamerad-nix schiessen . . .* we surrender – "

The burst ripped the length of his face. He heard the flesh burst. Bone splintered. Blood spurted from his shattered nose. Suddenly everything went black. They'd blinded him. A moment later he went under.

Systematically the speedboat curved round and round the rest, machine-gunning them mercilessly until they were all dead, floating away down the great river into eternity . . .

Faintly, O'Rourke could hear the chatter of that machine gun, as he crouched, with Colonel Sterling at his side, a couple of hundred yards from a tumbledown farmhouse, with a couple of morose black-and-white Holstein cows trying to graze on the short grass outside. The house was occupied, he could see that. There was a lazy curl of smoke coming from the chimney and once they had seen a fat woman, with a yoke from which hung two pails of corn coming out of the door and disappearing around the back of the farm, presumably intent on feeding some animal or other there.

"That's our lads, Colonel, O'Rourke whispered, not taking his gaze off the farm for one instant." They've bumped into trouble, probably down b – "*duck!*" he hissed urgently as yet another Fieseler Storch came winging its way across the damp fields.

As one they ducked, keeping their faces hidden, as the

cows panicked at the noise and went lumbering across the meadow, udders swinging back and forth.

Then the spotter plane was gone and O'Rourke could continue. I don't think we can get across the river just yet," he said. "My plan is to take over that place. So far I've only spotted the woman. Even if there are any men, I'm sure the half dozen of us," he glanced around at his weary, unshaven, muddy troppers confidently, "can manage them."

Sterling nodded his agreement. God, what wouldn't he give for a real rest now, he told himself.

Mind made up, O'Rourke got to his feet. "Four to the right of the house, four to the left. Colonel, you keep close to me."

Swiftly, his men unslung their weapons and broke into two groups. In single file, every man alert and watchful now, they advanced on the tumbledown farmhouse, hoping it did not possess a dog which might bark and alert the old woman. But there was no dog and as they got closer to the house, which smelled of manure, sour milk and human misery, there was no sound save the clucking of the chickens to the back of the place.

O'Rourke paused by the door. Cautiously, he turned the handle. The old door opened with a squeak. Fetid, stale smells assailed his nostrils. Gingerly, he stepped inside. His boots seemed to make a devil of a noise on the bare stone flags of the hall. He progressed deeper into the place, followed by a tense Colonel Sterling, clutching his Colt pistol. Still there was no sound save that of the logs crackling in the green, tiled oven which reached right up to the sagging, cracked ceiling.

A few moments later they had searched the place; four or five rooms leading off from the hall, with the door beyond leading to the part of the house inhabited by the animals. It was empty. O'Rourke forced a weary grin. "Just the job, Colonel. Take a pew," he indicated the battered wooden chair next to the stove. "Take the weight off your plates o'meat."

Colonel Sterling didn't know what "plates o'meat" meant,

194

but he *did* know he needed a rest. He sank gratefully into the hard chair.

In that instant, the two groups of troopers entered, pushing the angry-faced old woman in front of them. "Sez it's *verboten* to come in here, sir," one of them explained. "I showed what's forbidden or not. I gave her a light kick in the arse." He grinned.

Sterling told the woman in German. "Now, Granny, don't worry. We won't harm you. All we want is some rest and a bit of food if you've got it."

The old woman's tension vanished. She pushed back a strand of loose grey hair and croaked. *"Ich habe nur Bratkartoffeln. Kein Fleisch."*

"That would be excellent," Sterling reassured her. "She's got no meat," he told the others. "But she's got fried potatoes."

O'Rourke said; "All right with me, Colonel." He turned to his men. "We won't post sentries outside. They might be spotted by passers-by. So I want two of you to keep watch. Get up in the attic, knock off a couple of tiles back and front and stand lookout. Arrange it by yourselves. You, Smith, keep an eye on the old biddy."

"Sir!" Smith said smartly, but the usual smile was absent from his handsome young face. He was still thinking of his old pal, Bookhalter, abandoned to his death in those killing fields.

He turned and watched casually, as the old woman busied herself at the sink beneath the dirty kitchen window, slicing the already boiled potatoes into the frying pan. But her back was to him and he did not see the look on her face, as she gestured to the hayloft to her immediate front.

Peering through the weathered boards, her grandson knew immediately that *Oma* Krueger was in trouble. He had deserted from the Rhine front a week before. Somehow he had managed to avoid the "chain dogs", was the German military police were called, because of the silver chains of office they wore round their necks, and reach the family farm. His grandfather had died in '40 and his father had been posted missing in '42, whereupon his mother had run off with another man. Now *Oma* Krueger worked the place on her own. She had been delighted to see her grandson. Peasant that she was, she valued the muscular power of a young man, who just happened to be her grandson, who would work simply for his food and board.

Now the 18-year-old deserter was placed in a quandary. He had recognized the enemy uniforms at once. What the Americans were doing here so far north, he couldn't comprehend. If they were parachutists, dropped behind the German lines, the *Wehrmacht* would soon be coming to look for them. If he stayed and was captured with them, the authorities would think that, not only was he a deserter, but that he was a traitor, too. They'd shoot him out of hand. What was he to do?

In the confusion of the retreat from the Rhine, men did get separated from their units. Could he convince the authorities that he had lost his unit during the retreat and in a state of confusion had made his way back to his grandmother's farm? He scratched his long, lank blond hair – like all the other men of his unit he had been lousy for weeks now and wondered if the chain dogs in Billstedt, the nearest town, would buy his story?

While he agonized in the barn, it started to get dark. From the direction of Hanburg he could hear the first thin wail of the sirens. He knew what that meant: the Tommies would soon be coming in to raid the ruined port city yet again. Once more everything would be confusion. The new homeless and the frightened would be streaming out of the city into the country, clogging the roads and creating chaos wherever they went and he knew from past experience at the front that at such moments, people didn't want complicated explanations and details. They wanted quick, straightforward statements. It would be an ideal time to tell his tall tale. His mind made up at last, he retreated to the back of the hayloft and started prying out the planks there, unseen from the house. Ten minutes later he was on his way . . .

NINE

"Right," Al Gorey commanded sharply. "*NOW*! He launched himself from the thick cable which ran over the river and went winging down to the rear deck of the slow barge. He hit the wooden deck with a thud. He gasped. His legs felt as if they had been driven right into his stomach. Behind him the others came falling out of the air, too, including Goldstein, his eyes tightly pressed shut, who had suggested the idea.

At first they thought they might be able to cross the Elbe by the stout cable which was about thirty feet from the water, to allow clearance for shipping. But in the end, Al Gorey had vetoed the idea. It would have taken too long and they might well have been spotted by one of the passing barges.

It was then that Goldstein had come up with his idea. "Listen," he had exclaimed urgently. "It looks as if we don't have a chance in hell of getting across that damned river. So why don't we sail *along* it?"

"What do you mean?" Gorey had asked in bewilderment.

"Well, if we could shanghai one of those barges going downsteam, and get away with it, we could sail the thing until we came to our First US Army's zone of operations below Magdeburg on the Elbe. We've just got to find the right barge, one going downstream and without any other barges in sight."

Gorey had hesitated for a little while, but Goldstein had pressed him with: "I'm sure there won't be any police and military checks on barges. Why should there be? They're sailing in German territory and they're doing an essential job, helping the war effort."

After a while, he had then said: "You're right, Goldstein.

197

It's risky and we'll have to work quick. But it looks as if it's the only way out of this jam. Let's do it!"

Now, flinging a quick glance behind him to see if all his men had landed safely – they had – a winded and shaky Al Gorey crept forward, pistol at the ready. Without turning, eyes intent on his front, he indicated that someone should have a look at the hold.

He could see the outline of two figures quite clearly on the forward bridge: a man in a cap steering the barge; next to him a hatless youth busily engaged in talking. Gingerly, ducked low, he crept up the flight of steps which led to the bridgehouse, praying that the youth who was doing the talking didn't look out of the side window and see him. He didn't.

Al Gorey took a deep breath and flung open the door. The youth reacted with surprising speed. He seized the club lying on the ledge next to the wheel and slammed it right across Gorey's face. Lights exploded before his eyes as he stumbled to his knees. Next moment the youth kicked him savagely in the teeth. He went out like a light.

Behind him, Goldstein fired instinctively. The youth screamed shrilly. He was lifted off his feet by the impact of that rage. He slammed across the bridgehouse. He slapped into the wall on the other side. Slowly he slid down it, trailing blood down the wall, two spurting pits where his eyes had just been.

"*Hande hoch*," Goldstein rasped, trying to conceal his horror at what he had just done.

The skipper's hands went up at once. His fat jowls trembled with fear, his face suddenly ashen. "Don't shoot . . . please don't shoot, sir!" he quavered.

Behind Goldstein, two of the troopers carried Gorey and laid him on the deck, while another went round the wheelhouse, opened the door on the other side and pulled out the dying youth.

"All right," Goldstein said, realizing suddenly that he was in charge. "You can put your hands down now. Behave yourself and nothing will happen to you."

"Oh, I'll behave myself, sir," the skipper assured him hurriedly and dropped his hands.

"Now what's your destination?" Goldstein asked.

"Magdeburg," the skipper answered, taking up the wheel. Cargo of scrap for the factories there."

Goldstein nodded his approval and was about to ask about the rest of the crew when a trooper, face wreathed in a huge grin, interrupted him with; "Come and have a dekko at this, sir. Gor, ferk a duck! Never seen anything like it in all me born days."

"Well, all right. What is it?"

"Wait and see. It's rear hold, sir."

Stepping over poor Al Gorey, who was still unconscious, despite the fact that someone had thrown a pail of cold water over him, Goldstein followed the chuckling trooper, who, for some reason was now walking on the toes of his feet, as if he didn't want to make too much noise.

The trooper gestured to the open hatch of the hold. "Just have a shufti inside there. Bugger it, some blokes do have a bloody good war!"

Slightly puzzled, Goldstein peered over the edge of the open hold. He gasped.

Down below in the gloom of the hold, lying on a pile of blankets, lay a naked man, a beatific smile on his lips, as he snored. At each side of him was a huge woman, similarly naked, furiously playing with his flaccid member, breasts wobbling like puddings as she wrenched and tugged at it.

"What a way to go, sir," the trooper who had summoned him said in admiration. "Two judies working their balls off, trying to do a little good for an honest working feller."

Goldstein was inclined to agree, though he had his doubts about falling into the hands of those two naked Amazons. But for the time being he had other things on his mind. "Is that it?" he snapped.

"Yessir," the trooper replied, raising his voice when he realized that the two women were so preoccupied with their self-imposed task to have noticed his presence above. "Just the two female wankers – and poor old Fritz down there."

"Kay then. Batten down the hatch and see that someone is placed on guard on it. We don't want them realizing what has happened and shouting their heads off. I'm going back to see how Captain Gorey is getting on."

By now Gorey, a bandage wrapped round his damaged head, had recovered somewhat. Supported by one of his men, he asked a little weakly. "Everything under control?" He groaned. "That Kraut bastard certainly packed a wallop."

"He's dead now," Goldstein said. "Yes, everything's under control. We've taken over the old tub." He looked at the darkening sky. "At this speed I reckon we'll reach Hamburg by eight this night. With luck, there'll be a raid and we can slip through in the general confusion. Our destination is Magdeburg, as we had hoped. I think we're gonna do it, Al."

"Good show," Al Gorey affected a British accent and smiled. Next moment he wished he hadn't. It felt as if someone had just hit him over the head with a heavy object. "All right, you're in charge. I think I'd better lie down for a while."

Goldstein nodded to the SAS trooper and the latter raised the officer gently and led him away to find a bunk where he could rest, while Goldstein watched the dark shadows of approaching night slide silently down the valley of the Elbe. Now, for the first time, he heard the faint wail of air raid sirens coming from the direction of Hamburg. "Good show," he said to himself aping Gorey. "It looked as if their luck was in. Hamburg was going to be raided soon . . .

Now they were sailing through the outer surburbs of Hamburg. Most of them were in ruins from the raids of the previous years. Now, as they chugged on their way, they could see the ruined houses and apartment blocks, silhouetted a stark jagged black against the flames of the new fires being started by the RAF. The flak was in action everywhere. The guns belched fire, peppering the night sky with bursts of dark brown smoke. The searchlights combed the heavens trying to cone in on the bombers.

Fire engines and ambulances raced through the streets, their horns blaring. All was chaos, confusion and sudden death.

But the watching SAS troopers were happy. Nothing could cover their progress through the great city better than the RAF attack. Al Gorey, his head muffled in a thick bandage, said: "The poor bastards are really taking a beating."

Goldstein, standing next to him, sensed that the other American felt some pity for the Germans. He snapped curtly; "The Krauts shouldn't have started it. Remember London and Coventy and all the other places in England they knocked the shit out of. They're getting what they deserve. I think – " the rest of his words were drowned by a bomb exploding only fifty feet away.

Blast slapped them across the face like a blow from a flabby wet hand. Shrapnel, glowing red-hot and lethal, hissed everywhere. On the bridge above them the terrified skipper cried: "Gentlemen, I can't go on any further! It is too dangerous." He started to turn the wheel. "I shall heave to."

In a flash an angry Goldstein whipped out his pistol. "If you do, you're a dead man!" he shouted above the roar and thunder of the bombs and guns.

"But – "

– "No, buts." Goldstein stopped short. A small motorboat was chugging straight towards them and in the sudden flash of an exploding bomb, Goldstein caught the name painted in white on its side. "*Wasserpolizei*"

"Water Police," he said urgently to Gorey.

"Oh shit!"

"Well, what do you do?" Goldstein rasped, "You're the leader of men.

"Well, I'll tell you this. We're not going to be taken at this stage of the game." He peered through the glowing darkness. "The boat's got a radio aerial. So we don't do anything till they board us."

"And then?"

Grimly, Al Gorey drew his finger across his throat.

A minute later the motorboat stopped its engine and a gruff voice called: "*Kontrolle. Wir kommen an Bord!*"

Again the skipper looked terrified. Goldstein dug his gun harder into his ribs and hissed: "Tell them to do so."

The skipper cupped his hand about his mouth and shouted above the noise of the barrage: "*Jawohl. Ist in Ordnung.*" He slowed the barge down even further.

Ponderously a heavy-set man in a leather overcoat, followed by another carrying a battered briefcase came up. Gorey crouched down behind the bulkhead with half a dozen of his men and told himself they would be easy. But there were others in the motor boat perhaps? There was a helmsman. He could see him behind the wheel. Somehow they had to take him out – and possibly others, too, before he – they – could sound the alarm.

"You lot," he hissed urgently, "take them out when they're on board and out of the sight of that guy at the wheel. But gimme a couple of minutes before you start anything. Clear?"

"Clear, sir." they answered as one.

Hurriedly, Al Gorey scuttled across the deck, crouched low, the pain in his injured head forgotten now. He lowered himself into the water. It was freezing. But he had no time to take in the fact. Swiftly, he swum round the hull of the almost stationary barge, coming in to the rear of the police boat. To both sides of the river the guns continued to belch fire at the raiders and some poor swine of an RAF pilot had been coned by the searchlights. As he swam, Gorey, told himself that he wouldn't survive for long now.

Now he was about six feet from the police boat, rocking gently in the water. Up above, shells were exploding all around the luckless RAF bomber, as its pilot tried desperately to escape from those killing lights.

Now Gorey could see the helmsman quite clearly. He was craning his neck trying to get a better look at the trapped bomber. Suddenly, the Halifax exploded in a great ball of blood-red fire. The helmsman cheered. It was the last sound he made on this earth. Gorey was over the side, down the passage, and had his hands around the man's throat stiffling his cheers even before the man knew what had hit him.

Gorey grunted and applied maximum pressure. The police-man twisted and turned wildly, while all around the bombs fell and the guns bellowed. But he couldn't shake off that lethal grip. Suddenly, he stiffened, then his body went slack. Gorey counted up to sixty before he released his grip. The dead cop slithered to the floor.

Gorey felt no pity. He knew the cops would have shot them on the spot if they had been captured. He looked for one instant at the dead man's cruelly contorted face with the tongue piking out of his gaping mouth like a piece of red leather. Then he completed his self-imposed task. He fumbled around the floor of the little boat until he found what he sought – the stop cocks. Hurriedly he twisted them wide open. The boat with the dead man started to sink at once. There was no more time to be wasted. He went over the side and headed back to the barge, while Hamburg rocked, burned, and died.

One hour later they had left the city behind them, a red flickering glare on the horizon, heading south towards the advancing American First Army.

TEN

O'Rourke sensed something was wrong. It wasn't only that the old biddy was clearly nervous, her gnarled old hand going constantly to her mouth in the manner of women who were worried, it was something in the very atmosphere.

O'Rourke thought nothing of the professional Irishman with his drinking, his cheery "top o' the morning t'ye", and all that Mick crap, but he did have that Celtic sense of second sight; that awareness that something was going to happen before it did. Now he felt it again and he didn't like it. It had been his plan to set off as soon as the air raid on Hamburg was over, when the city would be at the height of its confusion, but the raid was lasting too long and he wanted to be out of this place. Twice he went to the door and stared out at the glowing darkness. But the fields which surrounded the house were empty. Even the chickens had gone to sleep by now. About eleven, unable to restrain his nervousness, he ordered; "Those of you who've still got debollockers, plant 'em to the rear of the house in the ground." As Smith and a couple of the other troopers hurried out to execute his order, O'Rourke called to the lookouts in the roof: "And don't go to kip up there. Keep yer eyes open."

"You're worried, aren't you, O'Rourke?" Colonel Sterling said quietly, as they sat at the bare, scrubbed kitchen table, now cleared of the big pan of fried potatoes which the old woman had made for them.

O'Rourke nodded and admitted: "I am. The raid's lasting too long. I wanted us to be on our way by now."

Sterling smiled reassuringly. "The flyboys will be gone soon," he said, "and it's still only eleven o'clock. We've got a good six or seven hours before first light. With a bit of luck we'll be over those Elbe bridges by then."

"I suppose you're right," O'Rourke said after a moment's thought. I've never been a particularly patient man," he added. He grinned suddenly, displaying a set of crooked teeth. "It was impatience that got me into the SAS. After Dunkirk I should have stayed in England. I might have got on the staff. Instead of that, I'm in with the cloak-and-dagger boys and I know for certain that the War Office'll pack up this regiment as soon as the war's over. They don't like unconventional forces. Where will I be then? I'm a regular soldier, you see."

Sterling shrugged. "Where will we all be?"

"But you're a professor or something, aren't you Colonel? That's a good job now. Me. I'm a regular NCO, who's a temporary officer and gentleman, thanks to the war. SAS and a former ranker. Not a good combination for a glowing future in the post-war British Army."

"Something'll turn up I guess," Sterling said reflectively, looking at O'Rourke's tough, hard face in the flickering light of the oil lamp.

"Ay," O'Rourke said in that bitter Ulsterman's way of his. "*The dole*! Just like it did for my old man when the shipyards fired him in the '20s. Never worked again in his life. Drunk hissen to death and – "He stopped short, face suddenly very businesslike and tense. "What's that?"

"What's what?" Sterling snapped, turning his head to one side in order to her better.

O'Rourke didn't answer; he was concentrating.

Up above in the roof, Smith whispered; "Sir, I think I just saw something."

O'Rourke rose to his feet urgently. "Tell the old biddy to get under the table and keep her trap shut, Colonel. Quick! Lads, outside – at the double!" He waited until Smith and the other lookout dropped to the floor. Then he blew out the light. Now everything was tense urgency, as the troopers filed noiselessly into the night.

Outside O'Rourke bent low and then brought his gaze

up slowly. It was the old trick for trying to spot objects at night. Yes, there they were. Dark objects against the lighter background of the fields. There were men out there all right and he didn't need a crystal ball to tell him they were Germans.

"Move!" he hissed and stood there, half crouched, sten gun in hands, as they hushed by him like silent ghosts. Sterling halted. "I'll stay with you – "

The rest of his words were drowned by a sharp crack followed by a howl of sheer agony. Someone had stepped on a debollocker. Next moment, angry fire started to stab the air. Windows shattered in the farmhouse. Slates came tumbling from the roof. Wood and brick splinters shot everywhere.

"They think we're still in the house," O'Rourke said to Sterling. "That poor old biddy. She'll be pissing in her pants now. Come on, Colonel!"

Suddenly a flare hissed into the air. *Crack*! It burst, bathing the scene below in a hard, frozen white light. A German shouted something. The direction of the firing changed immediately. Bullets came winging their way. "Scatter – into the trees!" O'Rourke yelled urgently. He turned round and, without aiming, ripped off a burst. Several of the running figures fell heavily, but the others came on in a ragged skirmish line. It had to be, at least, a company, O'Rourke told himself as he whipped out the empty magazine and thrust another home into the little sten gun.

At his side, Colonel Sterling grunted abruptly and was spun round. "I think," he began. Next instant, he pitched forward without any further sound.

O'Rourke knew he was dead. He didn't need to look. Instead, he concentrated on whipping off another burst, firing from the hip, swinging from side to side like a western gunslinger in some pre-war Hollywood movie.

Germans went down everywhere. The line faltered for a moment.

O'Rourke seized the momentary pause. "Back off," he called, "Spread out – and move backwards – "

The bullet hit him with a tremendous blow in the right thigh. It was like a kick from a mule. His thigh was paralysed and numb immediately and he guessed the bone had been broken. He sat down abruptly. Brown dashed forward as if to help him, but he cried urgently: "*Get out*! But sling me a couple of sten mags before you do."

Brown fumbled with his webbing. He pulled out two long magazines and threw them to the grass where O'Rourke sat, feeling sick and a little confused.

"Can't I help you, sir, *please*?" Brown pleaded, his face twisted and agonized.

"*No*," O'Rourke shouted. "Save yourself. Go on, bugger off."

"But sir – "

– "No buts. Do you think I'd have fucking well stayed behind with you? *GO!*"

Brown hesitated, then he turned and started to run after the others.

O'Rourke gave a deep sigh. Awkwardly, he pulled himself behind the dead American's body. "Sorry, old friend," he whispered. "But it's the only way." He tugged out Sterling's pistol and laid it in his back. Next to it he placed the two magazines that Brown had thrown him. Finally he rested the sten gun on the body and waited.

He was feeling faint again. The blood was pouring from his wound and his eyes kept closing. Angrily he shook his head and everything came back into focus once more. Now he could see them, silent figures stalking off to the right, trying to outflank him. He chuckled. They thought they hadn't been seen. "Well, you have," he said, talking to himself like all lonely men did. He squinted down the sten gun and pressed the trigger. The little automatic chattered violently. There was the acrid stench of burned cordite. Men screamed shrilly. A grenade came hurtling his way, but fell short.

It exploded with an angry roar. In its violent light he could see a group of Germans halted in their tracks. It was an ideal target. He let loose another rapid burst. Men tumbled to all sides, arms threshing the air, screaming shrilly at the outrage done to their bodies. He kept his finger on the trigger until there was a dull click. The mag. was empty!

A German realized what had happened. He came racing forward at full speed. O'Rourke could see the glint of his bayonet. "Thought yer caught me with my knickers down, did ye?" he chuckled, half crazy with pain and the loss of blood by now. He raised Colonel Sterling's big Colt pistol. He pulled the trigger. The Colt erupted. Flame shot from its muzzle. The impact at such short range lifted the German right off his feet. Next instant his chest blew apart and disintegrated.

That did it. The enemy went to ground again, sniping at him as they did so.

O'Rourke laughed and ducked behind the body, as the slugs wacked into Sterling's flesh. With fingers that seemed suddenly, strangely clumsy, as if they were enclosed in boxing gloves, he fitted a new magazine into the little automatic. Now he had exactly one magazine left.

"Gie's a penny, mister," he said suddenly, with a voice of the Belfast working class child he had once been. Of a Saturday they'd always gone up to the better parts of the city to beg from the better-offs. Then it'd be off to the cake shops for "a hapoth o'broken biscuits, missus – and don't be light-handed with scales, missus."

The dying man's tough face cracked into a weary smile at memory. It had been a good childhood, even when the old man pawned his boots at Ikey's to buy drink. There'd always been enough bread and marge with a little sugar sprinkled on it and as much "tay" as he could drink.

"*Oh Danny boy*," he began to sing in a hard cracked voice, "*the pipes are calling . . .*"

**"Mensch, der Tommy is vernuckt geworden,"* a voice across the way called in astonishment. "*Nein,*" another voice commented scornfully, "*der ist sternnagel blau!*"

O'Rourke shook his head. Slowly things began to drift back into focus again. He looked at the green-glowing dial

* The Tommy's gone mad . . . No, he's drunk as a lord. *Transl.*

of his watch. He'd give the lads another ten minutes. That should give them a head start.

Across in the trees, a voice shouted: "Throw down your weapons, Tommy. For you ze war is ofer."

"Ger on, shit in ye cap!" O'Rourke sneered, the British officer's accent he had adopted during the war completely vanished to be replaced by the harsh Belfast accent of his youth. 'Come and frigging get me – "

– A bullet slammed in Sterling's body, inches from his face. Slivers of wet flesh flew past him. But he didn't fire back. He had to conserve his ammo till they rushed him again.

For a few minutes nothing happened. Then he strained his ears, turning his head to one side so that he could hear better. Someone was buckling on a heavy pack – he could hear the jingle of metal quite clearly – and among the darkness of the trees he could see a sudden small blue flame. What was going on?

"Your last chance, Tommy," a harsh voice shouted.

"Go an' fuck yersen;" he yelled back.

"*Los!*" the harsh voice commanded.

From both flanks men started forward, ducked low, firing as they came.

O'Rourke laughed and swung back his head, his red hair flying. "Now then lads," he yelled crazily, "say a nice little prayer for what you are about to receive." He pressed the trigger. The sten gun erupted into frenetic life. To the left the Germans were bowled over like skittles as the burst slammed into them; screaming and cursing, limbs flailing widly. Almost immediately, O'Rourke switched his aim to the right. He fired again. The angry lead stopped them in their tracks. They went down everywhere. Carried away, cackling like a madman, O'Rourke couldn't take his finger off the trigger. Long after they had all been hit or gone to ground, he kept on firing, crying: "*Up the Irish!*"

The dry click brought him back to reality. The mag was empty. He dropped the sten gun as if it was red-hot. He grabbed the Colt. But already it was too late. He recognized that long dry hiss, as if some primeval monster was taking its first first breath. His face contorted with horror. He raised the Colt. A rod of angry red flame shot out, searing all before it, filling the night air with the cloying stench of burnt oil.

He buried his head in Sterling's body, which turned an instant black. "No," he quavered, "please not that. *PLEASE.*"

The flame thrower hissed again. Once more that cruel flame shot out. Flame engulfed him, drowning his screams of absolute, total agony. The screaming seemed to go on for ever, as the flame rose higher and higher, shrivelling the two men's flesh, reducing their bodies to those of charred pygmies, fused together as if for eternity.

"Operation Dare and Win" was over.

ENVOI

"Life, to be sure, is nothing much to lose,
But young men think it is, and we were young."

Housman.

Each March, the private executive jet, with single golden letter "G" painted on its black sides, lands at Hamburg-Fuhlsbuttel. There it discharges its cargo of white-haired old men. As always the two stretch Mercedes, beautifully polished and immaculate, are waiting for them. They are whisked into the heart of the city and deposited at the swank *Hotel Vierjahreszeiten*.

There in the early evening in that same small dining room where *Hauptmann* von Witzleben last viewed the Nazi *Prominenz* and thought they were like the passengers on the doomed "*Titanic*", they dine. It is a strange meal for grand hotel's excellent chefs, but the foreign gentlemen tip exceedingly well at the end of their stay, especially the Jew, so they are glad to prepare unusual fare.

It is always the same: battered corned beef, fried, baked beans straight from the Heinz tin, and dehydrated potatoes, followed by fruit cocktail, again from the Del Monte tin, covered by Carnation milk. Invariably the meal, which makes the chefs shudder, is greeted by both the Americans and the English with a phrase that the waiters do not understand, but which they take to be of approval. It is: "Cor, what luvverly grub!"

It is washed down with various drinks which they refer to as "wallop". Once one of the waiters looked the word up in Langenscheid's big dictionary. According to it the word meant "a blow" or "to beat". Thereafter, the waiters decided not to attempt to understand the strange English used by these elderly gentlemen out on their annual spring spree.

Flushed a little with drink, the old gents are then driven

213

to the city's red light district, the Reeperbahn. These days the Reeperbahn isn't what it used to be when they had first started coming to Hamburg, twenty-odd years before. The Eros-Centre is now a refugee asylum. The water beds have vanished to be replaced by bunk beds, with up to twenty refugees packed into the former "love chamber". Hamburg's most famous brothel, "Max und Moritz", on the Hans Albers Platz, had gone too. In its place there is a fake Irish pub selling weak and expensive beer, "Pat O'Briens". But there are still a few jolly middle-aged tarts hanging around, with their time-honoured call, "*Hey big boy – look at me, handsome!*"

Not that the old men are much interested in sex these days – most of them have prostate trouble. But, as former Trooper Brown, now confined to a wheel chair, always maintains fondly: "But it's nice thinking about it now and again, ain't it? As long as it does get out of hand," which is always the occasion for a bawdy but not very funny joke.

Next morning, usually slightly hung over, they are picked up by the stretch limos once again. Now they are formally attired – the casual clothes of the previous day have vanished. Now their shoes are shined so that you can see your face in them. All wear smart blue blazers with a winged dagger insignia on the pocket in white and blue. Swiftly the limos take them out through Hamburg's dingy suburbs through the one-time villages of Oststeinbek and Glinde, which have become virtually part of Greater Hamburg.

The thick woods of the *Sachsenwald* where they once hid have almost gone now. A new super highway cuts through the fields that had formed their DZ on that fateful March dawn in 1945. The factory has been re-built and it now makes roofing tiles, though there is no one who works there who can explain the battle scars left on the buildings which survived the attack. "Perhaps something to do with the bombing," they say.

With Smith in the lead, pushing his wheelchair with difficulty across the little road which is still cobbled, they form up at the edge of what fields that are left. No one seems to know who owns them (for once the "G Organization" as it is called had tried to buy them) and in all their years of being here they have never seen as much as single cow graze on them.

For a few silent moments they gaze at the fields where it had all started half a century before – and ended for many of their comrades. Then Al Corey, the senior survivor, now bent and white with age, calls out: "Lieutenant Goldstein."

"Sir," Goldstein, now head of Goldstein Securities, one of the largest firms on Wall Street, responds smartly. Inspite of his bulk, for he has grown enormously fat in the intervening years, he steps forward, as Al Gorey barks, "the American roll-of-honour."

Eyes already filling with tears, Goldstein yells out the name of his old professor, "Colonel Sterling, R, Silver Star and the British Military Cross."

"Trooper Brown," Al Corey commands.

"Sir."

"The British roll-of-honour."

Brown does not need the sheet of paper with the names of the dead written on it. They have been inscribed on his heart these many years. In a clear youthful voice, he begins, "Trooper Bookhalter, E . . . Sergeant Jenkins, R . . ."

By now the tears are streaming down all their aged, lined faces.

Finally Brown comes to the last on the list. "Major O'Rourke, Rory, Victoria Cross . . ."

That's it. A last salute. Damp-eyed and in silence they return to the stretch limos. There the German drivers, as puzzled as always by these old men and their ceremony in the empty field, stub out their cigarettes hurriedly. They shuffle inside. Without another word, each old man wrapped up in a cocoon of his own thoughts, they are driven away. With luck they'll live to come another year. Behind them they leave the killing fields, shrouded in the heavy gloom of a March morning . . .